CIRCLE OF 7

CIRCLE OF 7

Juanita Tischendorf

Copyright Page

First Edition

Library of Congress Cataloguing-in-Publication Data has been applied for.

ISBN: 978-1-928613-97-8 Circle Of 7 (Hardcover)
ISBN: 978-1-928613-95-4 Circle Of 7 (Paperback)
ISBN: 978-1-928613-93-0 Circle Of 7 (eBook)

Dedication

In memory of my son, Erik Saxton. You left fingerprints of grace on our lives and you shan't be forgotten

Acknowledgement

Storytelling sells books because people get caught up in the narrative. As a self-published author, I no longer try to get the attention of a trade publisher because there are too many well-known writers competing for their attention. I am one of the new breed of independent book publishers aiming for Amazon and other online bookstores. They're publishing print-on-demand books and eBook editions for the Kindle, Nook, and other eBook readers. Each year as I publish my next book, I learn new and inexpensive ways to promote it. Each year brings new hope for reaching a wider circle of readers, with my aim to have my books be read and enjoyed. If you are reading this, my aim has been accomplished

Preface

Rochester, New York, sitting on the shores of Lake Ontario is the city where Xerox and Kodak were born and like many other cities it has another claim to fame. It has its share of hauntings and ghosts.

The origins of our superstitions are lost in time. Our beliefs that have survived are often relics of ancient cultures and long-vanished ways of life. However, they remain within us and demonstrate themselves as outward expressions of the tension and anxiety that test humanity. Be it called superstition, magic, folklore, chance, luck, or a curse; it is still the same.

We admit to the existence of an external power controlling and visiting our minds. And consequently, life grows more complicated, and for some, more frightening. No one can understand or explain it. But our 'reality' of life remains an impenetrable mystery dancing to the rules of a sane society. But what controls the other.

The power! Some call it good and evil. Others see it as god and the devil. Then there are those who label it white magic and black magic. But what is it for sure? There are those who retain their sanity by saying that this power can be summed up in the single connotation of 'luck'.

It really doesn't matter; does it? The aim is always the same: good must survive over evil. But to reach this end it will take more than willpower alone. It will require belief. Yes, a mental and physical belief so that we can arm ourselves with the power to fight off the evil spirits.

To turn our back in denial of the existence of supernatural powers would render us useless in combat and this, my dear reader is what, really, life is all about. One must find a way to accept that which is; or isn't.

CHAPTER 1

Ned Log

The day he learned of his parent's death Ned was beyond consoling. He had lost them both and no one knew exactly what had killed them. Ned was named after his father and they were kindred spirits. His mother doted on him, but he could not think of one thing they had in common except he loved her dearly. His family told him that his mom and dad both came down with a mysterious illness and died. They had been taken by ambulance to the hospital where his mother expired first. After her passing, hospital staff reportedly planned to transfer his father by helicopter for additional treatment, but he died shortly before they could make the arrangements. All they could determine was that his parents had died from an illness, though the exact type still remained unknown, and authorities were working with Health Ministry to investigate the matter and conduct additional testing. The autopsy report for his parents had been completed, but no report had been issued and the forensic investigation of areas of their home and places they frequented had yet to be received.

That had happened when he was still quite young and naive and the pain over their loss was all consuming, but as the years progressed, he learned how to channel that pain into the deep recesses of his existence. What he

1

thought most of was his father's wish that he remembers he was 'golden'. Though he never understood exactly what that meant or had a chance to have his father explain it to him, he later decided on it meaning his father wanted him to better himself.

After the passing of his parents, Ned's siblings determined it would be best for him to move into the home of his oldest sister who lived in Salem, New Jersey. Her husband had a decent job and they would be best able to provide for Ned.

Ned never had a say so in this discussion nor did he care. He trusted his siblings to make the right choice even though it felt strange to know he would be leaving Bartlesville, Oklahoma, a place that had been his home since his birth. As he thought on it, he realized that beyond a distance of thirty or so miles, even Bartlesville was foreign to him. Thus, the little part of Bartlesville compared to this opportunity to see more than he had ever dreamed he would see felt like a blessing.

When his oldest sister, Alba arrived in Bartlesville, there was a flurry of activity in the house as things were packed and distributed. That evening he listened as his family discussed the trip ahead.

They pored over maps and estimated out the cost of the trip for gas alone to run about one hundred and fifty dollars. To Ned this sounded like an impossible sum to accumulate. After figuring the quickest route they turned to mapping out the stops. All this was discussed so that the family could help Alba and her husband with the expenses.

And thus, it was that Ned moved from Oklahoma to New Jersey -- lock, stock, and barrel. As the car pulled away from the one-story, ramshackle home, Ned turned around in the back seat of the car to take one last look. The house was one story and sat at an angle in the middle of a small lot. The front porch where his parents often sat could

2

barely fit two chairs, but the overhang shaded them from the heat of the sun. From the cinderblock base to the asbestos siding that had once been white, the need for repairs was evident even before entering the front door. Inside the floors slanted toward the back of the house, with ripped wallpaper, threadbare carpet, and chipped wood around the windows. The house had only 2 bedrooms and one bathroom for their family of seven, but somehow his parents had managed to make it work. Ned whispered a final goodbye to his father, his mother, and the life he knew.

The drive was long and tiring, but never having gone outside of Bartlesville, it became an adventure for Ned. They were on the road for at least six hours that first day before stopping off at an inexpensive motel to stay the night and eat barbecue ribs and mashed potatoes prepared for them by the family. The next morning, they were up before the sun and after taking showers and going through their morning rituals they were back on the road again. They would make two more overnight stops before finally reaching their destination, traveling 1300 miles, and crossing through Missouri, Indiana, Ohio, and Pennsylvania before finally reaching the border of New Jersey.

When they pulled into his sister's driveway Ned couldn't help smiling. The house was a mansion to Ned. It was two stories with a red door that set in a frame of red. Off to the left was a large window with its own little roof that matched the color of the door. On the upper level there were three windows and off the driveway there was a total of five windows. The one thing missing was a porch, but it had its own driveway. Though it was in need of a paint job, it looked majestic to Ned.

His sister's husband came out to greet them and while they hugged and chatted about the trip, Ned walked into the house. His mouth dropped as he moved slowly through the family room, into the dining room and through to the kitchen. The floors were wood, solid wood and each room was large and inviting. He opened a door off the hallway to reveal a bathroom and stepped inside, looking for a tub, but there wasn't one. When he stepped out his sister stood waiting for him.

"So, what do you think. Can you be happy here?"

"Wow, yes, I can be very happy here."

"Come upstairs and we'll put your things in your room."

Ned stared, dumbfounded. "I get my own room?"

Alba smiled. "Yes."

She walked in front of Ned and turned to point out each room. There were three bedrooms in total and a full bath in the hallway that would be just for him as they had a bathroom in their bedroom.

He paused and stared at Alba. "Oh, Ned, it's a bathroom attached to our bedroom. Let me show you." He followed her down the hall and she opened the door so that he could step in and check it out.

"Well, get settled in. Take a nap if you want. I'm going to get some things from the store."

That was his first introduction to Salem, New Jersey. It was different in many ways to what he was used to, but he had no complaints. Maybe it's his quick wit, his physical features or his undeniable self-confidence that makes it easy for him to fit in.

The people who met Ned would say he was sensitive, soft-spoken, and very generous. He eased into his new lifestyle appreciative of every moment and

4

constantly expressing that to his family. It was hard to believe that a child who had known hard work from the time he was ten and had experienced two tragic losses before reaching the age of thirteen, would be ready to fight back at the world. But this was far from the type of person Ned was then or would be in the future. He had watched as his father had literally worked himself to death to keep clothes on his children and food on the table so they could concentrate on school. Then once they were older, he had encouraged them to find part time jobs and save their money. And from that upbringing Ned had learned early how to do without in order to have the things that he needed to survive.

This did not make Ned bitter, but instead taught him how to face work as a challenge and school as a necessity. Moving from Oklahoma to Salem during his freshmen year, did not discourage Ned and his sister reveled in his ability to adjust to just about anything. Many times, she would say that, "He has a light soul and glorious outlook all the time."

Ned was well liked and had many friends even though he never had much time to spend with them. Perhaps it's the disarming smile or his magnetic personality that made Ned so appealing to others or maybe his fondness for telling jokes was what drew them to him. What with his studies and work which he would not consider shortchanging, there were few "free" time hours to share with his peers. But this did not seem to matter. People just naturally liked him and could be seen helping him get his work done just so they could be around him.

Yes, Ned was happy. All Ned knew during that long drive to New Jersey was that he was on his way to a new life in a whole new area of the country and that his path of destiny was now being paved. All he had to do was wait, work, and learn.

5

CHAPTER 2

Enolai Ceps

Salem, New Jersey was all Enolai Ceps ever knew. This town with a population of around 5,000 was comfortable for her because she had a hard time being around a lot of people. She was reserved to the point of appearing cold, but really due to her excessive shyness. She had desires of being strong and supportive, but her outward nature was of one needing these characteristics from others. Sweet, innocent, and kind were the adjectives that would best describe her, but she was dominated by forces beyond her control, which would lead to people thinking her "strange". Many days she would find her way down to the Salem River and sit on its banks, wondering why no one wanted to remain friends with her. On this day she was thinking as she set on the riverbank that finally she had found a friend in Dr. Reb Memer. She never understood why her peers deserted her one by one when she needed them most, nor did she care to understand. She didn't need them now. She had Dr. Reb Memer and her father who were more than adequate replacements.

Enolai knew that her brothers also thought her strange. She knew that the children in school felt the same way. But this did not matter. Dr. Memer was helping her to understand and believe that she wasn't strange at all. She

6

was just going through a change that would eventually dissipate. Or at least this is what the doctor alleged. Enolai thought that her mother, May, would say differently if she ever had the inclination to speak to her daughter about the spells. But, Enolai never had a conversation with her mother where they talked about their spells because May didn't want to discuss it at all.

When Enolai was to see Dr. Memer for the first time, May and Neves had gone to meet him first. At that time May had opened, a little, and told the doctor that she, as well as Enolai had been born with a veil. This had astounded Dr. Memer, since being born with what is medically called a caul occurred in fewer than 1 in 80,000 births. Having a mother and her child born with one was unheard of. Even before meeting Enolai, Dr. Memer's interest was piqued by this extraordinary phenomenon. He had no way of knowing just how deeply he would become involved.

Even though Enolai trusted and loved Dr. Reb Memer, she never felt like she should tell him everything about her spells. She wanted to, but just couldn't. Yet she had told him enough so that he thought he knew how to help her. It was during one of their later sessions when Dr. Reb Memer asked if she mind being called Nola. Enolai had thought about it and liked the idea and from then on, she was known as Nola.

When she was turning eight Nola had shared with Dr. Memer about her birthday incident. It was a very hot July day and Nola had been looking forward to having a party with her friends from school. She tried to ignore the fact that the feelings of her friends towards her had changed, that she had changed. Instead she thought about when she had turned seven, she had a big birthday party with all her family, neighborhood kids and school friends.

7

It had been a joyous occasion with lots of food and laughter. Even though this was her mother's birthday too, May never celebrated. Within a week after the celebration, something had shifted in her that made people stay away.

Accordingly, on her eighth birthday, Nola found herself sitting with her family, eating cake, and talking too much to cover up for the lack of her peers around the festive table. There were no games, and no laughter like before. Her eighth birthday was the last time she invited her peers to celebrate with her.

But now Nola was fifteen; a shy and quiet girl. No semblance of the happy, cheery little girl of her youth remained. She could see the hurt in her father's eyes. Neves wanted that child back, but it was beyond his power as well as Nola's to help that lost child surface once again.

Nola had at first blamed the changes in her life on her mother. She had determined that her mother was jealous of her closeness with her dad and that was why she was so standoffish and quiet. Never once over the years did she feel there could be another reason.

But lately Nola had begun to wonder again, probably because of Dr. Memer who felt that there was a deeper connection between Nola and May that only May could disclose. The only help May had offered was to tell the doctor that Nola had been born with a "veil" over her face. When Dr. Memer shared this with Nola she asked him, "What did that mean?"

"Well, Nola, it really isn't a veil, but a caul. A caul happens when a piece of the sac breaks away during gestation or during the birthing process and attaches itself to the baby's head."

Seeing a strange look on Nola's face, Dr. Memer quickly added. "Many cultures consider a baby born with a caul a sign of good luck."

8

He could see the wheels turning in Nola's head. "Does it happen often?"

"Oh, no. Birth with a caul is rare. The caul is harmless and is immediately removed by the physician or midwife upon delivery."

Dr. Memer could see Nola having problems with accepting this so he added, "Many belief systems hold that being born with a veil is a sign of special destiny and psychic abilities, or good luck."

Sensing that this might perchance lead to Nola opening more, he added, "Most who are born with a veil are female and believe themselves to be psychically gifted, while others show no advanced abilities nor interest."

Nola looked up and gave Dr. Memer a half smile, started to say something, but closed her mouth tightly.

Trying to encourage her, he continued. "To be born with a caul, may go more to being Born with a Calling and where that takes a soul. It was considered an omen that the child was destined for greatness."

At that Nola smiled.

"Guess what?"

"What"

"Your mother was also born with a veil."

The minute he saw the change in her expression, he knew he had overstepped. From the glowering look on her face, he misread it to mean this unsettled her, but instead it was because it made her want to ask if he knew anything more, but she was too timid to question him, even less apt to question her mother. Ever since the change, or the arrival of the powerful visions, Nola felt she was not her own person and that made her feel inferior.

May had seen the change in Nola. She had seen her daughter change from a happy, carefree little girl into a shy,

9

quiet girl. Neves felt that the change could be something that little girls go through, but her mother had spoken up then, saying that this was not so. That was all she could say as to say more would reveal her secret, and that secret she could never reveal to anyone.

It was after having one-sided conversations with May that Neves felt it necessary to get his daughter outside help. That was how Dr. Reb Memer came into the picture. Dr. Memer did seem to offer Nola some outlet, but May knew, just like she couldn't tell everything, Nola was probably unable to tell Dr. Memer any more than the entity would allow.

Both May and Nola were struggling alone to understand. And there was a lot to understand. Neither knew if there were two entities or only one in their visions. Neither knew if the entity was good or bad that came to them, or if one was good and the other bad. Too much concentration brought on another spell so neither spent much time trying to sort it all out. But more monumental, neither confided in the other.

CHAPTER 3

Enolai Ceps Meets Ned Log

And then for Nola something wondrous happened. Ned Log entered her life. Ned, with his cheerful disposition reminded May so much of Neves and that set well with her. Ned being so full of life and happiness that he could not except sadness in anyone could only help their daughter.

Nola was swept off her feet. May and Neves began to see flickers of the little girl, Nola. Whenever Ned was around, Nola was radiant and happy. She didn't have to add much to the conversation or share much to attract Ned. It was a comfortable relationship with Ned offering all the support while Nola reveled in his attentive presence. It didn't take him long to realize that Nola was not aware of how attractive she was. She stood five feet eleven inches in height, towering over most men. She wore her long black hair straight without a semblance of curl and back off her small, heart-shaped face. To Ned, her face was in total alignment with her small, aquiline nose, perky mouth and dark mysterious eyes that broke from the symmetry as they were large, black, and shining. If she had a mind too, she could have succeeded in the world of glamour, but this was not in Enolai's nature.

Ned would talk for hours about his dreams and ambitions. At the time of his meeting Nola, he was enrolled in a local school studying to become a computer engineer and would talk endlessly about his studies to Nola. Nola listened though she understood not even half of what Ned said. She was just happy that he wanted to talk and spend his time with her. Nola knew that several of her classmates had more than a passing interest in this Oklahoman, but she was the target of his attention. Somehow this made Nola feel exceptionally good.

Not only did Nola recognize a change in herself, but also it seemed that her mother had changed since Ned had appeared. May seemed more talkative and friendly toward her daughter.

Yes, Ned was a breath of sunshine in the lives of the Ceps woman. Even Neves had become attached to Ned though he tried not to show it too often. Inside Neves knew that Ned would be the one to take Nola away from him and this was not a cause of celebration. Yet Neves could not help liking this carefree, well-educated boy.

Therefore, it really did not come as a surprise to May or Neves when Ned asked for Nola's hand in marriage. But it was a surprise to Nola. Nola had looked upon Ned as a shepherd trying to gather in the stray sheep. She had felt that Ned's attentions were like that of a brother and not those of a future husband. She had never dreamt that Ned could love her as deeply as she loved him. Nola not only loved Ned but needed him far more than she could ever have told him or shown him. She didn't hesitate to accept his proposal.

Nola and Ned didn't have a lot of money and were pleased as punch when a neighbor down the street offered to let them use a vacant house, they owned just steps away from the Ceps resident. From the minute Nola stepped into the house, built in 1890, she felt something, but she shook it off as she walked through the expanse of the interior. It was a massive three-story colonial with hard wood floors throughout. Once she had accepted the offer, she was given the keys and a few instructions. When Nola asked how much, the neighbor said, "consider it your wedding gift." May joined her daughter and was pleased as punch. It would do just fine.

From that day forward, Nola was joined by others as they went about cleaning the place. The house had been vacant for some time so there was a lot of dust to contend with. But the structure was solid and in great shape. On the day before the wedding, Nola and her mother stood back and looked at the transformation. Not only was the place clean from top to bottom, the decorations they had accumulated, along with the borrowed tables and chairs had turned the place into a fairy tale. Even the paper tablecloths looked elegant, with their blue paper napkins and blue bordered plates. All of this was in the front two rooms, while the enclosed porch behind another living area were decorated with streamers and kept open for dancing. Nola turned and smiled at her mother. It had been some time since the two of them had done anything together and now, after everyone had left, they were overwhelmed with joy, as they hugged each other firmly.

Nola flinched as a weird sensation went through her body. Her head lifted and she saw a form out of the corner of her eye. Panicking, she squeezed her eyes shut, then slowly opened them to look over her mother's shoulder only to see that whatever was there had vanished.

Her mother released her as though sensing nothing and Nola took a quick glance around. Seeing there was nothing nor anyone there she decided that it was just the light playing tricks on her.

It was the end of October when the wedding was held. Luck was on their side as the day dawned bright and clear with little chance of rain, so Nola and Ned were able to say their vows outside on the house lawn. Nola wore a crimson red heart on a gold chain belonging to her mother that she had admired since she was a little girl. She also had a white gold bracelet lent to her by Ned's sister and a blue garter demurely hidden under her wedding dress.

Nola had never thought anything could be as beautiful as her wedding dress. It was all gossamer and lace that flowed around her, making her feel wonderfully beautiful even though she would have to return it the next day. When she was dressed and ready, she walked on air to be at Ned's side.

With the flickering of strings of small white lights hung across the lawn, they said their vows in front of family and friends. Ned had included a special moment in the ceremony where they moved into a semicircle and joined hands with friends and family while the celebrant read aloud. "These are the hands of your best friends and family, the hands that will hold your children. Nola you hold the hand of the one who will care for you always, the hands that will still reach for yours when you are old and grey." The Celebrant paused and said, "I pronounce you husband and wife. Ned, kiss your bride."

His kiss said it all. That he would love and protect her for the rest of her life. And then, to end the ceremony, Neves laid down the broom that he and May had jumped many years ago. They watched as Ned and Nola joined hands and jumped the broom.

Ned and Nola moved to the door to the house and greeted their guest as they entered the transformed interior.

It was when they were making their way into the house that what looked like a swirling mist appeared. It moved swiftly only several feet off the ground. Nola pulled back on Ned's arm as she watched the mist transform into a shadowy figure before it finally disappeared.

It was only then that Nola heard Ned saying, "Darling, what is it?"

At that point she realized he hadn't seen anything. With an effort, she smiled and replied, "It is nothing."

The rest of the evening passed with no nonentity interfering with her happiness as she danced and ate an endless assortment of food until she thought the seams of her dress would burst. That night as she lay beside her new husband, Nola was totally, undeniably happy. The warmth of his body next to her seemed so natural and she gave herself to him in sheer joy.

From that moment forward their life together was blessed. They were inseparable and every want and desire became attainable.

CHAPTER 4

Birth Of The Twins

Ned worked hard and Nola kept house. Their first home was an apartment in a modest area of town, but it was adequate for their needs. Ned worked all day and then came home and worked some more. He was constantly reading and writing down things that he wanted to try, his brain never quiet. But whenever Nola entered the room his book would close, and his pencil would be put aside. Her presence seemed to force his actions, without him even being aware of it. Ned couldn't put his finger on exactly how to describe his attraction for Nola. It was like she had an inner power that controlled him. Ned who had always been in control and had liked the feeling, did not mind this mental control Nola seemed to have over him. In fact, it made him love her more.

If ever two alien forces were blessed with a union of oneness, it was to be the union of Ned and Nola. On the surface the two seemed to have nothing in common beyond their love. Yet, if one were to look closer, there was indeed a level of commonness in them.

Nola was content. So was Ned, only he wanted to do more than just make it in the world. He wanted to grab the world by the tail and swing it in his direction. He had to live up to his expectations as his father had said he was the golden child and that meant golden child not only the one favored in the family, but also at work he should expect to be held in high esteem by others, and be the one for whom there are high hopes.

Ned was really doing "notably" well and people in high places were buzzing about this young protege. Here was a man who showed dedication, capability, and an outstanding personality -- all the ingredients needed in an executive to head their new plant opening soon in New York. There was little hesitation and much agreement among the higher ups to approach Ned Log with an offer.

While this plan for Ned's future was growing, Nola was also growing with the anticipation of their first child, the product of the complete union of Ned and her as one.

Strangely enough, Ned felt he could pinpoint exactly when their child had been conceived as it was burned into his mind. It was the most unforgettable experience of his life.

The evening had been the same as many evenings passed. Nola prattled about the kitchen doing last minute preparations for their dinner. She had seemed on edge from the moment Ned had come home which had also happened before, but somehow her edginess seemed different; almost frightening.

Ned, a devoted husband, decided to keep an eye on her. Between Dr. Reb Memer, who had also taken a liking to Ned, and Nola herself, he knew of her spells, visions, or whatever you cared to term them.

Nola eventually had to explain herself to Ned when she had one of her spells and returned seeing that anxious, worried look on his face. She tried her best to be honest, but make it seem normal, afraid she would alienate him. So, she said it was a foggy feeling in her head when her

17

brain goes blank sometimes in mid-sentence and her mind swept her away.

Not sure he understood, Ned had asked her what caused it and she said that was what Dr. Memer was trying to find out.

Ned sometimes knew when Nola was about to have one of those spells and prepared himself, knowing that she would go to a place in her mind that he could not go with her. Only this time it would be distinctively different.

Ned knew it was about to happen. Nola sensed the same. She could feel a wave coming over her that snuffed out the present. No matter how hard she fought, she knew she could not win. She also sensed that this time it would be different, somehow. She couldn't understand how it would differ, but just knew it would be. This fact did more than terrify her.

Ned followed Nola with his eyes and kept up a prattle of conversation, hoping he could keep her with him, but Nola could only half hear him no matter how desperately she tried to keep in touch. Suddenly dinner seemed the furthest thing from her mind as a desire to touch Ned and be close to him swept over her. The feeling was best described as a need to possess Ned.

Ned felt it too. A strong urge to hold Nola in his arms. A need to have her take charge of his body and his soul.

Dinner was forgotten as Nola and Ned clung to each other in their tidy little apartment kitchen. The walls, the furniture, all seemed to close in and unite with them. The air was thick with the ecstasy of their unexplainable passion.

Later in the confines of their bedroom they quickly undressed one another and laid down on the bed in anticipation of what was about to happen. But neither could have predicted this outcome.

18

For hours on end Nola's chants were repeated to the incessant sound of beating drums. The rhythm seemed to increase as their need for each other grew. It grew loud and fast, drowning out all sounds beyond that of the drums until everything around them changed. Their perspiring bodies moved like dancers, visible in the night by a glowing fire in the forest clearing that now surrounded their exhausted bodies. They whirled around, arms flailing, eyes glazed with excitement, mouths contorted with exertion and ecstasy.

Suddenly all activity ceases. Only the flame flickers in movement. Then abruptly a figure in black clothes and a top hat emerges from the shadows of the trees to join the two dancers. His face is painted white and in his hands are a rope and a skull. He lifts his head up and the sound of Nola's screams pierce the night. The drums are silenced as Nola falls heavily onto Ned's chest in an enchanted faint. Then it was over.

Nola loved their tiny apartment in Salem, New Jersey and Nola finally felt complete. Ned never felt comfortable in their little apartment but being with Nola was all that matters. They survive that first year of marriage admitting that it went so easy with the help and example of May and Neves Ceps.

Even in the early days of their marriage, Ned had noticed something strange about May; something that he couldn't explain beyond she seemed to look through him instead of at him.

Nola was like an extension of May and they certainly couldn't have made it alone. That was proven by the need for Nola to keep her last name, not that he would have balked at it, but that she was so shaken when she realized marriage would give her a new last name. It was like she hadn't expected it or thought it until it was

19

happening.   Who gets worked up about something like that?

As the days progressed, he had his work, and life didn't change much for Nola who spent a lot of time with her family. Nola still didn't feel comfortable sharing her innermost secrets with Ned and he accepted that since she did have Dr. Memer.   There was a personal connection between Nola and Dr. Memer, a closeness as though he was a member of the family. A closeness like a daughter to her father and the person she went to when things went awry. It felt strange when returning home from work Nola met him at the door saying, "I have something I want to tell you first. Before I tell anyone else." If it hadn't been for the smile on her face, Ned would have felt uneasy, afraid she wanted to talk about something else that he feared he could not handle.

"Honey, we are going to have a baby!"

Ned's mouth fell open as he stared at his lovely wife, not knowing what to say. This was big, really big and he didn't know how to react. Ned, the planner was happy, but equally anxious. Immediately his mind went to the need to find a new home, buy a safe car. "Honey aren't you happy," he heard Nola through the racing of his brain. "Yes, oh yes, I am more than happy." As he hugged her, looking over her shoulder he continues to think about what he needed to do. That night they shared the news with the Ceps who were elated, taking turns hugging her.   Ned noticed how Nola, at first hesitated before allowing her mother to clasp her in her arms.

May wanted to know when they would become grandparents, but Neves was all about making sure Nola sat down and relaxed. Ned stood there trying to catch up with all the excitement around him, until finally as they all sat down for dinner, he calmed knowing that it would all work out.

Ned, advised by Nola, waited the appropriate amount of time before he shared the news at work. The first thing that happened when he announced his wife's pregnancy is coworkers congratulated him. The next thing they start telling him how it will go and what he should do. Those with children just arched an eyebrow and said "Hmmm." By the end of that first day, he was a mess. What he was thinking, and feeling was not rational, but it is normal. It's just that no man ever talks about it and that was something he was used to dealing with.

The months went by quickly. For Nola, it couldn't go fast enough. She was exhausted most evenings and quite irritable, though she tried to cover up her irritability. Most days May would be at the apartment preparing dinner or cleaning up so that Nola could rest; especially when the doctor announced they would be having twins!

Not one, but two babies. How could they manage. He felt overwhelmed and confused wondering, but again, May and Neves eased his mine. Life settles in and the Ceps are blessed with twins. They name them Jonathan and Joy Ceps-Log.

From the minute the babies arrived in the world, Neves and May were right there to help them settle into parenthood.

Now they were never alone. If Nola's parents weren't with them, they spent their time changing and feeding the babies. Each day it got easier and though Ned still worried about finding a larger place, they seemed to make it work.

The years went quickly with Ned and Nola watching their twins grow. Each day faded into the next as Ned worked hard and spent his time at home being a father to his twins and a good husband to Nola. One night when the twins were past the toddler age and easier to handle,

Ned and Nola took some time for themselves. They were seated in the Living room talking quietly when Nola asked, "Ned, have you noticed anything different about Joy?"

Ned turned to look at her and could see she was worried. "What? Did you notice something?"

Nola was silent, then thinking better of it she closed the subject saying, "Oh, it's nothing, really. Probably how little girls are."

That little conversation had Ned's mind going back. He hadn't thought about it in years, but now it was like it was yesterday, that first time he had shared the vision with Nola, the night he was sure Jonathan and Joy were conceived. A shiver ran through him.

Just like the shared visions with her mother May Cep, Ned and Nola never really spoke about that evening, each afraid to speak aloud such a strange event, for fear that the other would confirm the incident and make it become more real than fantasy.

CHAPTER 5

A Change Of Scenery

The day came when Ned was approached at his job about a promotion. The staff secretary came to his desk just as he was hanging up the phone. Ned had been conversing with Dr. Reb Memer at the time and relayed to him that Nola was having a spell and needed someone to talk to. That's all he said, it's all he dared to say as he just couldn't bring his mouth to form the words that he had somehow participated in the vision. But then, he wasn't sure of this, was he?

"They want you in the front office, Ned,"

"Thank you, Sheila."

Ned didn't linger but got up from his chair and was close on the heels of the secretary, heading in the direction of the front office. There had been rumors about the opening of a new branch, consequently Ned, like his fellow employees were aware that this meant one of the top executives would be transferring and that would leave an opening in their office to fill. He felt confident as he joked with colleagues as he made his way up the line toward the big double doors. When he reached the entrance to the office he turned and winked at his co-workers. They in turn gave him a "thumbs up" response.

Ned entered the executive office and was asked to take a seat. He sat down at the closest chair. Instead of promoting him to an opening in the New Jersey office, they wanted him to head the new branch in New York.

At first Ned was speechless. This was so beyond his expectations that he had to take a moment to regroup.

"Wow, this is not what I expected!"

"Why not, Ned. One of the most impressive things about you is that you strive to continually improve. You listen to feedback from your manager and co-workers—and actually use it. I guess what I am saying is that you are a leader, and everyone knows it, and, just as important, everyone likes you because you don't draw attention to yourself for the sake of showing off. It's like there is someone or something guiding your life to the finish line, if you know what I mean."

Ned looked at his boss, James Masterson as if seeing him for the first time. He stared at him wondering what he meant by that last statement that seemed close to the truth. Did he know? Because now Ned knew that there was something special about his marriage to Nola. He could see that whatever they desired, seemed to happen in their life.

"Ned? Are you still with us?" James asked.

"Oh, yes, it was a shock, to say the least."

"Are you saying you want the position in New York?"

"Yes, I do. I really do."

"Then, congratulations. Let's go over the details then. You will be the president and answer to the CEO. You will be responsible for providing strategic leadership for the company by working with the Board and other management to establish long-range goals, strategies, plans and policies, just like you have been a part of here. You

24

will be responsible to plan, develop, organize, implement, direct and evaluate the organization's fiscal function and performance."

Ned listened, barely able to digest all that was happening and when the salary was mentioned, he had all he could do to not fall off his chair.

"Do you need me to explain anything? I just went over the surface because it's in line with what you have done and seen here."

"No," Ned responded trying to punch down the excitement before speaking. He had to remain calm and not act like a fool, or as if he didn't deserve it.

"Okay, here's your package on the job and this one," he added extending another folder, "covers the transfer package. First, a trip, including transportation and hotel costs, to the new location to find a future home suitable for your family will be paid for. We will also cover the costs of selling your home and purchasing a new home. This includes closing costs, real estate commissions, and other expenses normally incurred when buying or selling a house."

Ned's head was spinning. "We'll also provide job search assistance for your spouse."

"Does that sound fair, Ned?"

"Yes. More than fair. I don't have a house to sell as we live in an apartment."

"Well, if any family member is intending to join you and have a house to sell, we will apply it to them."

Ned made note of that because he knew that Nola would want her parents with them, and they would want to be near her.

"We'll reimburse all travel expenses for the move and since we are hoping to have the plant up and running in a short period of time, we will provide expenses for a temporary furnished rental or a hotel for a certain period. Oh yes, the cost of a moving truck and other related expenses are included. That part my wife liked," James reminisced. "She loved that the logistics of the move included that the movers would pack up our house and transport it to our new home, where they unloaded, and in some cases unpack, the boxes where she wished."

James smiled, recalling the transfer he made from Indianapolis to New Jersey to run this office. "Do you have any questions, Ned."

Ned shook his head.

"Would you like to talk it over with your wife? This will be a big move."

Ned started to say, Yes, but stopped because there was no need to tell Nola. He couldn't explain why this wouldn't be necessary, so he just said. "She'll be as happy as I am. Thank you."

Ned sat, remembering how he had done a google search on the Golden One because of his father's reference those many years ago. He had read that the Golden One is haughty and proud and adores his special one. He is strong and sharp. At the start woman feel subservient to him almost immediately, but he seeks one who feels his equal and will not become his total possession. Because of this the Golden One is nevertheless superior to those around him because he suspects that there is more to the world than the collective equality enforced in the society and this makes him stand out from the faceless, nameless masses. He had read it and like his boss, James, had said it was like there was someone or something guiding his life to the finish line and that was Nola. He couldn't explain it but just knew it, like he knew Nola had already saw and knew about the promotion and move. Accordingly, he accepted the offer of the executive position for the New York plant without hesitation.

Ned had been offered the rest of the day off to advise his family of his good fortune, but he declined. Ned told them he had work he wanted to complete and after work there would be time to talk with the family.

Closing the door behind him, Ned smiled at the pool of anxious faces awaiting his exit. He paused just long enough to build the scene to a climax, then he raised his hand and gave a "thumbs up" salute.

The chain reaction of congratulations, back slapping and laughter filtered through the double doors where a group of men sat around the table nodding their heads at the obvious seal of approval leaking into the room.

Ned headed down the aisle shaking hands, joking, and trying to act modest. Everyone knew how hard he worked and felt he earned the promotion. But once Ned was seated at his desk the aural of the dedicated employee again surfaced and he plunged into his work. His attitude, always recognized as the standard, caused the jubilant employees to follow his lead.

At the end of the day, Ned did a little research before facing the family. What he already knew was that the salary was more than double what he was already making and that this income level was far above that of the average New Yorker. They would be able to afford a large home and have more than a comfortable living style which now was important as they had a baby on the way. With no home to sell, and few personal friends, there was nothing standing in their way.

Ned had reviewed the package from his boss and knew they would cover his expenses to move, along with a sizable amount for a down payment on a house. With all the details for the job and move covered, it was now time to think about the other. Telling Nola and her family that they would be moving would require his full attention. He wanted to make it as easy on everyone as possible. He didn't want this career move to cause anyone anxiety.

CHAPTER 6

Preparing the Family

By the time Ned pulled into a parking space in front of the house, he still wasn't sure how to handle telling the family. He knew they would be happy for his promotion, but the move, well, that was a different matter. Resignedly Ned got out of the car, reminding himself that if there's one thing in life that's certain, it's that plans can and will change. More importantly, he couldn't find an easy way to share his news and would have to deal with whatever happened. He was as ready as he could be to make his announcement.

Over their dinner they talk about the weather and plans for the weekend. Once the dinner dishes were done and the kitchen in order once again, it was time. "Nola, I have something important to discuss with you."

He could see the uneasy feeling growing on her face, giving Ned a need to soothe her, but he had to tell her.

If only Ned could read Nola's thoughts, he would know that she thought he wanted to talk about the night of her vision; the night their baby was conceived. Nola had seen the scratches and bite marks on her husband and dreaded the day he would ask what had happened to her that night. She had learned to accept her visions as her own and not jeopardize her sanity by trying to understand what they meant, if anything. To openly discuss them meant that they were not just visions.

Ned guided Nola into the Living room and took a seat in his chair, pulling Nola down on his lap. She needed closeness as much as he did at that moment.

He could sense Nola's uneasiness by the tenseness of her body against his and taking a deep breath he braved forward.

Not wanting to make her suffer he delved right in. Ned related the day's event of being offered a promotion. He tried to explain what this meant in terms that Nola would understand. There would be money to buy their own home, a much-needed car, and lots of extras that he was not able to provide with his present level of income. Why they would even have money to tuck away for the future. All of this in Ned's mind meant that he had taken the first step up the ladder of success, but he didn't think that this would mean much to Nola.

Ned paused for a moment to give Nola time to absorb the situation. Then he asked her how she felt about pulling up stakes and starting a new life in a new state.

Nola didn't speak right away. She leaned back against Ned's shoulder without saying a word. She thought about her family. She thought about Ned and her life and then she spoke. Nola told Ned that night that she wanted a better life for them. She wanted Ned to have every opportunity to fulfill his dreams, which were her dreams too. She paused and then added that she wanted her family near her, no, she needed her family near her.

There was silence. Nola thought through what she wanted to say. She told Ned that she would go anywhere that he wanted her to go and would be happy. She paused again and then decided that it would be best to just say what she was thinking. "Ned, honey, can I ask my mother and father to come to New York with us?"

Ned smiled and nodded his head.

The bond was growing strong between them and Ned had his first inclination that eventually they would become as one unit in mind and soul. What this would mean he could not fathom a guess, but this did not scare him. No, not yet.

Ned and Nola turned off the lights and locked the apartment door as they left to go over to Nola's parents' home. They climbed into the dilapidated car that they had so carefully chosen with their budget in mind and closed the doors. Ned started up the car and they were on their way to the rambling old building that May and Neves Ceps called, home.

Dr. Reb Memer was a part of their family in every sense of the word. He had become part of the Ceps family when Nola was a little girl in much need of help. This thought was running through Nola's mind on the drive to her parents' home. She had to tell Dr. Memer and let him know he was welcomed to come with them too. Nola decided that she had best tell Ned this now and she did.

Ned looked over at Nola. The last thing he wanted was to have Nola experience a loss, but he began to feel that he would not be able to keep this from happening. It was a possibility that her mother and father would come with them either now, or maybe later. Nola was there last child and the only one still living near home. But Dr. Reb Memer! He had his own medical practice here and other clients besides Nola. He couldn't even kid his self into feeling that Dr. Memer would want to move.

Dr. Memer was attached to the Ceps' family--he knew that, but he couldn't just throw away his profession at his age and start all over again in another state. That was absurd! But that was what Nola was hoping. Of this Ned was sure. Ned said nothing since he didn't think that Nola was waiting for a reply.

Nola seemed content enough the rest of the way. She leaned back against the torn seat cover and said nothing more.

Ned did talk. He tried to paint a picture for Nola of the City they would be living in. He tried to include a replica of what he envisioned their home to look like. He even went as far as to try and describe the car they would purchase.

Nola listened. There was something she could have said but felt it best to leave it unspoken. She wasn't ready yet to tell Ned that she didn't need the words because she could visualize his thoughts, somehow. She had noticed this new extension of herself happening from the moment Ned had arrived home this evening. This was new and a little scary, but she could live with it.

She had noticed something else too. If she thought over Ned's thoughts, she was able to read what he was thinking. This she had done earlier this evening because of her fear that Ned wanted to talk about the events of the previous night.

She felt certain that Ned would understand this if she told him. As for anybody else, well they would either think it weird and fear her or call it a gift and be scared of her. Either way she would be seen as "different" and she could do without that. Anyway, outside of her family and Dr. Reb Memer, there was no one that Nola knew that she would talk to about herself. She had no real friends. Her family and Ned were her everything.

The minute her daughter and son-in-law entered the house, May knew their life was about to change. She could sense it even before either one opened their mouth.

At Nola's request, May and Neves sat at the kitchen table with them. Every now and then May got up to refill coffee cups and pull away to think on her own. She knew this would happen eventually. It had happened with each of her children. They married and then they moved away. Only this was different. This was their little girl, their last child, who was leaving now. Though she never spoke it aloud, she knew that this child was more a part of her than any of the others. She had the visions and somehow May felt that Nola would be the one to remove what May had always referred to privately as the "curse". She didn't want Nola to go, yet she had so much faith in Ned's determination and care of her daughter that she knew if Ned thought this was a good move, it would be so. And there was something else too, yet May could not place her finger on it just yet. It was only a feeling that she had that Nola knew something else that she was not sharing with them. Shaking her head May dismissed the idea.

While May was sorting all of this out, Neves was doing pretty much the same thing as he sat listening to Ned at the table. As usual, Ned was the spoke's piece for himself and Nola. Neves thought about how often he had tried to get Nola to speak her fears or even her happy thoughts with him without success. He felt sure that she loved and trusted him, but just could not bring herself to talk to anyone, about them. That's what made this news so hard. Neves knew that Ned was the best thing to happen to his daughter and he could not stand in the way of either of their happiness. Yet, Ned had said that he and Nola wanted them to go with them to New York. Could he leave New Jersey where he had been born and raised? He had lived all his life in this house and community. Could he let it all go now? Would he regret losing a part of his very soul?

Because that's what this place had become to him, a part of his soul.

Ned, and Neves, talked late into the night. May and Nola made a comment here and there but remained pretty much quiet, just listening to the two men. Ned told May and Neves that they did not have to make up their minds right away, but that he and Nola wanted them to have time to think about all of this.

May finally had something she wanted to say. It seemed to have come from out of nowhere. She didn't even know she was going to say it, until the words came out. It wasn't meant to be an obstacle in Ned and Nola's plans--it was just something that she felt she had to ask and that was what about Dr. Reb Memer.

Ned and Nola looked at each other in surprise. May had never showed any attachment, barely a mention of Dr. Memer before, except as a person that was engaged for Nola to talk to. May did not believe anyone could help Nola. No one had helped her. Of course, she had not let anyone try. But now, while she thought about what Ned was proposing to them, Dr. Memer had come to mind.

It was Ned who spoke next. He told May that Nola had already decided to ask Dr. Memer if he wanted to come with them to New York. They planned to talk with him the following evening to give him a chance to decide what he wanted to do.

Neves' thoughts ran along the same lines as Ned's. He doubted that the Doctor would even consider a move. Of course, he would miss Nola and would regret losing her as a patient and friend, but to move; no. He would probably recommend a doctor in New York for Nola to see.

May on the other hand felt as Nola did. This seemed logical to her that Dr. Reb Memer would want to go where Nola was so that he could continue to help her. Why this seemed logical to May, she did not know. She didn't even feel that this was her own thought she had spoken, but that was too silly to dwell on.

Ned and Nola got up to leave and May and Neves went out to the car with them. Ned could see the indecision on their faces as they gave each of them a hug and a kiss. He felt bad about having to lay so much in their laps, but he had no choice if he wanted to fulfill his and Nola's dreams, they had to make this move.

They pulled away with both thinking about all of it and wondering what the final decision would be on May and Neve's part. Neither one of them spoke. There were no more words to be said on the matter. It was all out of their hands as far as Nola's parents were concerned.

But there was the matter of Dr. Reb Memer now to think about. They planned to call him the following morning and visit with him that evening.

Ned was not looking forward to this visit. He felt sure that where Dr. Reb Memer was concerned there would be an answer given immediately. He knew that Nola would be deeply hurt when Dr. Memer had to decline their offer to come to New York.

Nola on the other hand felt confident that everything would go all right. She was sure that her parents would call tomorrow to tell her that they would start planning to go to New York. She was confident that there would be one other person making the move with them and that was her beloved doctor and confidante. She could no more give up him than he could give up her. After all, he had shared in parts of her 'spells' ; to use his term, and though she had not yet gotten to telling him everything, she felt that even knowing parts of them over so many years, he would be unable to dislocate himself from her.

This last thought was another new revelation to Nola. Why did she think this? She didn't know but couldn't help believing that it was true. Somehow their talks about her vision had made them inseparable.

CHAPTER 7

The Session With Dr. Reb Memer

Nola's call the next morning did not surprised Dr. Memer. He had been thinking about calling her to see how she was doing. Ever since her marriage to Ned, Dr. Memer had seen less of Nola. He assumed that this was because she now had someone else, she could confine in when she needed to talk. In a way this made Dr. Memer feel strange; sort of like he had lost something very special to him. Nola was like his child since he had been her companion from her childhood days. At first, she had been like any other patient who needed special medical assistance in understanding something happening in their life. But over the years this had changed. Nola's problem was indeed different from any he had dealt with in his 56 years of practice, something too that no one would believe.

Oh yes, he had seen patients who had suffered from strange dreams, but nothing like Nola's. Nola's were not dreams. This he had determined long ago. Dreams were unconscious thoughts that could be dealt with in one way or another and resolved to some extent in a year or two of sessions. Nola's problem he had termed "spells" because they were more real than a dream. He even fancied that they took place as a reality.

37

Dr. Memer was all too happy to accommodate Ned and Nola that evening and he even looked forward to it.

Right on time the two appear on his doorstep. They ring the doorbell and Dr. Memer hurries to answer the door. When he swings it open, there is a smile on his face.

"Good evening Dr. Memer," Nola says as she moves into the house in front of Ned. "This is my husband, Ned."

"Good evening Ned. I feel I know you as we have talked several times on the phone. Please come in."

With the introductions out of the way, Dr. Memer leads the two through the office waiting room and opening the door at the back of the room, they see a long hallway. "Come in," Dr. Memer says. As they walk down the hall, they are confronted on the left by pictures of happy family outings, some taken a long time ago identifiable by the style of the clothing. On the right there are pictures of various sunsets, trees, and beaches in assorted frame types.

Nola looks around, surprised. "I didn't know you lived here."

"Yes, I do. I love this house. It has been in my family for many, many years and I can't bear to move elsewhere. Besides it's a guarantee I'll never be late for work." He adds this with some humor.

Nola and Ned both sense the change in each other. This last confession from the doctor places doubts in their heads. He has a personal attachment to the house as well as with his patients.

Dr. Memer has prepared some hors d'oeuvres and offers them wine. They accept and following his lead, giving them a brief, incomplete view through the rooms until they are on an enclosed porch area, looking out on the most beautiful garden Nola has ever seen. It is expansive with many flowers. There are pink flowers. There are purple flowers. There are small flowers. There are big flowers. There is also a fountain with water spraying outward and forming little sparks of light. Nola moves up against the screen for a better glimpse while Ned nervously sits thinking as they wait for their host to return. When Dr. Memer joins them, he hands them their drinks and offers the tray of hors d'oeuvres and though full, they graciously accept. "So, what do I owe this visit to?"

Slowly, thoroughly, and right to the point, Ned explains that he has been offered a big promotion at work and he has accepted it. The only downside to the promotion is that they will have to move to New York.

They watch as Dr. Memer's face changes. Nola had always liked the kindness she saw in his face. Now as she looked at him sitting comfortably, she studied him. This five-foot nine-inch, healthy looking man was like her mentor and a giant in her eyes. From his thick head of blonde hair, sprinkled with gray to his inquisitive clear blue eyes below dark lashes they were features so familiar to her. There was something very special about Dr. Reb Memer and she observed how their news had unsettled him.

Ned started to speak, but Dr. Memer held up his hand to quiet him. They watched as the doctor got up and walked across the room to stare out the window. Ned and Nola held hands, waiting with a sense of alarm until finally Dr. Memer turned around.

"Okay, I understand. I really do." He paused and surprising them both by adding, "You want to know if I will go with you to New York?"

"Yes," Ned replied, startled by Dr. Memer's remark. "That's what we wanted to ask."

"Good, because I want to go."

Nola was beside herself as she walked hesitantly toward her doctor and reached out to touch his hand.

"You see, I have to admit that there is something I can't explain drawing me into your family and I can't not help you, Nola."

"I'm so glad."

Ned, always the reasonable one finally spoke. "Dr. Memer, can you practice in New York?"

Dr. Memer explained that it would be easy to transfer. He needed to apply for a license to the American Medical Association to practice in New York and he would do that right away as it could take up to two months to receive the license.

"What about all of this," Ned added reaching his arms out."

"Well, Ned, like I said, this house is a part of me, but it's a house. You are people and you are now my family. One must be with family, don't you think?"

The rest of the evening was relaxing as they chatted about Ned's new position and what it would entail. At the end of the evening they got up to leave and Dr. Memer saw them to the door. All three were happy with the way everything had transpired.

That evening, before turning in for the night, Nola called her parents to share the good news.

CHAPTER 8

The Move

Dawn arrives and brings the first light of day and Ned and Nola Ceps-Log are up and ready. Over the previous months they have been busy packing and helping her parents get ready for the move. Luckily her parents' home sold quickly so they would be going with them.

They had also found a house in Rochester, New York where they would be living. Located in an area known as Irondequoit, and with the help of a local realtor, Ned and Nola had managed to tour through many homes that would meet their needs of space for future children and their parents. When they had settled on two, he invited the family to make the choice. This 1950s home had been brought into the future with lighting on a smart system that Ned could control from his smartphone. But for Nola it was the kitchen with its stylish breakfast area and custom cabinets packed with upgrades, organization enhancements and a user-friendly space for dining. The kitchen looked clean, painted a soft white with tons of storage. She had to even appreciate the smart solutions that included a mixer lift and trash chute, though they were not necessary.

Coming from a one-bedroom apartment that had a living room and kitchen in seven hundred square feet, everything about this house was dramatic.

Even her parents couldn't help but fall in love with it. Though their home had been run down and small, it was part of them, and they didn't want to find they liked this home better. The in-law apartment on the first-floor level was very stylish and comfortable with their own luxurious bathroom and sitting area, as well as a kitchenette that was twice the size of that in their old home.

They wandered through the rooms peeking into every nook and cranny. Six bedrooms, six bathrooms, a butler pantry, two outside porches and beautifully landscaped gardens with lots of trees and bushes. It all sat on an acre, giving them privacy. It was a dream come true.

They moved very little furnishings with them since the home was offered for sale furnished and they liked what they saw. Nola was surprised how easy it was for her to settle into this new home and this new city, but then, everything that made her life what it was, came with her.

The day of the arrival of the Ceps-Log to their new home was the day that Jolene Mann had a vision. In her vision she saw seven heavenly bodies. The Sun, Moon, Mercury, Mars Venus, Jupiter, and Saturn and seven faceless figures floated with her in space. Upon waking from the vision, this was all she could remember as she tells her husband and asks him what significance did he think this vision had. Edward Mann just stares at her.

Jolene Mann was just slightly over five feet in height. She had a head full of massive red curls that surrounded her porcelain complexion. She seemed to have a knack in applying her makeup to highlight her rather small, amber eyes. She once told her husband she wore blush to give the appearance of better bone structure than she was born with when he had informed her that she really didn't need it. Only Jolene disagreed and thought the results presented her at her best. And now as he tried to appear serious in front of her dancing curls and beautiful face, he knew he couldn't. As Jolene looks back, she watches as the first hint of a smile appears and then unable to hold it back, he starts laughing. Confused, Jolene frowns, but then joins him.

It was after breakfast that day that they noticed the activity at the empty house next door. Edward was the serious type, a lawyer by trade. He joined his wife as she stood staring out the window, his jet-black hair with an early touch of gray at the temples contrasted her mane of unruly curls. He turned with a question on his lips. "Yes, Edward, someone bought the house next door. I think I'll fix something, and we can take it over to them this evening. Edward squeezed his wife and kissed the top of her head before heading out to his car.

Curiosity was brewing on the other side of the Ceps-Log's new home too. Ted and Nan Safer watched the new neighbors moving in. Nan, her neatly coifed gray hair turned her sparkling blue eyes toward her husband Ted. Ted and Nan were the elderly couple on the other side of the Log's home. Ted was in his sixties and his wife shortly behind him. They were of the age of the grandparents; May and Neves and squinted out, hoping that the new occupants would be close to their age. Ted had a thick head of white hair topping his weather-beaten face. Deep creases gave character to his face and he was known as the most understanding and caring person that anyone could ever know.

All of this was happening around them, but neither Nola nor Ned had noticed that morning as she rushed about getting breakfast for her husband before sending him out the door. She moved quietly, not wanting to wake her parents who usually rose early but were tired out by the moving day activity.

The day went by fast as Nola and her mother went to get groceries and then go for a drive around the neighborhood. It felt strange to have her own car and a nice one at that. Ned had insisted that she have a car as well so that she could get mobile during the day while he worked. They located a deli, a dry cleaner, and a butcher shop before turning into a plaza known as I-Square just doors from their home. Several time people waved at them and May would turn toward her mother and smile. People were indeed friendly.

When they arrived back home, Neves was up and sitting at the kitchen table with a cup of coffee. May and Nola joined him. Later Nola went back to unpacking and washing clothes and May did the same.

They didn't have to speak to know what to do. Even though there was a kitchen in their quarters, May knew that Nola would want them to cook and eat together so they went about checking the cabinets and trying to decide on what to have for dinner. They were still in the process when Ned returned home. They could pinpoint the minute he opened the door as there was a light breeze entering with him and they stopped what they were doing. May looked at Nola who was staring at her, paused in getting things out for dinner. "No need." They said in the same breath, frowned and turned to face Ned.

Minutes later the doorbell rang, and Ned turned around and went to answer it. Standing on the stoop was a bubbly redheaded woman and a somber looking man carrying a covered dish.

"Hello neighbors. We're Jolene and Edward Mann. We live over there. Jolene turned and pointed to the house on the right side of theirs."

"Please come in. Come in and meet the family."

They were in the midst of introductions when the doorbell rang again. Ned excused himself and went to answer it. This time there was an older couple standing on the stoop. Both had gray hair and twinkling eyes.

"Hello, we are Ted and Nan Safer. We live in the house next door to you. This time, Nan, her gray hair swinging as she turned to point to the house on the left of theirs.

"Please join us," Ned said as he moved aside. Spotting the other neighbors, they moved quickly into the room. "Hi, neighbors they said, greeting Jolene and Edward. "Looks like we all had the same idea. Each had brought food. Ned guided them all into the kitchen where each member of the family introduced themselves. Nan and Jolene went over to help Nola and May set the table and put out the food. There was baked lasagna, and a chicken and rice dish. Nola and May got out the fixings for a salad and a loaf of bread. They decided to set up dinner in the dining room so they could all fit in. "I was wondering about the size of this room and if we would really need it, but now I'm glad it is here. Thank you all for your kindness."

By the end of the evening they felt like best friends. Jolene told Nola she would take her around to meet the neighbors, while Nan made plans with May.

Later at the door as they were seeing their guests out, Jolene hugged Nola, withdrew quickly, and gave her a puzzled smile. Nola smiled back feeling a closeness to this woman who she had just met. Something had passed between them during that hug, but as usual, Nola dismissed it.

CHAPTER 9

Things Are Changing

Months pass and Nola is busy putting away cereal from the twins' breakfast when her husband joins her. She fixes him a cup of coffee and Ned says, "Thanks" before sitting down at the island. Several minutes later, May joined them in the kitchen and accepted the cup of coffee Nola offered her.

The silence dragged on until May spoke. "Okay, I'll say it. Doesn't anyone want to address the elephant in the room?"

Trying to look puzzled, Nola gave May a raised eyebrow in response.

"Okay, how long did we live in our homes in Salem, New Jersey?"

"A long time."

"Right. And, how many drop ins did we have over the years?"

It's quiet again with no one wanting to say the obvious.

"I'll say it! None! Not one person ever dropped in. This place is no different, yet our neighbors come to welcome us and are constantly stopping by. Is that a coincidence, you think?" May meditates before letting it

46

all out. "I think, no, I know, something is happening. I don't know if it's a good thing or a bad thing, but something is happening. I know you know what I am talking about Nola. I think you felt it too."

May gets up and goes over to her daughter. She grabs hold of her shoulders to try and turn her around. During the motion, they are taken away together in a vision.

They stand in a dilapidated room with peeling paint and debris everywhere. Hanging on to each other they move carefully across the littered floor to stare out the grimy window. They are inside the halls of a crumbling building. Fear takes hold as they move out into the darkness of the hallway, trying to find a way out. The hall seems endless as they try not to look inside the doorways they pass, hearing cries and shrieks as they hurry along, sensing people watching them as they go. Then up ahead a figure appears, and May moves forward, only to feel Nola pulling her back. "No," her daughter yells, repeatedly. And just like that they are back in the kitchen, with both Neves and Ned staring at them.

Neves is the first to react. He gets up and goes around the island to hug May who is shivering. "You're all right baby. You're all right," he says comforting. Ned just sits staring not knowing what to do When he sees his wife crumbling into a chair, he snaps out of it and goes to her. He holds her silently waiting for what he doesn't know. Finally, Neves speaks. He moves over beside Ned and asks, "Don't you two think it's time to fill Ned in?" May and Nola lift their heads and stares at Ned seeing the confusion on his face.

Ned looks over at Neves, afraid to look directly at his wife. There is an uncomfortable silence as he waits for

47

someone to speak. Just when he thinks he can't wait any longer, Nola begins. "Ned, remember that night when our babies were conceived? I know it was that night and I think you know it too. That time you were part of what I call my visions. You participated in it and because you were able to, it means somehow you are connected with us, beyond just being married to me."

"I don't understand."

"Well, we don't understand it all." Nola looks at her father and then her mother. All we know is that there is something between us that goes deep; something that seems to mean we are to do something together, maybe."

"I don't..."

"You can't understand when we don't understand either. For a long time, we refused to talk about it or even think it was happening, but ever since I noticed something in our daughter, I decided we can no longer ignore it. We need to start trying to understand. That is when mom and I spoke about our visions...yes, my mother has them too. We talked to Neves and now I'm glad we did. This time is the first time that my mother and I shared a vision together."

"What? You mean our Joy? What did you notice with Joy?"

"Joy is having visions too, but hers are being shared with people outside the family. She was playing with Jennifer Mann the other day and when they grabbed hands to swing around, they both see something in the distance, something that frightens them so bad that Joy said they couldn't move or breathe. At first Joy is afraid to reveal that she has seen something that she knows is not real, but when Jennifer snatches her hands away, Joy realizes that she has seen something too. She asks Jennifer what she saw, but Jennifer doesn't respond. She backs away from Joy already thinking that what just happened was because

48

of Joy, so she runs home. She tries to tell her mother what has happened, but she can't get the words out except to say she doesn't want to play with Joy anymore. As a result, Jolene, being the friend that she has become, calls me, and tells me what has happened. It is then that she mentions that she felt something go between us on that first evening we met; something she couldn't explain."

Ned is having trouble following the conversation as he sits there listening. He must admit to himself that he had felt something strange was happening. Clearing his throat, he spoke. "Has it all just started since...since I married Nola?"

"No, it's been going on since May gave birth to Nola..." Neves paused realizing that to be true. Yes, since the birth of Nola, exactly. I guess it had a lot to do with why we didn't socialize much because we didn't want anyone to think May or Nola was strange. But we did realize early on that it was affecting Nola and we didn't know what to do so we eventually found and contacted Dr. Memer. It was like he fell in our path. One minute we were walking down the sidewalk saying that we needed to get Nola some help and then this man walks by, his shoulder brushes against me. He stops, looks at me to apologize but then asks what did I say. From there the conversation got weird, but it ended up that he was a psychologist and had an office just up the street. We ended up following him there and once in his office, we shared our need for someone like him to help with our daughter. He told us his name was Dr. Reb Memer and he would try to help Nola. He also asked if May would like to talk with him, but having kept it silent for so long, she declined."

"You see, May's visions were less frequent, but she felt Nola's. I mean she knew Nola was having a vision, but she wasn't a part of them. Nola had visions on her own."

When Neves stopped talking, Ned ran his fingers through his hair, trying to understand all that he had heard. Finally, he can speak. "So, just now, what exactly happened?"

Nola looked up and begin sharing as best she can, what May and her experienced. She tried to be open and not worry about how weird it sounded as she shared the vision. It was hard to do this with the family since the only one she had ever talked to about the visions was Dr. Memer. Dr. Memer knew she wasn't crazy, but she couldn't be sure of that with anyone else. When Nola finished, she looked up at Ned who was still standing by her chair.

"You never have to worry about telling me anything, sweetie. I know you and I love you deeply. I love all of you," he added looking around the room. Nola stood and hugged him close. When she let him go, Ned continued, "I think from what you are saying that this has always been something that happened between Nola and May. Only now you are seeing others become part of the visions and that to mean that whatever is being prophesized by these visions is getting closer to a conclusion. That's the only thing that makes sense to me, too."

Ned paused before adding, "I think you are right. I feel something is different now."

While they talked, May Cep told of some visions of the past that had been so bad that she needed Neves to keep her sane. Ned asked if Dr. Memer knew of this and all three shook their heads.

Over another cup of coffee, Ned asks Nola what visions she has shared with Dr. Memer.

Nola concentrates for a bit and then begins to tell him one. She tells him about the time she was getting ready for bed at her father's house. As she undressed, she thought she heard her mother's footsteps near the door. But when she opened it, the corridor outside was empty. She looked along the hallway and there, standing silently at the head of the stairs she saw a woman in a long, black dress, holding a handkerchief to her face. After a few seconds the woman descended the stairs. The hall light went out and she saw no more. During the next seven years the phantom in black was seen quite frequently and she began to accept it almost as part of the family. On one occasion she watched it for half an hour, then touched by the figure's obvious distress, tried to speak to it. She received no reply, and it vanished, its head pathetically bowed.

Dinner could be an unnerving affair for Nola due to the figure's appearing to her while remaining invisible to the others. Sometimes it would suddenly stand between two guests who were oblivious of its presence and would go on gaily chatting. Try as she might, Nola was unable to prevent a certain flagging in her own conversations. Dr. Memer in trying to understand had accounted this to maybe a mistress of the previous owners of the house.

She saw the lady again in the new home. She awoke one night to see a woman silhouetted against her bedroom window. She was dressed in black with her head bowed and she appeared to be sobbing quietly into a handkerchief held to her face. When she cried in alarm, the figure vanished. Often now she would see her flitting down the staircase or wandering through the rooms, weeping piteously into her handkerchief. Obviously, time had not assuaged her grief; but why she should have changed locations was a mystery because she had seen this woman originally in her parent's home in Salem, New Jersey.

CHAPTER 10

Sharing It All

From that point on, every spare moment that Ned had he and Neves tried to figure out what was happening with the Cep women. Neves told him that Enolai had been born with a veil and what that exactly meant, and Ned had a feeling that it did play a role in all that was happening. But that was just the surface. There was way more to it than that. With Nola's permission, they went to see Dr. Memer and together they talked about what each of them knew, hoping to find the underlying cause of it.

This would be the most eye-opening conversation that Dr. Memer had in understanding Nola for she, nor her mother shared more than a coating of their visions and feelings. It had been the same for Neves and Ned until their wives had finally let them in. Hopefully it wasn't too late to help them. Ned began the conversation and not holding anything back did his best to describe the night he knows that the twins were conceived. He ignored the expressions that appeared during his confession because in his heart he knew it was time to be open and honest. He even referred to what had encouraged him on several occasions to call Dr. Memer concerning a spell that Nola had that scared him. He ended by expressing a truth that he hadn't wanted to believe. It was the union of him and Nola that made everything attainable. When Dr. Memer asked what that meant he said. "Whatever Nola or I want or desire, it comes to be for not only us, but for our family."

Neves was a little skeptical about sharing all he knew, but with a little encouragement from his son-in-law he opened up sharing May's spells and the fact that she too was born with a veil. Not only that but all the Ceps women were born in the seventh month, on the seventh day and the seventh hour. He would hesitate during his recitation and would have to be spurred on because of all of them, he knew the most important details that may come in handy. Dr. Memer was especially alert when he shared the fact that May refused to celebrate her birthday from the age of seven because that was when she felt a change in her that in her mind made her different. He had witnessed firsthand the change in Enolai when she turned seven. That bright happy child he had known, just disappeared.

When it was Dr. Memer's turn he had something to share that neither of the husband's had known. He told them about the two hooded figures and the crying lady, letting them know that May nor Nola were able to tell him much about them except they don't speak and they come together with the one in white robes ahead of the one in black robes. Nola had said they aren't even sure half the time of what the spirits look like or which is the 'good' of the two, which was the first instance she actually remembered there being two different spirits in her visions. He told Ned that like him, Nola sensed that the power of them together was where their "fortune" laid and what brings about all their spoken or thought of desires.

From that point on as years passed the men continue to meet and talk, sharing even the most personal details to help them to discover what needs to be done. Not only the men, but the Cep women find it easier to share what is happening with their husbands and with each other. All of them keep a watchful eye on Joy.

Nola now, more comfortable with what she experiences, talks to Joy, hoping she will bare her soul and not suffer through it alone. Yet, she understands her need to hide it. Thus, Nola does not push, only lets her know she is there for her.

As the years progressed, Joy knew that what was happening to her was not the immature mind of a child playing tricks on her. Many times, she wanted to share what was happening with Jonathan, but she shied away from telling him just as she did with her parents, afraid they wouldn't understand. As she struggles alone, it eventually becomes unbearable as the visions take over most of her waking life. It happened while in school, or even just walking around the yard. No place was safe from the visions and the power of them became more real each day. And then it happened. No longer was only she a part of the vision. It was she and her mother together, captured in the visions.

When this starts happening, Nola, always hesitant about talking about her visions because she didn't want to influence Joy in that way, now was there beside her, or so it would seem. But Nola didn't accept that. She at first forced her mind to believe that she manifested Joy in the visions.

Joy knew better. As this union began, Joy knew that they were sharing the visions and that their physical contact would pull them out of the visions and then something happens to change that.

Joy and Nola are picking up a few items chatting about their day. They both are pushing the cart together with hands side by side on the handle. Their free hand stretches out to pull needed items from the shelf. It's a game to see who can reach the shelf without moving their other hand. The aisles are narrow so it's easy at first, then Joy reaches for the cereal and the display falls, knocking several boxes to the floor. Not thinking, she releases the cart handle to stoop and pick up the boxes. Nola is on the verge of laughing and telling Joy she's won, but only the laughter comes out, then stops. Joy looks up at her mom to say something and stops as the grocery store attendant, Sara Chambers hurries toward them.

Sara Chambers is a pleasant, middle aged woman who is always friendly and helpful to the customers. Hearing the boxes fall she has come to help and is at the head of the aisle when it seems like dirt or something blows into her eyes. Joy and Nola who are several feet away see Sara, but only for a minute before they are thrown into a visional journey.

Joy is running through a forest thick with trees and underbrush calling and calling for Nola. Nola is frantically running in the opposite side of the woods and yelling for Joy, but neither can hear the calls of the other. They run and run toward each other, but not hearing. Then suddenly there is a condensation of a soft blue smoke, sort of like the sky falling in amongst the trees. When the smoke lifts, the forest is gone, and they are in a field of daisies and see each other and hear each other calling. They finally are close enough to touch and they reach out their hands to each other and hold on tightly.

Then they are back in the store. They see Sara Chambers as she approaches, wiping her eyes and telling them not to worry about the knocked over display, a stock boy will take care of it for them. And with that, Joy and Nola prepare to leave the store, neither speaking to the other about having shared the vision.

Joy began having trouble sleeping and would toss and turn all through the night. The next morning, she was zombie-like, bumping into things and responding oddly to questions asked of her. It was then that Nola decided it was time to have her see Dr. Memer.

At first Joy balked at the idea, telling her mother it would put a black mark on her record if anyone found out she was seeing a psychiatrist. "Mom, I have enough trouble getting along without that hanging over my head!"

Nola saw that as her opening. "Joy, baby, I know you are having visions. I have them too and so does your grandmother. Just like you, we kept them to ourselves, but now we can see we can't do that any longer. It is not going to stop going down the line of Ceps women until we do something about it. Dr. Memer doesn't have all the answers, but he has helped me to accept the visions and each piece of information I share, helps him to understand and, maybe be able to put it all together so that he can help in eliminating them."

Eventually, Joy gave in and went to see Dr. Memer. Eventually, just like her mother, Joy begins to look forward to the comfort of talking with him.

Session after session, Dr. Memer listens and takes notes, realizing that he is hearing the same things from Nola. He keeps it to himself until it becomes clear to him, he must tell them. On that day he tells Joy that he wants to have a session with her and her mother. There is something he needs to share with them both. Joy thinks it is a good idea and as she stands to leave, she turns back around and faces the doctor. "Do you think that whatever it is that happens is going to kill us in the end?"

Shocked by her question, Dr. Memer quickly responds. "No, definitely not. I think it's a purpose you are to perform." With that they parted ways.

Later at home, Joy told her mother that at her next appointment, Dr. Memer wanted them both in attendance. Adding that he has something to share with them both.

56

After all these years, Nola feels confident that he is finally getting somewhere beyond keeping her sane. Maybe he can explain it all since he knows everything.

That evening they are expecting the Manns over for dinner. As Joy helps set the table, Nola hears her mother prattling about in the kitchen. She goes to see what the fuss is about and finds May staring out the window.

"Mom, what's wrong." May turns around slowly to face her daughter. "I'll tell you what's wrong. Everything. I feel it in my bones. And, you know what, I think that this Jolene and Edward Mann have something to do with it." Reading Nola's expression, May adds, "Don't look at me like that. I like the Mann's, but something, can't put my finger on it, something is going to happen. Mark my words!"

In a soothing tone Nola tries to calm her mother down. "Here, let me help you finish in here. Joy has the table set." Just then the doorbell rings. Nola hears Ned talking to their guest. She puts her arm around her mother's shoulders and together they walk into welcome Jolene and Ed.

Never at a loss for dialogue, the two families sit down, and conversations flow easily between them. Only May adds nothing to the talk, but that's not odd. May and Neves are closer to the Safers and see very little of the Manns who spend more time with Nola and Ned. Now as she brings forks full of food to her mouth, she watches them closely. When there is an opening in the conversation, May looks up and somewhat stiltedly says, "By the way Jolene, I haven't seen Jennifer in a while. Is she all right?"

Jolene chokes on her food, takes a sip of water and forces a smile. "Yes, she's fine. She's been busy is all."

With dinner out of the way, Jolene helps Nola clean the table and they join the rest of the family in the den for drinks.

"Nola, did I tell you that Rochester has some of the most haunted places?" Nola, who has been pouring the wine, pauses and tilts her head to the side. "No, you didn't."

"Well, the famous ones, most of which have been done as episodes on the Sci-Fi channel and movies are, George Eastman Museum on East Avenue, The Valentown Museum in Victor, New York, but the most famous one in my estimation is Durand Eastman Park right here in Irondequoit. Jolene bites her lip as she tries to remember. Oh yes, there is also the Auditorium Theater on East Main Street, downtown. Then there's the Holy Sepulchre Cemetery on Lake Avenue in Greece. No surprise there, huh.

Nola finishes pouring the drinks and sits down beside Jolene. "Well, that's quite a few hauntings…"

"Oh, but that's not all." Jolene tosses her red curls and then taking her hands, she pushes them back into shape. "Okay, now, there's Main Street Armory also on East Main Street, The Rush Rhees Library on the University of Rochester on Library Road. Then there's the Rochester Public Library on South Avenue downtown. Taking a finger Jolene taps her chin. "Oh, yes, surprise, surprise. There's the abandoned Rochester Psychiatric Center on Elmwood Avenue." Jolene leans back, a pleased expression on her face.

There is silence while they all take it in. "Is that it?" May inquires.

"That's the ones I know. I'm sure there are others, but these are the most famous."

"What do you mean they were on the Sci-Fi Channel?"

Jolene sits on the edge of her seat, takes a sip of wine, and looks at Nola. "Just that, they sent a crew down to inspect the buildings and the final declaration was that they are haunted. The crew saw, heard, or experienced paranormal activity. What do you think of that?"

"I think that's interesting. How do you know all this, Jolene?"

"Well, I have an interest in haunted places. I believe that places and some people are haunted."

Nola clears her throat. "Do you see things or feel thing."

Jolene looks innocently at Nola as she says, "I sense things."

The conversation is getting uncomfortable, so Nola thinks fast and says, "You said that the most famous haunting is at Durand Eastman Park?"

"Yes, it is. It's quite a story."

"Tell us, please."

Jolene has the attention of everyone in the room as she begins her tale.

"Let me first paint the picture of Durand for you. It's a peaceful and picturesque location on Lake Ontario. The waters are usually calm and reflective as if nothing, but wonderful things happen there."

"Sorry, Jolene, wait a minute. Does anyone want another beer or more wine?"

"Yes, Nola, please." While Nola goes about refreshing drinks, May follows her with snacks and whispers in Nola's ear. "This is going to be a long night." Nola smiles and returns to her seat.

Once everyone is seated, Jolene starts again. "There are two small lakes that run off Lake Ontario and they are named Durand and Eastman; the two men who donated the land for the park. It is said that in the early

59

1900s Dr. Henry S. Durand owned a summer camp here and was friends with George Eastman. One day the men decided that there was a need for a public park near the water so the common citizen would have rights to nearly a mile of public beach and adjacent lands on the Lake's shoreline. Not ones to sit back, they began buying up several farms along the Durand property and when they had a sizable amount of acreage, they offered the land to the City of Rochester. That was sometime in 1907 and the result was a tract of land of about 484 acres situate in the Town of Irondequoit on Lake Ontario,". A year later the land was transferred to the city, and on May 22, 1909, Durand Eastman Park was formally dedicated."

Jolene takes a sip of her wine. "Okay, to adlib a little, I think that for a man like Dr. Durand to just give up his summer camp in Irondequoit that abutted Lake Ontario willingly, I have to believe Dr. Durand knew something was not quite right. Maybe something terrifying…"

"Durand-Eastman had to be highly engineered as it was a swampy, almost tree-less, farmland area. And here's where the story begins. According to legend, the troubled spirit of a farmer's wife still roams the area. The woman's name is Eelissa, who has been wandering this area since the early 1800s in search of someone who did her wrong. Through generations, pieces of the story have been lost and there are now a few different versions."

Jolene gets up and stretches as she goes to fill her wine glass. She smiles at her captive audience before sitting and continuing her tale. By now, Joy and Jonathan have joined the group in the den to listen to the tale.

"Like I said, there are several versions. In one, Eelissa was the victim of an abusive husband who left her for another woman. Blinded by jealousy, she kills them both. The ending result is that her ghost stalks the roads of the park. She mistakenly sees any unfortunate young

60

lovers in cars as her husband and his mistress whom she seeks to slay repeatedly. She is doomed to re-enact her crime with fresh victims over the centuries."

"A ghost that kills?"

"No, no, I don't think she has killed anyone, only appears to them."

Again, Jolene pauses as if trying to heighten the telling of the tale. "In other versions of the story, Eelissa searches for her long-lost teenage daughter. It is assumed that the daughter either ran away with a boy, or she was abducted by another local farmer. In the end her daughter is discovered to have been raped and murdered."

"No matter which is true, in either case, Eelissa has a mistrust of any men. She discouraged her young daughter from socializing with boys. And her ghost is now said to attack any man she encounters."

"She physically attacks them?"

"It's only what I've heard, but never has it been reported that someone was attacked by what she has become known as the Lady in White."

Jolene leans back satisfied with her story. "Jolene, do you know what the ghost looks like. I mean, what shape does it take."

Jolene is thoughtful. "Eelissa's ghost takes various forms and goes by a few different nicknames… Some call her The Lady in White, or The White Lady, and Lady of the Lake. Sometimes she appears as a thin, ugly old woman, who walks along the shores of Lake Ontario with a pair of dogs. Others see her as a youthful spirit who coalesces from the mists of Durand Lake."

It's quiet as the group takes in the story. Ned wonders how much is true, while Nola wants to see for herself.

CHAPTER 11

The Vision

After seeing their guests off, Nola has an uneasy feeling that she cannot shake. As she prepares for bed, she decides to tell Ned about her feeling, but when she enters the bedroom, he is fast asleep. With a shrug of her shoulders, she climbs in next to him and moves over to give him a peck on the cheek before pulling the covers up and turning on her side. Several hours later she is still wide awake and gives up trying to sleep.

Joy is restless and finally gets up to go to the kitchen. She is surprised when she finds on entering the kitchen that her mom, Nola is already there. At first, she stands in the doorway and watches her mother. Then she strolls over and before going to sit on one of the chairs at the kitchen table, she lightly touches her mother's shoulder to let her know she is there. The touch sends them off on another journey.

They are in a damp, dark, foreboding room of a large house with high ceilings. The room has the bare necessities of furnishings. From the few furnishings they surmise that they are in a living room of some sort. Nola is in front of Joy. Joy, behind her mother, clings to her arm as they look around the room, looking for a way out. They notice that there are no doors anywhere. It is like the room is shut off from the rest of the house. Driven by the same desire to find a way to leave this room, Joy and Nola look frantically around. There are no windows either. Almost instantaneously their eyes are drawn to the vocal point of the room. The fireplace. The fireplace is very large and made of stone. The mantle above the fireplace holds only one object, a picture. Nola and Joy move closer trying to see the picture. Closer they move until finally they can see it clearly. It seems strange, but it is no doubt a picture of May Ceps on the mantle in this strange room. They move closer. As they do, all the time looking up at the picture, the picture begins to change. Now it is a picture of Jolene Mann. The picture keeps changing as they draw closer from first May and then Jolene Mann. When they are right up to the hearth of the fireplace, the picture changes one more time. First it is a picture of both women and as they stare unbelieving, it becomes a picture of both May and Jolene together for a short time before the blood starts spurting out of their eyes, their mouths, their ears. Nola doesn't even think what she is doing next as she enters the fireplace with Joy still clinging to her arm. And then they are back in the kitchen of their home.

Joy stares at her mother, looking for any hint that she knows what has just happened and she sees it in her eyes. "Mom, what was that?"

"I'm not sure. Did you see a pic…"

"Yes, I did. What does it mean?"

"I'm sorry, Joy, but I have no idea. I think we need to write it down so that we can ask Dr. Memer about it."

"Have you ever had a vision about family before?"

"No, Never."

63

Neither one went back to bed that night. Instead they sat in the kitchen drinking coffee and waiting for the rest of the family to join them. This was not right, Nola thought to herself. Why would they have a vision about May and Jolene Mann. It didn't make sense. As Nola thought about it, she decided that she would go see Jolene and maybe something she did or said would help her figure this out. The visions that were about no one close to them were scary enough, but this one made her blood boil. Something was happening and they needed to find out what.

As Nola went about getting ready for the day, she had made her decision. She was going to give Jolene a call and see if she would take a tour with her to the so-called haunted places in the vicinity. Maybe it had nothing to do with them, but more with the city itself having such a vibe and her being open to it.

Later that day when she called, Jolene was excited. She said there wasn't a tour per se, but they could drive to the sites and probably find information. That along with what she already knew would give her a good bit of haunting history.

Nola told Joy what her plans were for the day but cautioned her not to tell her father or her brother. Joy swore she wouldn't. With that, Nola got ready, glad that Jolene hadn't insisted on going at night. Nola only wanted to see the locations and hear the tales, not witness them for herself.

At Jolene's insistence, they would be starting in the downtown area and saving Durand Eastman for last. When Jolene pulled into the drive, Nola was ready. She climbs in the car and sees a smiling Jolene. "Let's find us some ghost!"

Nola wanted to tell her about her vision, but held back, thinking maybe later. Maybe something would help her understand what happened. She already knew that Jolene had felt something when they had hugged that first day they met. She didn't want to scare her newfound friend away so she best keep it as normal as possible.

Our first stop is at the George Eastman Museum, the home of George Eastman. The mansion is breathtaking in size and design. As we approach the doors, Jolene says that the man was an entrepreneur, a philanthropist, and the pioneer of photography and motion picture film.

I ask about his life and she told me that the family moved to Rochester in 1860 and shortly thereafter his father died leaving them short of income, so George left school when he was 14 to support his mother and his two sisters.

"When he was 23, he took a camera on vacation and thought the equipment too bulky and awkward for use. That and the cost to develop the film led him to seek a way to better the product. In three years, he did and with financial backing he was able to start his company, changing the photographic world forever."

"I like that story, but it doesn't seem to warrant there being any ghost in the house."

"Well, when I tell you that on March 14, 1932, George Eastman committed suicide by shooting himself in the heart. The cause was a painful and degenerative spine disease which made it difficult for him to function normally. He left a suicide note which read "My work is done – why wait?"

"The ghost is nothing to be afraid of here. It's a peaceful ghost," Nola says as they walk through the hallways and up and down the stairs feeling and seeing nothing out of the ordinary.

They pause once more hoping to feel or see something. "Well, no action here. Okay, on to the next." Nola can't hold back a chuckle as Jolene swings her curls walking quickly and smiling over her shoulder.

The next stop is The Auditorium Theatre which was originally built in 1928 as a Masonic Temple. Broadway shows come to the venue, considered to be one of the most haunted locations in Rochester. We find out no more than Jolene tells me. There are several ghosts that have been spotted in the theatre including an elderly gentleman and a man in a red coat. The apparition of the older man hangs around backstage and has been known to move some things around from time to time. The apparition with the red coat only ever appears in the lobby and it is often after hours. Some have reported hearing strange voices inside the theatre. For us there is nothing to see or hear except the sounds of the living. We move on.

We drive over to take a short look inside The Main Street Armory and find a pamphlet telling us it dates back to around 1905 when it was built by the United States Army with the intention of using it to train and process soldiers joining up for the first time. It was still in use in 1990 but thereafter was vacant for several years. In the mid-2000s it opened as a live music venue. People who went to hear the music reported seeing apparitions in old style uniforms.

As we climb back in the car Nola turn to Jolene. "This is interesting even if there are no ghost." Jolene laughs. "What do you expect. It's early afternoon. Ghost don't come out until night."

Turning her face toward the car window, Nola silently whispers, "That's what you think."

"What do you say we stop for the day, grab some lunch and head home. We can do the rest tomorrow."

"Sounds good. I am hungry."

66

We talk about the places we have seen. Jolene tells me that once, not long ago, she thought she had seen something when she had attended a production at the Auditorium Theater. She had been standing in the lobby with her husband during the intermission and she saw, no saw through, a man standing just three feet away. When she turned to tell Edward, out of the corner of her eye, she saw the figure disappear.

"You are sensitive to this sort of thing?"

"Yes, I am. I think you know that already."

Nola didn't respond. The two women drove home enjoying the scenery. "I can't get over so many trees," Nola said. "It's like we are living in a forest!"

In no time they were back, pulling into Nola's driveway. "Come on in and I'll fix us something cold to drink?"

"No," Jolene replied. "Let me take a rain check. I need to feed my family and rest up to listen to them tell me about their day. She looked at Nola and smiled. "I'm sure ours was better."

Before parting, they made plans for the next day.

"If anything, Nola, you are becoming familiar with the city."

"Yes, that I am."

Over dinner that evening Nola shared what she had seen with Jolene. And when the obvious question came, she replied, "No, we didn't see or sense any spirits."

The following day was more of the same. Jolene took Nola to The Rush Rhees Library in the University of Rochester on Library Road. Opened in 1930 the library is said to be haunted by the ghost of a construction worker who died after a serious fall while the library was being built in 1929.

They next went to the Rochester Public Library, said to be haunted by the spirit of a young woman who is believed to have drowned when she fell into a nearby aqueduct. Her body was swept away and became wedged in a tunnel that runs under the library. Sightings have been of her wandering among the stacks. Another spirit, that of a former librarian called Frank died from a heart attack while on duty at the library. Their presence is reported by unexplained noises including moans and phantom footsteps or shadowy figures peeking around the stacks. They watch a clip from security footage showing a heavy door opening and closing when there was nobody in the building.

That ended their tours for the day and Jolene informed Nola that she was busy the rest of the week, but they could go again in the middle of the following week. That was fine with Nola.

Having gathered a bunch of pamphlets during their trips, Nola spent the next few days looking up as much information as she could about the haunted places in Rochester and tried to find events by people who were experiencing or seeing anything weird. She couldn't find much of interest that even came close to what had happened to her.

CHAPTER 12

Jonathan Goes Missing

It was Ned who suggested that it might be fun to spend the day at the beach during the upcoming weekend. He had driven down by Durand Eastman with a friend from work and thought it would be a great place to have a picnic and watch the boats coming and going. "Too bad we don't have small kids. They have a merry-go-round there too."

Nola told him it sounded like fun. So that evening at dinner they presented the mini vacation idea to the family. Everyone was in, for different reasons, of that Nola was sure.

That weekend was beautiful. They called to see if Jolene and her kids wanted to join them. Even with her hand over the phone, she heard Jennifer in the background say, "No way." When Jolene came back on the phone, she said that everyone was otherwise involved, but thanked her for the invite.

Patiently they waited for everyone to gather their things and once each member of the family emerged and climbed into the van, Nola slid in the passenger seat and Ned moved into the driver's seat. They backed out of the driveway and continue to Kings Hwy S to Lake Shore

Blvd. In less than ten minutes they arrived at their destination.

It seemed like everyone in town had the same idea as they pulled into the crowded parking lot and looked out at the beach that was filled with sunbathers and lots of folks walking along the boardwalk.

"It's too crowded," Nola said to Ned.

"Yes, here it is, but not where we are headed."

Ned opened the hatch and soon had their picnic basket swinging on his arm. Nola joined him, reached in, and got out the umbrella, while Joy and Jonathan grabbed the beach chairs and cooler. May and Neves gathered the blanket and towels and after a quick check to make sure they had everything, they followed Ned.

It took a while to find a place in the Durand area, near the Durand and Eastman Lakes where it was less crowded, but they did.

They set about setting up the chairs and spreading the blanket. May took out her book that she had in her beach bag and Nola did the same. They watched Joy and Jonathan as they surveyed the area for friends and seeing none, moved out a bit and threw a frisbee back and forth.

They had been at it for at least an hour when May and Nola gather the fixings for the food which most had been prepared ahead of time so that everyone could eat at will.

Jonathan and Joy announce they were going for a walk down one of the trails. "Kids, take your cell phones, please."

"No worries, we've got them."

Nola then watch as they went on their way.

May is the first to speak. "So, how was the tour of the haunted places, really?"

Nola laughs. "Mom, just like I said. We didn't see or hear anything strange at all. The places were beautiful and historic. I really enjoyed seeing them. If you want to go sometime, I will take you."

"No, that's all right. I am not up for hunting for strange things."

They both laugh.

It felt good to clear their minds and relax. With the sound of the waves and the heat of the sun, it is a warm balmy day and they spend most of their time sitting in their beach chairs, reading. When Joy and Jonathan return from their walk along the trail, Jonathan sees some friends near the water and goes to join them.

Joy stays on the beach with her mother while Ned and Neves get up to go off to find the golf course. A breeze blows up and sand is deposited in Neves and Ned's eyes. Joy and Nola lift their hands to protect their eyes. There hands brush each other on their way up and that is enough to start the vision.

They see a lady dressed in white walking on top of the water. She heads toward Jonathan who is not aware of her. Once she is near him, she begins talking to him, but Joy and Nola are too far away to hear what is being said. They see Jonathan nod his head, saying yes to her and he grabs the lady's hand. Paralyzed with fright they realize that the lady is taking Jonathan away. Joy automatically reaches out to Nola as she says we must stop her, she has Jonathan. They make contact and the vision disappears.

They turn to Ned who is in the midst of rubbing the sand out of his eyes. He lowers his hand and smiles over at them, then sees the panic expression on their faces before they turn and head toward the water. Ned barely heard what they say as he looks out at the water and the quick moving figures headed in that direction. He hears himself say, "Where is Jonathan?" He tries to remain calm as he runs down to the water and stares up and down the beach, but he can't find his son.

"Where did Jonathan go?"

He can hear the panic in her voice as Nola says, "She took him. She took Jonathan."

He doesn't ask anything more as Nola and Joy stand beside him. Soon others ask what's wrong and Nola gasps, "She took Jonathan."

People rush about trying to find him. They dive into the water to see if he is there, while others walk up and down the beach. Several people pull out their cells and dial 911. Soon the peaceful atmosphere is filled with activity, but Jonathan is never found.

This event leaves the Ceps family shaken. They answer questions and listen to the promises to keep looking until they find him, but Nola and Joy know they never will. When they finally gather their things and leave, Nola leans into Ned and says, "Joy and I have something to tell you when we get home."

Ned doesn't question but instead gets everything loaded and takes the family home. Once in the confides of their living room, the family sits down together and listens as Joy and Nola tells them what they saw.

Silence fills the room until finally May speaks. "I told you. I tried to warn you that this would happen."

"Mom, the Manns had nothing to do with this. They weren't even there.

"Sure," May replies.

Ned has been thinking and finally he says, "Nola, Joy, you need to call Dr. Memer. You need to tell him about the vision you had just before Jonathan disappeared.

CHAPTER 13

Death of Jolene Manns

Jolene sat before her computer searching restlessly for something. She didn't know what, but something that would help explain what was happening with the Ceps family. That first time she hugged Nola, she felt as though there was a connection between them and in that feeling was the sense that not only was Nola hiding something, but whatever it was she hid, it was becoming stronger and dangerous to her and her family.

As she puzzled over it, she came to one conclusion and that was she had a role to play. It was important that she figure out what to do to help her. If only Nola would talk to her about it.

Night after night she told herself she needed to talk to Nola and maybe they could figure it out together, but Nola ignored every opportunity to share. The visits to the haunted places had been to give a signal that she had an ideal what was bothering her. The mention of her being sensitive to things, was another, but Nola would not speak freely, even though she sensed that she liked her and considered her a friend.

Hearing a noise in the kitchen, Jolene looked at the time on the bottom of the screen. It was after midnight. A smile appeared on her face, as she fondly thought, Edward must be looking for a snack.

Jolene shut down the internet and rubbing the back of her neck, headed toward the kitchen. The house was silent and dark as she felt her way until the glow of the night light in the dining room helped light her path toward the island in the kitchen. It wasn't until that moment she realized, there was no light on in the room. As her eyes adjusted, she moved over to flip on the light switch. There was no one there. Softly she whispered, "Ed? Are you in here?"

Nothing, not a sound. She shook her head doubting herself now. "That's what you get girl for looking up all that spooky shit at night." She reached over to turn out the light, but it went out before she could touch the switch. Paralyzed she squinted trying to see in the darkness but could see nothing. Jolene shook her head back and forth, reprimanding herself as she started to turn away.

Halfway during the pivot, she saw something, and it was coming toward her. Her eyes grew big as saucers and her heart pounded frantically in her chest as she watched the shape slowly float across the room until it was right in front of her. Jolene tried to scream, but nothing came out.

Not only could she not scream, she couldn't move her body. It was like her feet were stuck to the floor. All she could do was watch as the figure came closer and closer. She felt warm liquid running down her legs, but that was of no concern because at that moment she was blind, unable to see anything. It felt as though a dark drape had been placed over her head. She was helpless unable to protect herself. She felt something like a hand press down on the top of her head and then her thoughts were not her own as her mind raced with images and words in fast forward, making her dizzy.

Just when she felt her head would burst, it stopped. The veil of darkness dissipated, and she saw the shadowy figure moving in reverse until it disappeared. Weakly, Jolene started and fell to the floor.

Silence dominated the room as she continued to lay there motionless until slowly her body began to move at her command. Never one to faint, but finding herself seated on the floor, the only hypothesis that worked was that she had fainted. Slowly she worked her way up to a standing position, turned and went into the office, ignorant of the fact she had wet herself. There she pulled out a piece of paper and began writing.

With thoughts captured in her head, Jolene started Word and studiously began typing information into the program, pausing now and then as she figured out the translations from her sheet of paper. She was leaning close to the screen when Jennifer called out, "Mom, have you been up all night?"

Slowly Jolene turned, at first not recognizing her daughter, but when she does, a smile covers her face. She turns back around. Finishes what she has written and sends it to the printer.

"Good morning, Jenny. Is everyone up."

The next few days, Jolene felt different. She couldn't put her finger on it, but something had changed. She just didn't feel right. She tried to shake it off as she was never one to be sickly. Whatever was throwing her off her game had to be something simple and would pass, consequently she just ignored it.

When it started to get worse, she didn't tell Ed as she didn't want him to worry, but the odd sensations began to include burning in her chest, added to fatigue, neck pain, and a tendency to sweat profusely after just a short workout. Not an idiot Jolene resolved she needed to get a checkup.

Before entering the examination room, she was asked if she could pee in a cup for them. Jolene covered her mouth as she started to laugh. When she could control herself, she said, "Sure, that won't be a problem."

Jolene remembered only two things that happened that evening and it was that she might have fainted, and she had peed herself.

Back in the reception area, she heard her name called and she was taken back to an examination room.

Dr. Matthews had known her since she was a little girl, thus his family history questions were just routine. "Has there been any new developments and changes in your health history."

"No."

"What about your job and relationships, medications, allergies, supplements, or any recent surgeries?"

"No."

"Okay, get undressed and put on this," he said handing her a paper gown. "I'll be right back."

Jolene took off her clothes and started to laugh, thinking that there had been a development beyond that she thought she had fainted; which was what she had shared with the doctor as the reason for the checkup. Yes, she could also have told him she had wet herself. She couldn't hold back the laugh as it escaped her mouth.

There was a knock at the door. "Come in."

Dr. Matthews entered with a nurse by his side. They helped her up on the examination table. The nurse placed a blood pressure cuff on her arm and reported that her blood pressure was fine. Dr. Matthews listened to her heart and respiratory rate. "Everything sounds excellent, Jolene."

The nurse stood by as the doctor ran his hands around her head, looked into her eyes, pushed in on her chest and abdomen. That done he checked her hands and wrists for any musculoskeletal problems.

"So far so good," he said. "Can you repeat, peter piper picked a peck of pickle peppers."

Jolene smiled and recited it back to him.

"Good."

Okay, let's see you walk

The nurse helped Jolene get off the table and they watched her walk across the examination room. She held the back of the gown together with one hand as she performed for them and turned and walked back to the table. The nurse assisted in getting her back up on the table.

"You seem to be steady on your feet. Nurse, please draw blood for the lab to tests and it won't hurt to prick her finger for a diabetes analysis."

Dr. Matthews turned to Jolene. "When she is done, get dressed and come to the office."

"Okay."

Jolene had to admit she was worried as she walked into Dr. Matthew's office. She needed have worried. He told her he had scheduled an x-ray for her down the hall and that after the x-ray she should come back to the office. "They will give you an envelope to bring with you. Give it to the receptionist and wait for your name to be called."

"Okay, doctor."

Thinking this was a waste of time, she none the less did as she was told. When she returned to Dr. Matthews office, she handed the receptionist the envelope and then took a seat. Her wait was longer this time and she began to worry. But when she had almost worked herself up in a flurry, her name was called, and she was taken to Dr. Matthews office.

Once seated, Dr. Matthew said, "Well Jolene, all the test came back negative."

"Why do I feel so strange, doctor?"

"Well, Jolene, you have all the symptoms that prelude menopause."

Jolene looked aghast. "I'm not that old, doctor."

"The average age for menopause is approximately fifty-one for most women. However, it is possible for perimenopause to start in the late thirties and early forties. Which makes the average age for perimenopause around your mid to late forties. To ease the symptoms, we can give you something, but I know you prefer not to take anything unless it's really necessary. We checked the x-rays we did on your lungs, looking for pneumonia and bronchitis and they were clear."

Maybe he was right…sure, he was right. She was going through menopause is all. God, I'm getting old!

Already she felt better as she walked out of the office, glad that all the tests came back normal, but in the hallway as she was leaving, she felt it; a burning in her chest that felt like her insides were on fire. The pain was worse than before and she stood there unable to move. Seconds passed before she could manage to turn her body around and go back through Dr. Matthews office doors. She was almost up to the reception desk, steps away when she fell to the floor, grabbing her chest and then it all went black.

Death came to Jolene like a shot from behind. One moment she was gazing at the office door, breathing in air, the next she was gone. The attack gave her perhaps a half second of confusion and then it was "lights out."

This had never happened in all the years that the receptionist Sally had worked there, and she didn't know what to do. She could see the worried look of the patients in the waiting room but decided to buzz Dr. Matthew first. He picked up immediately and she told him that Jolene Mann had fallen on the floor in the waiting room. "I think she's dead!" Before she could finish the doctor dropped the phone and soon, she saw him using the exit door to the reception area. She watched as he got down on his knees and put his ear next to her mouth. She saw him begin chest compressions. "Call 911 and get a nurse out here."

It was like a movie on fast forward as Sally stood behind the glass watching as the lobby became a sea of white coats, ushering patients out of the area and making room for the stretcher, until the patients were ushered back in and everything returned to normal.

Dr. Matthew had to call her twice before she reacted. He asked for Jolene Mann's file. When she handed it to him, he carried back to his office. Before he sat down behind his desk, the phone rang. It was the hospital calling. He took a minute, then picked up the phone and dialed.

The knock on the door came shortly after Ed arrived home. He opened it to see two police officers with downcast expressions on their faces when they looked up to see him standing in the doorway.

"Good evening sir, are you Mr. Edward Mann, the husband of Jolene Mann?"

He stood there, looking at them with his mouth hanging open, unable to think of what to say. Finally, he managed to nod.

"Would you mind if we stepped in to speak with you?"

Coming to life, he pushed the door open. "Sorry, no, please come in."

The officers stepped inside, closing the door behind them. They followed him into the living room. "Please sir, take a seat."

He heard someone moaning. He stared fixated on the officers unable to believe what he was thinking. Then one of them spoke. "Sir, I'm sorry to tell you that your wife is dead."

Totally in shock, Ed's mouth dropped open. The officer moved over closer as if to comfort him. "No, there's been some mistake. My wife is at work. I'll just give her a call..."

"No, sir. She had a heart attack and she died. They were unable to revive her."

Even as he spoke, he was all too familiar with how thorough the police were before they would notify the family.

"Jesus, that's... that's ... I can't believe..." he tried to say.

The officer nodded, giving him time to digest the news before he added, "If you like, I can give you a ride downtown."

"Where is the bod... my wife."

"She's at the morgue. I think it is best that I drive you there and I can give you a ride back."

Ed was about to agree when there was another knock at the door. He quickly wiped his eyes, excused himself and went to answer it. It was Ned and Nola."

"Is everything okay? We saw the sheriff's car."

"No, nothing is all right. I'm glad you're here."
They followed him into the living room. "Officer, these are
my neighbors and our best friends." There is a catch in his
voice, and he paused. "Please, tell them what you told me.
Please. "

"Ah, Sir, Madam, I just had to inform Mr. Mann
that his wife died of a heart attack this afternoon."

"What I don't understand!" Nola broke down,
leaving Ned to handle the situation.

"Officer, this is hard to take in."

"I understand. I was just going to give Mr. Mann a
ride down to see his wife. I…"

"No need. We'll gladly take him. Just tell me
where we need to go."

The officer handed Ned a card with the information
and then followed as Ned walked him to the door.

"Take care of him and don't hesitate to call if you
need anything."

Ned nodded as the officer stepped out the door, but
he was still trying to process everything he had told him.

They wanted Ed to rest, but he insisted on going
right away. Nola looked at Ed then at her husband and
feeling quite sure he was doing okay, considering, she said,
"Maybe it's best we go now. The kids are in school and it
will be much easier if we go now."

During the drive, Ed stared straight ahead and
though Nola wanted to cry for her loss friend, she held it
back. Rochester General was a few blocks from the house
and in a few minutes, they were searching for a parking
space in the garage. As they circled around, Nola saw Ed
growing restless beside her. He kept rubbing his hands
together and stopping only to pound a fist on his thigh
before commencing with the rubbing once more.

When Ned finally pulled into a spot, Ed barely waited for the car to stop before he jumped out the passenger side. Nola quickly released her seat belt and stood next to him. Ned followed. "Listen, I'm going ahead and find out where we need to go, he said over his shoulder. "Meet me at the information desk."

"Are you ready Ed?"

Ed didn't respond. Nola held his arm making sure he didn't get run over as he didn't seem to be present at the moment. They made it inside without incident and easily found Ned.

"We have to wait here for someone to take us to see her." Ned had barely gotten the words out when they were approached by first Jolene's doctor who looked as shocked as they did. Behind him came a woman, dressed in a gray suit with a stark white collared shirt underneath. Her glistening black hair bounced with each step and her smile was just enough there, but not overdone. "Hello, I am Liz Kelly, the grief counselor from the Chief Medical Examiner's office."

Ned and Nola shook her hand. Dr. Matthew stepped forward and introduced himself as the doctor of Jolene Mann. As if not noticing Ed's lack of response, she touched his shoulder. "Would you like everyone to come with us to the office. We have some things to discuss.

Ed raised his head. "I want to go see my wife."

"We will Mr. Mann." Liz was by the book and knew she must bring the anxiety level down as much as possible. "I will be with you during the entire identification process. I know this is hard and I want you to know I understand. Dr. Matthew is here to help as well. Would you like your friends to come also?"

Ed nodded and they followed Ms. Kelly to the elevators, taking them to the lower floor. She stepped out first and guided the group to her office. "Can I get you something to drink? Water. Coffee?" Everyone shook their heads so she moved behind her desk and began telling them that she will take them to identify the body and that because she was young and in good health, both Dr. Andrew and herself would like to have them sign a permission form for a post-mortem examination.

Again, Ed nodded. Dr. Matthew reviewed the form and handed it to Ed to sign which he did, his hand shaking so that the signature was illegible. Ms. Kelly continued, explaining that the body will be laid out and kept in the hospital mortuary until they receive notification of the arrangement for someone to pick up the body.

Most of this was barely understood by those seated in the room. Thank goodness Dr. Matthew was present, Nola thought.

Ms. Kelly again expressed her sympathies, but said they needed to move quickly as Mrs. Mann had donated her organs. Ed let out an agonizing sob as he lowered his head to the top of the desk. Nola started to reach out to him, but Ms. Kelly shook her head. All were silent as they waited for Ed to gain control. When he did, he looked up with red eyes and choked out, "Please can I see my wife."

"Yes."

When they rose, he turned to say, "Please, I want to be alone with her."

They stepped back and watched Ms. Kelly take him down the hall. They were joined by a staff member who gave them a plastic bag containing Jolene's possessions. Nola looked over the contents. There was her clothing, shoes, purse, and jewelry. Knowing her friend, she was confident this was everything. She took the itemized receipt, signed, and took possession.

While Ed was gone, Dr. Matthews shared the events leading up to the death of Jolene. He stated that Jolene had told him she was feeling under the weather but was sure it

83

was nothing. He had given her a complete physical and didn't find anything. This heart attack, which is what the medical examiner claimed caused her death, needed to be investigated further. Because he had just finished examining her and had her other medical records, it was hard to believe she had a heart attack. He'd feel better having an autopsy performed to collaborate the cause.

Just them they heard a commotion outside the office. Dr. Matthew was the first to the door with Nola and Ned behind him. It didn't take them long to see that it was Ed. Ed had collapsed and fallen in the hallway. "Give him space, give him space." Someone was yelling as they hurried to the scene.

There was a flurry of activity as they checked his pulse and were ready when someone wheeled up a gurney and helped to put him on it. They crowded into the elevator to ride up with him. "Is he all right?" Dr. Matthews was checking him along with a nurse from the floor. They both spoke. "It's shock. Seeing his wife was too much for him. He'll be all right."

Ned and Nola were asked to sit in the waiting area while they did the paperwork to have him admitted. Several hours later they got word he was given a sedative and was resting comfortably. They told them to go home and they could come get him in the morning. Dazed and exhausted they left the hospital knowing that they had to handle telling the children not only that their mother had died, but that their father was in the hospital.

They had never done this before and didn't know how to proceed. Besides, they were still grieving for the loss of Jonathan. At least they just had to accept that Jolene had died, while where Jonathan was concerned, they had to wonder where, if not dead, was their son.

They turned to each other. "I don't think I can handle this, Ned. Can you?"

"No, but we have to."

Nola thought for a moment. "No, it is best someone help us handled this fresh loss." Once home, Nola placed a call to the only person she knew who could help.

CHAPTER 14

Facing The Loss Of Jolene

That evening Nola watched as Dr. Memer sat with Jolene's children, Jennifer and Matthew, their flaming red hair in competition with their faces. They did not hold back as they shook with sobs, hugging each other and staring in disbelief at first and then finally allowing it to sink in.

They were in shock. Dr. Memer waited patiently, allowing them to express their grief and then he spoke. "You experienced a great loss and you're still young, with so much life ahead of you. You are probably wondering how you can make it through the rest of your life without the parent who is no longer here. I see you struggling."

There was a distinct lessening of their tears as they listened to the soothing voice of Dr. Memer. "Eventually on the outside, you will hold it together. You'll smile again and want to embrace life. Every day will be a good day until a memory strikes you. And it'll happen fast. Something triggers your memory. It could be a song. It could be a picture. It could be a moment, a quick glimmer of a memory that stops you dead in your tracks and leaves you breathless. When that happens, just close your eyes, take a deep breath, and remember the memory. Because that is all you have now, memories. And the memories are what keeps your mother alive in your heads and your hearts."

When Dr. Memer finished, both Jennifer and Matthew had wiped their tears and seemed comforted as they thanked him.

Nola and Ned had remained at the Manns and now they thanked Dr. Memer profusely. The doctor had explained that the loss is so disruptive that recovery would take time. "They are overwhelmed with feelings of bewilderment, anxiety, self-reproach, and depression. It's best that they are given time now to absorb the reality that the world was about to change dramatically for them."

With console written on his face he added, "You know how it feels. You know how hard it has been to accept the loss of Jonathan." Nola started to speak, but Dr. Memer cut her off. "Hear me out. It is the same. After a sudden death, the loss doesn't make sense. The critically important understanding of what happened is missing. The sudden shock of losing someone we love without warning stuns us and we cannot comprehend what has transpired. Consequently, you repeatedly will have to go over it to try to make sense of the loss. The same as you have had to do losing Jonathan."

Nola nodded. They hugged each other and saw Dr. Memer on his way. Nola and Ned closed the door behind him and stayed with Jennifer and Matthew, giving them water, and inviting them to stay the night at their home.

After a bit, Jennifer said, "Thank you Ms. Log, but we want to stay here."

"I understand." She went over and hugged them and then as she and Ned departed, she turned and said quietly, "I will find a way to help them through this."

Ed was in the hospital overnight. Early the next morning the phone rang, and Nola went to answer it. "Nola, it's Ed. I need to come home. I need to tell the children that... Can you come and get me?"

"Yes, I'll be right there. I had Dr. Memer talk with the children."

"I'm so sorry I put all this on yours and Ned's shoulders."

"No, no problem. You two were there for us when Jonathan... I'll be there shortly."

Nola hung up the phone and called next door. As expected, Jennifer and Matthew were up. "I'm going to the hospital to pick up your father. Would you..."

"Yes, they said, the phone obviously being held between them so they could both hear. In minutes they were in the driveway, looking disheveled and sad as they climbed into the car. Nola was glad it was a short ride as she peered into the rearview mirror and saw their faces. She wanted to say something to ease their pain, but she didn't know what would help. Best to keep quiet, she thought. As they made their way to the hospital Nola could feel the physical and emotional shock building up as the reality of where they were going was where their mother died.

Once inside the hospital, Nola went to the front desk and asked directions to the elevators for the fourth floor. When she had the directions, she went over to the children and without a word, she started walking and they followed. They stood quietly waiting for the elevator to arrive and when it did, they stood back waiting for the people to disembark before climbing in. The elevator was full and that helped them keep it together. When the elevator stopped at the fourth floor, they excused themselves and got off.

Now Nola again took the lead as she guided the troupe to Ed's room. When they entered, he was dressed and waiting. As if on key, the tears and sobs began. Ed had both of his children grasped in a tight hold as all three of them wept, with Ed trying desperately to control his tears for the sake of the children. From the look of him, Nola was sure that just like the children, he hadn't slept much, but cried a lot.

As it was hospital procedure, a wheelchair arrived and Ed, protesting, finally climbed in so that he could be taken down to the car. One last swipe of the eyes and several deep breaths later, the group was back in control. As the nurse pushed him, Nola walked beside her, and Jennifer walked on one side and Matthew on the other side of the wheelchair. No one said a word as they waited for the elevator to arrive on the fourth floor. When it did, they waited until it emptied and then climbed in. Nola pressed the lobby button while Matthew and Jennifer moved to the back beside the wheelchair; each with a hand on their dad's shoulder.

When the doors opened in the lobby, Nola said, "I'll go ahead and bring the car around." The nurse nodded as she moved the wheelchair into the mass of people rushing back and forth; expertly making a path for them until they were on the sidewalk in front of the hospital.

Nola drove into the circle and parked in front of her passengers. She sat behind the wheel, watching as they climbed in. She checked to be sure everyone was seat belted in, and then pulled out of the circle to head home. Ed sat in the passenger seat but turned sideways so he could hold the hands of his children as they sobbed in the back seat. In minutes Nola was pulling into the Manns driveway and watched them climb out.

"Can I get you anything, or would you like me to come in for a while?"

"No, Nola, we'll be fine, you have done enough. You have enough on your plate as well. We'll give you a call later."

Now she could allow herself to let go. Nola backed out of the Manns' driveway and drove next door to pull into her own. When she walked into the house May was waiting as if anticipating what was about to happen. Nola looked at her mother and let the pent-up flood of her feelings go. Nola cried for the loss of her best friend. She cried for the pain of the Mann family and she cried for Jonathan. Where was Jonathan.

By the time Joy came home from school, she was all cried out.

CHAPTER 15

Shared Visions

Nola sat at the kitchen island drinking a cup of coffee while her mother, May stood in front of her. Nola knew her mother was waiting for her to say something, but she needed to think first. Nola didn't doubt that May knew whatever was bothering her was not something she could turn her back on. For some time now May had watched the change in Nola. It was subtle at first, but after the birth of Joy it was hard not to notice.

As she thought about it, she recalled the episode told by the old woman from the old neighborhood. She had come to May when Nola and her husband were planning the wedding in the vacant house. She had no reason, none at all to think the house was haunted, but she swore that the day she showed the house to Nola, she saw two figures. Both figures were tall and concealed every inch of their body in large ominous capes with hoods. The hood shaded their faces so that she could not even describe what they looked like.

When May asked if it was only while she was with Nola, she had said, "No." Once Nola left and she went about locking up the house, she felt like she was dreaming while awake. The two figures were fading, but she swore

91

they described themselves in a way that made her think one represented evil and the other good. The one who remained the longest actually spoke.

May was listening intently, waiting to hear what the woman had to say. When she finally did, she said simply, "The woman in the Ceps family are the chosen ones." That stunned May on many levels. First, this woman swore she had never experienced anything like that before. Second, the apparitions had spoken to her. When May was able, she had asked the woman exactly what that meant, but she couldn't tell her anymore because she didn't know.

May, waited for Nola to compose herself and when she did, she said, "I have something I want to tell you daughter." She then told Nola the story the woman had shared those so many years ago. She explained that she didn't want to ruin her special day, so she had kept it to herself. But she couldn't any longer.

Nola at first didn't know what to say. "Come on, daughter, it's me. I won't judge you or think something is wrong, but if we don't figure this out, I'm afraid more bad things will happen."

Nola decided to ease into it. "It was like visions, but about other people and places before. It wasn't until recently that all that changed." She leaned across the counter, resting her head on her hands. "At first it scared me, but I was so afraid to tell anyone because people already thought I was weird. Then, when Ned and I married I somehow knew that whatever we wanted or desired would happen. It would happen for us and those close to us." She paused again, trying to smile at her mother but it was only a slight facial change. "You know the saying. Don't rock the boat!" So, I just kept it secret. I wasn't even sure half the time of what the spirits looked like or of they were good or evil. But I must admit I figured out that they were behind our luck and good fortune. They

92

somehow made our spoken or thought of desires come true and I didn't want it to stop."

The women are quiet, taking it all in. This is the first time that Nola has been so open, and May wants to encourage her to continue. "Would you like some coffee?"

"Yes, mom, that would be nice."

"What's going on here and why wasn't I invited?" Joy was standing in the doorway looking at her mother and nana.

"Oh, I was just telling nana what has been happening." She sees her daughter's face, so readable at sixteen. Nola figures Joy has so much to hide that she didn't even try when it came to her. She watched as Joy went over and poured herself a cup of coffee, added cream and sugar and carried it over to the counter to sit next to her mother.

Joy said, "I think it is time we talk because I am scared."

"I understand. I'm scared too. But do you see the hooded figures."

"Yes, I do," Joy replied. "I think I always knew there were two figures fighting for power and existence. At first my visions were not scary, even pretty at times. But then they changed. I'm not sure it was because of the move, but I can say for sure it was the first time that someone was able to witness what I was seeing."

"What do you mean, Joy."

"Well, it was when I was playing with Jennifer one day that it happened. She won't admit that she saw it, I'm sure." Joy let out a nervous laugh. It was right after that she stopped playing with me, so I know she had to see what I saw."

"What did you see?"

"A pretty teenage girl dancing with her boyfriend when she suddenly burst into flames. It was like it was driven by an inner storm that this fire burst furiously from her back and chest, enveloping her head, and igniting her hair. In seconds she was a human torch, and before her companion could beat out the flames, she was consumed, and he had to back off. I watched as she disappeared into a pile of ashes."

"Ah, sweetie, I'm so sorry. What did Jennifer say?"

A weird look appeared on Joy's face. "Oh, she didn't say anything. She stood there with her brow wrinkled and her mouth hanging open. Her hands were halfway up as though she wanted to cover her eyes but couldn't. Then, when it was over, she never looked at me. She just stiffly walked away. She never played with me again."

Joy took a sip of her coffee and kept her eyes down. When she raised them, she looked at her mother. "What were your visions like, before..."

She didn't have to say it. Nola knew that she was going to say, before they began sharing them. "Well, most of them dealt with sorrow and tears, but were visions of other people. No one close to me."

She paused. "What about yours?"

"Well, just like that one that Jennifer witnessed, most are about fire."

Joy told of a vision where she was driving down the street with her mom in their car. She thought she saw her father pulled over at the side of the road doing something under the hood of the car. She rolled down the window and waved. They continued driving and a short way down the road she simply burst into flames. One time it was while she was in bed asleep and she knew she had burned to death. She could feel the intense heat yet nothing else in her room was burned. She laid their burnt and took in the areas around her. Her clothes, her sheets and blankets were not even scorched while still in the vision. The room was as it had always been, just she lay there burnt to a pile of cinders.

"I'm so sorry baby." She looked at Joy, wanting to take her in her arms, but afraid to. She watched as May came around the island and hugged her tightly. Unable to hold back, Nola slid off the stool and walked to her daughter's side. She waited to see if Joy wanted her to touch her and when Joy nodded, she gathered her daughter close.

Nothing happened. No shared vision captured them. Nola was smiling as she released her daughter. And then it happened.

The minute they are no longer in physical contact a shock goes through their body and they see the outline of a person before them, beckoning them. They both reach out without hesitation and force their bodies toward the outline ahead. But something pulls them in the opposite direction. Then, from nowhere, a bird falls from the sky and lands in front of them as they struggle forward. Joy reaches down and carefully lifts the hurt bird up in her hands, ever so tenderly. As she stands, she turns to Nola and moves her cupped hands out so that Nola can see the bird nestled there. Nola reaches her hands toward Joy and they make contact. With a force that takes their breath away, they return to the kitchen of their house, frightened, shaken, and confused.

All the time this was happening, May was yelling out their names, trying to bring them back. She couldn't see or feel what was happening to them, but she knew that vacant look seen so many times before, that they were caught up in a vision. When they finally returned, May rushed over to them.

"Oh, mom," Nola said, turning to hug her mother. "It is changing. Instead of us touching, it came when we released each other."

"Yes, that was different. I thought that when we both touched and I felt that shock, that maybe, just maybe, we were going to see Jonathan." Joy was sobbing now. May held her while Nola looked on.

Nola cleared her throat, getting their attention. "Listen, mom, one of the visions Joy and I had before Jonathan…before he disappeared, was of you and Jolene. We saw you in a picture. First it is a picture of you mom, then it changes to a picture of Jolene. It keeps changing back and forth until finally it is a picture of both you and Jolene together before blood starts spurting out of your eyes, your mouths and ears."

"Holy Christ," I don't know what to say.

"Neither do we. We don't know what it means, only that it was what we saw. We did share that with Dr. Memer too, but he hasn't been able to make sense of it, yet.

While the Ceps women are openly dealing with the visions, Dr. Memer is busy too. Desperate times call for desperate measures. Dr. Memer felt that this was indeed desperate times. Over the years of treating first Nola and then her daughter, he recognized a change. At first, they never shared a vision with them or allowed him to know much about their visions until of late when it got bad. The visions seemed to now be affecting the people they loved and were close to. The visions were not individual ones, but shared ones between mother and daughter.

After much research he ran across a name of interest. Going back through the records he realized that this woman was the grandchild of Kate Fox, one of the best-known Fox Sisters. Back in the day, Maggie and Kate had become famous for hearing raps from an unknown source. They had not only heard the raps but could get the raps to repeat a count at will.

Once their mother witnessed this, the Fox family deserted the house and sent Maggie and Kate to live with their older sister, Leah Fox Fish, in Rochester. That might have been the end of it except that some religious sects considered the Fox sisters were spiritual. Apparently, they could.

Maggie, Kate, and Leah Fox embarked on a professional tour to spread word of the spirits. It is understood that the promoters decided that they wanted more. Kate married a devout Spiritualist and continued to develop her medium powers until new practitioners seduced her to summon full-fledged apparitions. It was wearying, both to the movement and to Kate herself, and she, began to drink. Kate was chastised for her drinking and accused of being unable to care for her two young children. And it was one of her children that Dr. Memer has learned was considered to have the skill to summon spirits.

Dr. Memer gave Marguerite Fox a call. He is surprised when Marguerite herself answers the phone. He says that he would like to see her and tell her about a problem a family is having with what they call visions. He senses and urgency in helping them as they have already lost two people close to them. He didn't need to say more. Marguerite Fox tells him to come see her. "I'm available this afternoon if that is convenient for you," she says. Dr. Memer accepts.

That afternoon Dr. Memer knocks on the door, feeling slightly insane. A psychologist going to see a medium for advice. But what other choice did he have.

CHAPTER 16

Jolene & Ed Mann

Jolene would tell her friends that Ed had a face that stopped you in your tracks. Ed had met Jolene at the University where he had just completed his final semester and was ready to let loose before studying for the bar. He was seated on a half wall enjoying the warmth of the sun when out of the corner of his eyes he saw a flash of bouncing long red curly hair coming his way. The sun danced across her hair giving her a glow that washed away everything and everybody else on that campus. By the time she was close to where he was stationed, he knew he had to speak to her. He did.

Used to that sudden pause in a person's expression when they looked his way, he didn't see it in Jolene. He had met his match as she met his blue-eyed gaze with a crooked smile. Jolene was striking from the depth of her hazel eyes to the gentle expression of her voice. It was only later as they got to know each other did she tell him that he was the most beautiful man she had ever seen.

Despite all the opportunity that came his way he was a one-woman-man who prized genuineness and thoughtful conversation above lipstick and high-heels.

(

He loved how she openly shared her opinions and the way she would reach out to touch his hand when she thought he wasn't listening. Just that light touch, through all the years, still managed to quicken his heart and he would lose himself for a moment.

Ed awoke to find himself not in his bed, or even in the house. He awoke to find himself in another world, a world of suffering. As the numbness of sleep slowly faded from his limbs, he opened his eyes and gasped in a breath, but nothing came. He tried again and choked on his dry tongue. There was no air in this menacing world. His mind in a panic, in desperation he sucked in another breath. He could feel his heart beating against his rib cage, slowing every second before realization dawned on him. He was going to bury Jolene.

He tried to force air into his lungs, but none came. He felt his heart stop beating for an instant, and then there was nothing. He lay there trying to compose himself when he heard it. It was so quietly spoken he could barely hear the words. "Matthew, give the pages to Nola. Give the pages to Nola." Then he felt a light touch on his hand.

Fully awake, Matthew sat up and looked around. He was alone in his bedroom. The alarm went off, sending a chill down his spine. "Agh!" He said. Finally, he was back in control and reached over to silence the alarm. Ed was now fully awake.

Today he was going to bury his wife. Ed couldn't believe it. He somehow had managed to take a shower and get dressed, while his mind raced, searching for what had happened. He couldn't bring himself to accept the fact that his beloved Jolene would never call out to him to hurry up and get ready for breakfast or force the kids to put down their phones. It was all over for him. Ed's handsome face is distorted with grief. He seems unable to focus as he walks aimlessly through the empty house, feeling the loss of Jolene. He hadn't wanted to let Jennifer and Matthew go to stay at their grandparents, but he was in no shape to be around anyone at this point.

It was senseless and unexplainable how Jolene had just died. She was healthy and took care of herself so how could this have happened. "I can't understand. I just can't understand."

Finally, exhausted, Ed took a seat at the island, staring across the room until he heard someone at the door. Mechanically he pushed the stool back and stood. He took his hand and wiped it across his eyes before making his way to the door. When he opened it, he nodded his head when the driver said, "Are you ready, Sir?"

He didn't remember much after that as the limo drove him to the church and he was greeted by the rest of the family. They took their seats and he sat stiffly, trying to hold it together to reassure his children that they would be all right. They wouldn't be all right…ever.

After the service, Ed managed a weak smile to those offering condolences, before he climbed back into the limo; this time with his children and his parents. When his mother asked, "Ed, are you all right?" He let go.

"Explain why this happened, mom. Why did she die?"

"Death isn't kind, my son. I knew that. It snatches where it can, taking people who are far too young, far too good. It doesn't pretend to care."

His parents had gratefully planned to have close friends and family over to their house afterwards, making it easier on Ed. Being away from his home he seemed to function normally as he accepted condolences and managed to put some food in his stomach. Each time his children caught his eye, he managed an encouraging look that hung only on the surface of his being.

He was standing next to the sliding glass doors when he felt someone was near him. He turned and saw Nola and Ned Log standing behind him, hesitating to interrupt. "Ed, we are so sorry. If there is anything we can do, please don't hesitate."

Ed reached out and took Ned's hand and then released it as he turned to give Nola a hug. He had barely put his arms around her when it happened.

He couldn't believe his eyes and didn't want to. He never saw anything like that even in his worst nightmares. But now he was seeing something his eyes won't ever be able to erase. A kaleidoscope of colors surrounds him, with what looked like heads appearing and disappearing at will.

The adrenalin flew through his veins and he couldn't move a single muscle, not even to scream. The absolute horror completely paralyzed him, and the more he thought about pulling away, or simply moving a bit, the more he felt terror.

He didn't remember being this scared ever. Then suddenly all he saw was what he thought to be a spiritual vision of Jolene floating in front of him. Her head of red curls flowed out around her pale face, and at first her eyes were closed. Everything else fell away. He no longer heard the voices of the guests talking in the room. Every natural body movement was on hold until she opened her eyes and the voice of Jolene whispered in his hear, "Give the pages to Nola". As quickly as the vision happened, it disintegrated.

Nola was stepping back. Ed had a feeling she knew what had taken place and that was confirmed when she said to him, "What pages?"

All he could do was shake his head back and forth. "I don't know. I don't know what just happened."

CHAPTER 17

Nan & Ted Safer

Ted and Nan Safer were aware of all that was going on with the neighbors, since they were close friends with May and Neves Ceps. May often had to shake her head when she thought of being friends with Nan and Ted. They were used to having neighbors, but they had never been close to them; never saw them as being friends.

Nan was a gray-haired woman with young, sparkling blue eyes that were inappropriately set in her old, wrinkled face. Yet, to someone looking closer, they did fit for she had aged gracefully and appeared much younger than her age or appearance. Ted had long since passed his seventieth birthday. He had a thick head of white hair topping his weather-beaten face. Deep creases gave character to his countenance. Both had acquired the comfortable size of body so often seen in the older generation and widely accepted. He was the most understanding and caring person that anyone could ever know.

In the neighborhood they were the elderly couple who lived a peaceful, quiet, retirement spent in volunteering and socializing with their neighbors.

In contrast, there was the life of May and Neves Ceps. Neves had the appearance of having been a handsome young man. His hair was worn close to his head in tight frizzy curls that had turned from black to gray. His mustache was gray also. His skin was dark and rough textured but had very few visible wrinkles to speak of. His overall appearance was of a tough, not to be messed with character, but his heart was beating to a different drum than that of the outside. He was soft, kind and understanding in nature. May was close in coloring to that of her husband, but her skin was smooth and even. Her hair was of medium length, sprinkled with gray and worn most times pulled back in a bun. She looked all sweetness and peaceful on the outside. Both May and Neves remained thin in their old age.

Where the Safers had not been blessed with children, the Ceps had not just their children, but also grandchildren in their lives and they shared the experiences, to some extent with the Safers. That and their joy of playing cards. That the couples did at least once a week when they would go out to dinner and then settle in at the Safers or the Ceps to play cards. You might say that they had become family to each other.

Neves like Ted kept his family in balance, which for Neves wasn't easy. It helped to have someone to talk to, since he didn't want to lay his problems on May's shoulders. She had enough to deal with.

Nan became first aware of the strange happenings with May's daughter and granddaughter when she was at the neighborhood gas station. Peter Reed who ran the station knew everyone in the neighborhood as he was very personable. Everyone liked him and he liked them as well so when it wasn't busy, he himself would pump their gas. The only fault he had was he liked to talk. On this day as

Nan sat in her car with the window down, he walked over to her window and she immediately sensed something was wrong.

"Peter, what is it?"

At first, she sensed a hesitancy in him, but then he said, "The other day, Ms. Log and her daughter came to get gas and something weird happened."

"Weird how, Peter."

"Well, I was pumping the gas into their car when the light from the sun hit the rim of my cap, sending a blinding light into my eyes. And then something happened. I don't know what or how long it went on, but I remember that when I came to, the gas was spilling on my shoes and the tank of the car was full. Ms. Safer, I don't remember even putting the pump into the gas tank."

Nan was thoughtful for a moment. "That is strange. When you get to be my age, it will get stranger."

That seemed to relax Peter. Nan made a mental note to mention it to May.

A few days later, she and May met up for lunch at a cozy little bistro in I 'Square. After they had their food and were comfortably seated, Nan asked.

"May, you don't have to tell me if you don't want to, but I heard something strange the other day and I wanted to ask you about it."

May was chewing her food. She finished and took a sip of her drink. "Sure, what is it?"

Nan told her what Peter had said. For a moment, Nan was afraid that she had offended her friend and started to speak but May cut her off.

"You are my friend and I have learned over the years we have been living here that keeping secrets from friends is not a good thing. It stifles you and makes it harder on everyone concerned and I am beginning to think that everyone who has touched are life is a concern. I am going to tell you what happened that day to myself and Joy. I didn't know about Peter's experience until just now, but it supports the idea that this is about more than just my daughter and granddaughter."

"On that day Nola sat with Joy in the car. The same light flashes into their eyes through the windshield. The light brings them trancelike on a walk down the path in the light. The path is surrounded by foliage all green and healthy, with wildflowers scattered throughout, the two hold hands, smiling; serene, happy. Joy's hand slides from her mom's as she goes to the edge of the path to pick a flower there. On the path they see figures welcoming them ahead. Then shadow transcends seeming to rip its way through the ground and burning the foliage. As soon as their hands release, the sky that was bright turns dark, a wind rises, the foliage dies and they are again in the car, unable to recall or aware that they both have shared the vision."

Nan is thoughtful. "I'm not going to pretend I haven't noticed something special about your daughter and hers. I have noticed and felt a connection since the day we met." She paused. "I sense something more is going to happen beyond all that has taken place, the disappearance of Jonathan, the death of Jolene. I think I am somehow connected to you and have been placed here to help you so please, if there is any way I can help, tell me. Anything at all."

May smiled shyly. "Thank you, Nan. I wish I could tell you what we are dealing with, but we don't know. Besides that, I have a feeling that once you know, you may be in danger. Until we know how to, let's say, control it, it's safer not to know."

With that the friends parted.

106

CHAPTER 18

Marguerite Fox

Marguerite Fox walks down the hallway behind the glass entrance door, a flickering light illuminated her way. She is a little woman with an intriguing style and when she opens the door, Dr. Memer nervously introduces himself and holds out his hand. Marguerite looks at his face, then at his hand and barely touching it he draws back from the sensation of a high voltage shock coursing through his body.

Marguerite is dressed in black house pajamas and black low-heeled sling back pumps. Around her neck is a leopard-patterned scarf and wound tightly around her head a turban of the same material. Her skin is very pale. He can't see her eyes behind the dark glasses she is wearing and that frightens him. The eyes unveil truths and right now he needs to know that this strange woman is not going to harm him.

She speaks. "No, Dr. Reb Memer, I am not going to harm you."

He stops in his tracks, stares at the back of Marguerite for a moment before he can start walking again. Finally, she pauses and motions him into a room off the left of the hallway. He steps in and takes it all in. It is not as he expected. The room is well-lit and decorated with Chintz fabric curtains and furnishings. The curtains are open allowing the light to stream into the room. And at the doorway, his whole demeanor changes as he enters the welcoming environment.

"Please take a seat, Dr. Memer. Can I get you something to drink?"

"Yes, a nice cup of tea would be nice."

Marguerite excuses herself and while she is gone, Dr. Memer can't help himself. He stands and walks about the room peeking through glass cabinet doors and checking out the decorative touches on tables. The more he looks, the more relaxed he feels. When Marguerite returns, he is again seated, but he sees the knowing smile on her face.

He takes the tea that Marguerite offers him and places it on the coaster next to his chair. Marguerite sits across from him. Dr. Memer picks up his cup and takes a sip. It has a strange taste, but not that unpleasing. He takes another sip to try and determine what he's tasting, but he cannot.

"Marguerite, what is the flavor of this tea?"

"Well, it is black tea with Empirical Spirits from fir needles. It preserves the integrity of the raw organic tea leaves."

"Is that all," feeling hesitant to now drink the tea.

"Mr. Memer, it won't hurt you. It does encourage a person to open up their mind so that they share the experience without compromising it to their way of thinking. If I am to help you, help your patient and her family, I need to know the truth, not your truth. Do you understand?"

Dr. Memer nodded his head.

"Let's begin. Tell me about yourself."

"I'm not hear for me, but for my patient."

108

"I know, but I need to know about you as well. There may be something there worth sharing."

Years ago, during my grad school clinical internship in the late nineties, I was assigned a rotation on the locked unit of a mental health hospital in Massachusetts. I spent several months working on the unit, and while I have by now forgotten many of the details, my overall impression remains strong in my memory. The place was no healing sanctuary for the soul.

I remember thinking how ironic it was that the environment created for helping the mentally vulnerable was one of alienation, confusion, and helplessness—the very qualities that exacerbate such vulnerability in the first place.

Many years have passed since then during which I had no further involvement with the inpatient psychiatric hospital system. But recently, a relative of mine suffered a psychotic episode that I could not treat, and I had to have her sent to a private psychiatric hospital. I visited her and I was shocked and disturbed by what I saw. Nothing has changed. In fact, in some ways, things appear to have gotten worse. Consequently, that was when I decided that I would do everything I could to help a patient who came to me so that they didn't have to end up in any psychiatric ward.

"Thank you, doctor, that helps me to now understand you more. Tell me about your patient."

"Enolai came to me when she was just a little girl. Her mother and father were worried about her and needed my help. Though she never spoke about exactly what was happening, her mother did have a sense that she was feeling or seeing things."

"Tell me what her parents' names were.

"Her father's name is Neves and her mother's name is May. Their last name is Ceps."

"What has happened to bring you here."

Dr. Memer told Marguerite that just recently Nola, as Enolai is called, began to be frank with him and share the visions she was having. Not only was she having them, but her daughter, Joy, was too. Subsequently, he began treating them both, at first thinking it was just scary hallucination brought on by a period of intense stress and anxiety. But the more they talked, the more he realized it was much more than that. From individual visions, it became visions that they both participated in. The visions affected physically their life beyond the vision. They were seeing spirits, ghost, whatever we should call them, which is not odd for Rochester has it shares of ghosts. But then one ghost called, the Lady in White, took Joy's twin, Jonathan, and he has never been found.

When Dr. Memer finished, Marguerite stared through him and then finally she returned from wherever she had been. "Doctor give me your hand."

Dr. Memer hesitated, remembering the shock that he felt before, but finally gave in. For some reason he felt that this person had the answer. When she grasped his hand, his eyes flew open and he felt paralyzed. It seemed like hours that he couldn't move, but finally she released him, and it was if nothing had happened.

He could see the exhaustion on Marguerite face as she told him, "Seven."

"What did you say?"

"It is all tied up with the number seven. Something is happening and it is going to take a circle of seven to stop it."

"I don't understand?"

"I'm sorry, but that is all I can piece together from your mind. I would need to see the women to connect the rest of it together, but I think you need to tell them about

110

the number seven and maybe they will know what it means. If not, I would be willing to see them."

Dr. Memer nodded. I understand. I will talk with them and get back to you. He stood and Margarette rose waved a hand out to allow him to walk in front of her as they headed to the door. She opened it and he stepped over the threshold, turned and said, "Thank you so much for your time. It was enlightening."

And Marguerite smiled.

CHAPTER 19

Dr. Memer

Dr. Reb Memer was a psychologist first. That was his profession so for him to now be thinking that a soothsayer, or, what was it said on the sign. He paused in thought and then it came to him. Yes, a psychic. For him to now believe that the psychic was his only way of helping Nola and Joy, well that was unbelievable.

Dr. Memer stretched up his five-foot nine-inch height as if seeking some sort of power. He got up and looked in the mirror. The face that stared back assured him it was he. That was his head of thick blonde hair, sprinkled with gray. His eyes a clear blue below his dark eyebrows and lashes. He leaned in closer noticing a transparent look to his complexion. Had that been there before? It didn't matter, he was the same person, but his mind was now open to other possibilities. Maybe that had something to do with the drink she gave him. Dr. Memer nodded his head as if verifying this idea for himself.

Dr. Memer new the Ceps' family well. He had been with them since before Enolai was born and now he was treating her and her daughter, Joy. His understanding of this family went deep so why should he expect a stranger to be able to understand them more than he could. Again, it didn't matter.

Thoughtfully he knew that he loved the Ceps and would go to whatever extent it took to help because he had a feeling things were going to get worse; if that was possible and Marguerite claim to fame was she was precognitive, allowing her to know about or see future events before they happened. He could only work from conversations about something happening in the past or right now and that might be too late.

Dr. Memer sat down and made notes on a pad. He did have something from Marguerite. Her last words were, ""It is all tied up with the number seven. Something is happening and it is going to take a circle of seven to stop it."

That didn't help much since she couldn't tell him anything beyond that until she met with Nola and Joy.

Dr. Memer was at a lost as he sat staring at the pad before him. He tapped the pen against his lip for some time and then he started writing. He first wrote about how he had first met May and Neves and his impression of them. He jotted down the fact that May wanted not only her name to be hyphenated, but also her children to be known as Ceps-Log. Neves agreed to that. That might be important. He didn't know how, but he wrote it down.

Looking at what he had written so far, Dr. Memer decided to put this into the computer. He poured a glass of water and took it into his office where he started his Word program and began putting the information into the document. When done with that, he filed it so if something happened, he would have at least that much to review.

Next he wrote about how strange and quiet Nola had been at the beginning, but that she had later shared little tidbits with him, and he finally was able to diagnose her as not having dreams, but visions.

113

Dr. Memer paused looking at what he had written so far and then started again, noting the day that Enolai had told him he could call her Nola. Though he had never met Joy's twin, Jonathan, Nola had told him much about him. Where Joy who was so much like her mother, Jonathan was a bright, fun-loving boy with the luck of having the characteristics of Ned, including his good looks. He was very close to his father and had the ability to kid his mother out of her moods now and then and reveal the person of her youth. He only knew the changes in his mother and later is sister were the result of "spells". Nola seemed to lose touch with life and reality as did Joy but he loved them both.

Joy would say that Jonathan loved Nola for herself and her love for him. He loved his father because he could relate and understand him. He even seemed to understand his mother's desire to have her children carry her maiden name. He understood it to be a need to let the world know that this child belonged to her too.

From Nola's point of view, Joy was indeed a joy to behold. She was a perfect replica of her and her husband Ned. When Joy changed, she could see Ned's spirit drop. It was hard on him to see his happy, well-liked, and charming daughter turn into a lonely, sometimes frightened person that he could not figure how to help.

Joy would say that the change seemed to take place shortly after her seventh birthday. But it was not until around the age of twelve that she admitted to herself that she was not just dreaming, that there was a presence with her almost all the time. She somehow felt it to be more than one but was not sure of this. She had dismissed it and tried to deny its existence. But by the age of twelve the force was too strong to deny any longer. During that fateful year of her life she began to change while people around her began to alter their feelings toward her. Eventually there was only her brother Jonathan who would remain by her

114

side, helping her to laugh off her strange visions. But Joy had backbone and was determined to not be friendless and alone, so she had tried.

Joy had shared the time she had played with Jennifer Mann in the yard and had a vision. By Jennifer's reaction she believed that she had seen the same thing as her, but she never had a chance to ask her.

In Joy's mine the visions were a curse and her mother Nola would become "The One" who would eventually remove the forces that controlled the Ceps women.

Dr. Memer leaned back in his chair staring in front of him and now was more than sure he had not been picked by chance, but that there was a force behind the decision for him to enter the Ceps family picture. What his role would be, he was unsure.

Dr. Memer saved the document and turned off the monitor. He sat there a while longer thinking about how what started out as just pieces of info, helped him to see a lot more than he had before.

Dr. Memer was happy with himself as he leaned back in his chair. He decided that at the next meeting with Joy and Nola he would bring up the matter of meeting with Marguerite Fox and what she had shared with him. He would ask them if they were willing, he would like to set up a meeting between Marguerite and them. Having a plan in place, Dr. Memer was hopeful that they would find the underlying cause of what to do before anything else happened.

CHAPTER 20

Searching For Jonathan

For months now, Nola and Joy have been doing their research on the computer and on foot. There were many acres, 977 acres to be exact, that they needed to cover, along with many people to talk with who had seen the Lady In White. Each lead led them to another location and each recommendation had them going out late afternoon until long after midnight. On most of those late-night excursions, Ned joined them, staying up all night and then having to go into work the next morning, but he didn't mind.

Walking every piece of the area during the day and during the night, Nola and Joy returned unsatisfied. They made sure to check with people on the beach or on the walking trails, asking if they had ever seen the Lady In White and where they had seen her. When someone mentioned they had been near the stone foundation in the park, they camped out there all night to no avail. There were a lot who said they had grown up in Irondequoit and heard the tale, but they thought it was just a ghost story with no real truth.

They tried not to get frustrated; especially by the non-believers, because no one wants to believe in ghost or spirits. What was really upsetting was those who told them a different version of the story and there were many. The one that stood out was told by another who had grown up in Irondequoit and heard that the Lady In White's husband was a merchant shipper on the Great Lakes who perished at sea. She still roams the beach looking for his ship to sail by on the way to the St Lawrence River. That one they wish they hadn't heard because that would mean she could have taken Jonathan away from Irondequoit. If that were the case, it would indeed be an impossible mission they were on and that was something they couldn't deal with.

Joy and Nola had maps of the trails throughout Durand and they followed each of them from beginning to end without any success.

In between their search, Joy and Nola met with Dr. Memer. The last three times they told him everything, every detail of every vision, but nothing came of it. After the second visit, Nola, exhausted and scared said, "Dr. Memer, the episodes are frightfully clear, and we are afraid something is going to happen if we don't figure out how to stop it."

Joy chimed in adding, "I think that if we do figure out what we need to do, Jonathan will be given back to us. You have to help us."

It was then that Dr. Memer told of his visit to Marguerite Fox. The daughter of Leah Fox of the infamous Fox Sisters. "Have you heard of them?"

"We read something about them in our search about them being able to summon spirits."

"They were famous in the eighteen hundreds and it started when one night she had the girls stay in her bedroom, afraid of what might happen and as they lay there, there came a strange sharp noise – as of someone rapping on wood. Kate and Maggie then started talking to the source of the noises – calling it "Mr. Splitfoot", and

117

getting it to mimic their claps with knocks. Their mother began asking it questions, and the source replied. Using two knocks for yes, one knock for no. It was her premise that it was the spirit of a man murdered in the house. Then she asked it if it would continue to perform if she brought in outsiders. The spirit answered yes and so their fame began."

"How can she help us?"

"I had my doubts that Marguerite Fox could help you, but I was desperate. She was an honest woman who wasn't reading Tarot cards or looking into a crystal ball. All she did was talk with me and ask that I keep an open mind."

"What happened."

"She said that something is happening, and it is going to take a circle of seven to stop it."

There was silence in the room while Joy and Nola thought about what this woman had said.

"What does it mean, Dr. Memer?" Joy asked.

"Don't know and neither does Marguerite Fox. That is all she can 'read' through me. To get the answer, she needs to speak with you and your mother." Dr. Memer cleared his throat. I told her I would ask, but that it was up to you if you want to meet with her. I will take you and stay with you...." He let his words run off.

"Can we talk with the family and get back to you?"

"Mom, what if we miss the Lady In White. We'd have to skip an afternoon..." Joy added.

"Tell you what, I will ask Marguerite if it is possible to see you midday. Will that work?"

They both nodded.

Dr. Memer would be up all night going over the notes and tapes he had taken to try to have something to share with them and Marguerite. Before Nola and Joy departed, he tells them, "You are blessed, you must believe this if you are to have the strength to overcome." He paused and with a serious expression added, "I advise that you do not talk to anyone else about your dreams or it may be fatal. Remember what happened to Joy Mann and to Jonathan." Joy and Nola nod. "And, you need to think about the secret is in the seven, maybe what it means will come to you."

It was a quiet drive home that evening and when Joy and Nola arrived, they tried not to upset the rest of the family. With dinner ready, they went about helping May set the table and after dinner they excuse themselves as they clear the table and go to clean the kitchen. Their minds continually worked on what they had learned.

Reluctantly, with the kitchen in order, they went to join Neves, Ned, and May in the living room. That evening they share only what Dr. Memer has suggested. Ned, Neves, and May listen carefully and when Marguerite is mentioned, they agree that two of them should consider going to see her.

"But we need to be in the park looking for Jonathan," Nola says and Joy nods in agreement.

"Don't worry about that, we'll be there in your place. Just tell us where you want us, and we'll be there."

Joy gave her grandparents and her father a hug, thanking them and Nola did the same. They sit with them for some time and then Nola gets up. Joy follows.

Not a word passes between the two as they both grab a sweater and head toward the door. They walk silently down the sidewalk, admiring the quietness of the neighborhood. As they pass neighborhood homes, they see the soft glow of lights inside and wonder what normalcy is going on within. They continue walking taking pleasure in the serenity of the evening. The houses face a park that

119

runs along the other side of the street. It is where Nola and Joy walk often.

That is where their footsteps lead them this evening. Entering the park, a slight breeze rustles the leaves making them fall to the solid ground one by one. The air is warm, with the last rays of sunlight glowing on their skin. All about them are wildflowers concealing the green grass around the pathways made of dirt and random stones. The forest hums with life all around and they pause to enjoy the serenade of crickets and birds singing sweetly. Each breath is fresh and cleansing as they finally start toward home.

They both stop, listening. "Did you hear that mom?"

"Yes, I did."

"What is…"

"Shh."

The sound comes again, and Nola says, "This way, pointing off the path and into a wooded area. They walk gingerly, trying not to make too much noise as they approach. Joy is apprehensive, wondering if this is a good idea, but she stays beside her mother.

A smile of relief covers Joy's face as she sees a squirrel a short way ahead is the source of the sound they were hearing. "It's hurt," Nola says moving ahead of her daughter. "Mom, wait. It could have rabies or something…" she grabs Nola's arm to slow her down.

The touch quickly sends the two into another vision that continues their approaching steps toward the squirrel. Finally, they are very close, and the squirrel makes no attempt to run. They know it is hurt. Joy places her hand on her mother's shoulder to bring her down closer with her as they peer at the squirrel. She starts to turn and ask Nola what they should do. Neither one is aware that they have entered a vision that continued into the present. But as she starts to turn toward Nola she suddenly stops, and her eyes are captured by that of the squirrel. Nola is also entranced by its eyes and then they see its little face change.

As if receiving a mild electric shock, they jump back with fright. Joy losing contact with her mother, falls on the ground while Nola, stands petrified, trying to slow her breathing. She manages to say, "Did you see that?"

When there is no reply, she turns to look at Joy, then at the ground to see that they are back on the path. "Yes, I saw it. The squirrel had Dr. Memer's face. It had his face…"

Careful not to touch, and wondering if it matters any more, they make their way home. When they stand at the door, Nola turns to her daughter and says, "I think that was a warning."

"Yes," Joy replies, "Dr. Memer is in danger."

CHAPTER 21

Facing Reality

Shaken by the recent vision, Nola, and Joy hurry home where they quickly say their good nights and head upstairs. Sitting in the sitting area of Nola's bedroom, the two women look at each other, hoping the other can explain it. Joy stands, "I don't know about you, mom, but I need some water."

Absently, Nola replies, "Bring me one too."

When Joy returns, she expertly avoids touching Nola as she hands her the bottle. "Mom, I don't know what to do. If we touch it happens, and when we release that touch it use to go away. Now when we touch it happens and may or may not end when we release that touch or touch again. It's all topsy turvy. "

Nola just nods at first and realizes that it is important that she say what is on her mind. They can no longer hold back, or they will never figure this out. So, taking a deep breath she begins.

"For a long time now, we have had shared visions, but, and I don't know about you, I have also had some when I am alone, like when they first started when I turned seven. From the time I was seven I felt that your grandmother had hidden resentment toward me because of my closeness to Neves. Never once did I think that there could be another reason. Later I learned that the real reason was because she dreaded my future once I became obsessed with--IT. Her mother before her was born on the seventh day of the seventh month just like my mother. Therefore, she knew that I would dread the day I was born. She had gone through the same thing. The entity had entered her life at just, past seven years of age and she had tried to ignore its existence but failed. She had begun to see the change in me, her girl child, born also on the seventh day of the seventh month. She watched me turn from a happy, carefree little girl into a shy, quiet young woman. The change, as had been the pattern for so long, took place just after the passing of my seventh birthday."

"Mom," Joy began.

"No, please don't interrupt. I must tell you everything now. I had hoped since you were born a twin you might escape the curse, but obviously not so I need to tell you all I know and then you can share what you know and just maybe together we can solve the riddle."

"Okay, mom, I'm listening."

Nola smiled and continued. "Her mother knew and could not bring herself to tell of IT for fear of making it even more real than its existence had been. I swore I would never do that. But I tried to believe it when your dad placed the change on being just a normal reaction in little girls as they grew into womanhood. But inside I knew. You and your brother Jonathan were born on the seventh day of the seventh month, but it was you only who had been born with a veil, just like I was."

"A what?"

"The medical term for it is a caul. It is a shimmery coating over the head and face."

Seeing her daughters horrified expression, she quickly added. "The caul is harmless, and it is easily

123

removed. A caul over a newborn baby's head happens occasionally, though they are not especially rare, and a child born in this way is known as a caulbearer."

Joy has a look of despair as she listens. It sounds awful no matter how her mother tries to sway it.

Trying to put a positive spin on it, Nola says, "In medieval times the appearance of a caul on a newborn baby was seen as a sign of good luck. It was considered an omen that the child was destined for greatness and protected from death by drowning."

"Drowning…"

"What's important is that you were chosen just like I was since you too were born on the seventh day of the seventh month."

Nola stops with a look of sheer surprise on her face. "Oh my God. That's it. I think that this is what the number seven means." Nola leans back exhausted.

Joy is appalled by what her mother is telling her, but when she hears her mother's last statement she starts. "Oh, yes, I bet that is it. You've figured it out."

Joy smiles tensely, still unsettled by the caul thing which she is sure is what has caused her life to be thrown into turmoil. But right now, that isn't important. What is important now is open sharing is helping.

They continue conversing and neither one hears Ned come to the door. He peeks in and sees them talking together, turns around and goes back downstairs to sleep in the den. It is mind opening as they both speak and work on diagnosing their findings. Joy tells her mother. "I think having Jonathan disappear near the water may be partly a sign. He was my twin and my caul offered me protection against drowning and saw him as a threat, so he had to disappear…"

Nola didn't like where that was going but had to admit it was probably true. Only she told Joy that it could also mean that Jonathan was alive and that he was being protected in some way by the caul even though he didn't have one. Joy considered it. "Yes, that could be true, too."

"Mom, the one thing I can't explain is something that happened with Jennifer and me. We didn't have a fight of any kind and I know that both Jennifer and her brother thought I was odd, but she did try to be my friend until it happened."

"What happened?"

"Well it was more than seeing a pretty teenage girl dancing with her boyfriend when she suddenly burst into flames. I think Joy also saw the two hooded figures. The one in white and the other in black. The first time I saw them they were far away and the one in white stood way ahead of the one in black. It remained that way until the day that Jennifer saw them with me. Then they were almost side by side. I think the one in black is evil and is now gaining control over the one in white who is trying to help us."

Nola sat up straight on the chair. "I think you are right. I saw that change too. I see those two figures also and just like you said the one in white started out ahead of the other. Then my visions were simpler, not having to do with family or friends, but now, the power of the other is taking over and the evil forces are getting stronger while the good force is weakening."

Joy looks at her mother. Why did Jennifer see the vision? Is she like me, but able to control it more? It doesn't make sense."

Nola thought she knew. "Joy, back when we first met the Manns, I remember Jolene giving me a hug and withdrawing quickly. She had this confused look and I just ignored it, but I couldn't ignore a feeling of closeness to

125

this woman. Something had passed between us during that hug, but as usual, I dismissed it."

At that moment, the women were in harmony. "I think Jolene is the key."

Exhausted, but happy with all they had managed to piece together, they said goodnight. Shortly after Joy left for her room, Ned returned, unable to get comfortable in the small pullout in the den. He tiptoed into their room and stopped. "I thought you would be asleep by now. Can I get you anything?"

"No, honey, I'm fine. I was just talking with Joy."

"Anything important?"

"No, I'm exhausted. Let's go to bed."

CHAPTER 22

Putting It All Together

The following morning dawned bright giving Nola hope. As she dressed and made her way to the kitchen she was working on the pieces of the puzzle. A lot of things made sense now that were a mystery before. The fact that Jolene had taken it upon herself to try and expose her to all the haunts in Rochester was not just by chance. There was something more to it, but maybe even Jolene was not aware.

Then the fact that Jolene's daughter shared a vision with Joy. Well, that was, she thought impossible. Unless again there was something, they had missed that conjoined them beyond the friendship. Who was it that said, 'all things happen for a reason'. Well their coming here and finding this house next door to the Manns was a sign. The fact that Dr. Memer who had been in their lives for so long was willing to move to continue to be their doctor, was another sign. But what did it all mean? How did they all connect.

Nola went about putting on the coffee and was in the midst of putting a fry pan on the stove when her mother joined her. As usual May let her lead the conversation and Nola was ready.

"Good morning Mom. I'm about to fix some eggs and bacon. Would you like some?" May nodded. Nola headed toward the refrigerator but changed her path as she moved to the side of May and gave her a bear hug, whispering in her ear, "I'm sorry, so sorry."

May squeezed her daughter and then gently pushed her back. "Sorry about what dear?"

"I'm sorry I didn't understand why you seemed a little distant to me. I do now. You were afraid that if we did get too close spiritually, you would be in the same boat with me as I am now with Joy."

The fact that May remained quiet, Nola knew this to be true.

Neves was the next to arrive in the kitchen. "Ah, my two favorite women." May and Nola smiled. As he walked over to sit beside May, he rubbed her arm. "What are we having?"

"Well, I was about to fix some eggs and bacon."

"I'm in."

"You're in on what?"

The voice came from Ned who was standing behind the island. Nola offered him breakfast and he sat down beside Neves. They watched as Nola worked on getting the breakfast ready, shooing May when she tried to help. Soon they were all seated at the table enjoying the meal and that was when Nola started to tell them that they had sat up late, going over everything they had heard and had some clues as to what they should do.

Neves tried to keep the worried look off his face as he asked, "I hope it's not dangerous, sweetie. You need to be careful."

"Don't worry pops, I will. We are going over to see Ed this morning and I think it would be comforting to him to have you with me. He has been through a lot, but we need to ask him some questions."

"I'd be glad to go with you."

"Well, let me know when you're ready."

Nola got up from the table and went over to kiss her father. "Thank you."

While May cleared the table, Nola went in the kitchen to rinse and load the dishes into the dishwasher. In no time the kitchen and the dining area were back in order.

May was quiet. She was afraid. It had been some time since she had a vision and she didn't want to get involved now. All of this may make her visions start up again. She had a feeling that what she had seen was nothing compared to her daughter and granddaughter and it may be due to the fact they were direct descendants of the Ceps and she was one by marriage. May thought about that for a while. She had tried for so long to figure out who was the cause of this curse being passed on and because she had visions, she blamed herself. But now, she wondered about that.

May first saw the two figures clearly when she was in her teens. She and her dad had gone to take a helicopter ride around New Jersey. This was something they could never have afforded, but her dad had been given it as a reward for some idea he had offered at the plant that had ended up saving many man hours. Her Dad would have liked a cash award, but he was glad just to be recognized. May's mother didn't want to go up in any little squish plane as she called it, so he decided to take May.

May was so happy. If she had friends, she would have been telling them all about it, but she didn't have any friends. When the day arrived, she was so excited her mother had to keep reminding her to do things, like tie her shoes. Finally, they were ready and out the door.

They arrived early and stood watching as two men were using a power cart to jumpstart the helicopter. She didn't see anything wrong but heard one of them say it was acting erratically – moving up and then down. As they stood there they watched as the motion caused the main rotor blades to strike one of the men in the head. That was all she saw as she started screaming because there were two hooded figures blocking her view, coming slowly toward her and her father. She screamed and screamed until her father picked her up and held her close.

"May, what is it."

She had lifted her head from his shoulder and asked if the man was all right and her father asked, "What man."

Putting her down on the ground, May looked toward the helicopter to see the two men motioning them over. It had been a vision, a powerful one and she could not get on the helicopter.

She saw the disappointment in her father's face as he told the pilot that they would have to pass on the ride. When they asked if he wanted to reschedule, he told them, "No." May could hear the despair apparent in his voice.

That had been the worse day of her life. She had never seen such a cruel vision nor had one happened before to interfere with her family. She tried to block out the image of the figures that were there, but she couldn't, and she took it all as a warning. When her father had asked what had happened, she never told him. From that day forward she tried to let it go.

She can't remember seeing those figures or something so tragic again until after she and Neves married. There were several times she had to suppress her visions, which she learned how to do, or maybe it was more that she had passed them along to Nola. In any case, she didn't want to test her strength at pulling back.

CHAPTER 23

The Day After

Joy came into the living room to find everyone seated, watching the news. When she entered, Nola looked up. "Good morning. Can I get you something to eat?"

"No, I'll fix it. You relax."

Nola watched as her daughter went into the kitchen. She could hear her moving about, opening, and closing drawers and saw the light in the refrigerator as she stood staring in it, trying to decide. When she closed the door, Nola was seated at the island, smiling at her.

Neither one said a word as Joy continued to open and close cabinet doors and drawers. Finally, she had all the fixings on the counter. Each movement was precise as she first opened the box of cereal and poured some into the waiting bowl. Next she opened the carton of milk and slowly tilted it over the bowl, careful to not add too much. That done, she closed the carton of milk, meticulously rolled down the plastic bag of the cereal and with the clip she had taken from one of the drawers, she put it over the top. Her final movement was to reclose the carton by sliding the tip of one edge into the opening of the other.

Nola had a smile on her face as she thought that by the time her daughter finished, the cereal would be soggy,

132

and she wouldn't want to eat it. But, just as if she had read her mom's thought, Joy decided to leave the items out and just carry her dish to stand across from her mother.

Normally, Nola would tell her to sit down to eat, but she was sure her daughter had done this so that they could speak privately.

"What are we going to do today?"

"You are going to school. This is the last day of classes and I don't want you skipping."

"How about you. What are you going to do?"

"I am going to go with your father over to talk with Ed Mann. Hopefully Jolene shared something with him that will help us."

Joy thought about it for a moment. She would like to be present, but what could she do to help. Nothing really. Besides she knew that she made Ed nervous and he might not be able to remember anything if he was feeling on edge. Besides she had a plan of her own.

"I think I am going to talk with Jennifer..." Seeing her mom's expression, she added, "Don't worry, I'll be careful. I just want to talk to her and see if I can get her to talk to me and tell me what she saw that day. I think we need to know. Maybe her mother had mentioned how she had sensed a closeness with you and that they may share a little bit of what we experience. I'll be careful not to scare her, mom, just help her open up."

Nola thought that was a good idea. If she and Neves ran into a brick wall, she planned to tell Ned and hopefully he would be able to get Ed to share something. If Joy worked on Jennifer, she might not have to pull Ned into it at all. They were comfortable with that and Nola told Joy to text her if she had some success and she would do the same.

With their plans in order, Nola watched her family disperse. She kissed Ned goodbye as he left to go to work and then she said her goodbye to Joy as she headed out the door for school. There was only May and Neves with her now and Nola sensed that May was uncomfortable with all of it. Nola could understand since she had felt the same way. She too had thought that if she ignored it and kept quiet it would all go away. But it didn't and it had become worse. As much as she would have liked to turn her back on what was happening and hope it all ended, she couldn't. Not when she now knew it was becoming more powerful and was affecting those that she loved. She was not about to lose any more. She was going to fight it until her last breath.

With everything back in place downstairs, Nola went up to take a shower and get ready. She wanted to wait a sensible amount of time before she and her father went over to the Manns home. She figured that like their household, everyone would be settled into their day by around ten which meant she had two hours to kill.

To prepare for the confrontation, she decided to look over the notes she had entered into the computer so that she would hopefully know what to ask Ned. And so, for the next couple of hours she had her computer open, reading and when she got an idea, she added it and then surfed the net to see if there was something there. She thought about calling Dr. Memer, but it was too early. She decided that what he had told her was enough for now, along with what Joy and she had figured out.

Nola looked up at the clock on the dresser. She had been at it for more than two hours. It was time. Nola hurried downstairs and found May standing at the bottom of the stairs as if waiting for her.

"Nola, I have something to tell you." While Nola had been upstairs searching, May was downstairs thinking. She decided that she had to tell Nola about that time with her dad. For some reason it was a premonition to her now and she was afraid for Neves. She wishes she could explain it better than just telling her daughter she could not take Neves with her to the Manns house, that it was unsafe, but that was all she had. Unfortunately, she didn't get a chance to say anything because Neves stood behind her and looking up at his daughter said, "Shall we go."

CHAPTER 24

Going To See Ed Mann

Nola walked beside Neves as they made their way over to the Mann's home. The Mann's house was much larger than theirs and was set off in a border of trees on either side, making it feel as though it stood alone on the block. It was a beautiful red brick house with white trim and burnt red shutters. Nola had been inside many times and knew that it was just as impressive on the inside where there was a wide foyer to greet the guest before going through a wide doorway to enter the family room, dining area and kitchen. It was set up much the same as theirs, only more spacious.

She stepped up on the porch beside her father and watched as he pressed the doorbell. Several minutes passed. Nola was afraid that Ed wasn't home, and they would have to wait until later to do this, but just when she was about to tell her father what she was thinking, Ed opened the door.

It wasn't the man she was used to seeing. This was a different Ed, still handsome but not the same. His eyes peer out through a wild tangle of grey hair like those of a cornered animal. Nola began to think this wasn't a good idea. The man is suffering, and she was about to open up the wound again so that she could have some satisfaction. It wasn't fair. But before she can speak, she hears his voice low and monotone, say, "Hi Neves. Hi Nola, come in."

With those words Ed sealed his fate and they stepped over the threshold to join him inside. "I was just about to pour myself a cup of coffee. Would you like to join me?"

They both nodded though they had their fill of coffee that morning. They followed him into the kitchen and just like at their home, they were able to sit at the island. The difference was that their island had seating around a curve so that the individual on the other side could sit across from them.

Cordially they accepted their cups and waited until Ed was seated at the island before talking. Neves asked Ed about his golf game and that brought a smile to his face as he shared his latest accomplishment on the course.

They both listened intently, and Nola managed to smile at the proper time. When Ed asked Neves if he would like to go out again for a game of golf, Neves said he'd like that. Ed said, "Ned is turning into quite a golfer. Each time we go out, Ned scores better than me." He chuckled. "Yes, Nola, that husband of yours is quick to learn all right."

That made Neves laugh, and Ed joined in, while Nola remained silent.

"Okay, I have a feeling you both aren't here to share golf stories, so let me have it. Or should I say, Nola, what is on your mind."

Nola had been staring into her coffee cup and waited a bit before lifting her head and looking at Ed. She tried for a smile but didn't quite make it.

"I feel bad about asking this, Ed, but I have to. Joy and I have been able to come up with some information to help explain what has been happening because it is getting worse. It is now affecting those that we love so we must figure out what we need to do."

Nola is surprised that Ed doesn't look as though he thinks this is preposterous. It looks more like he has been prepared for this.

"Ed, did Jolene say anything that might help us figure out what we should do? Anything at all?"

Ed takes a sip of his coffee and sits it back down on the counter. He then looks across at Nola. "Yes."

"Yes?"

"Yes. She did."

Nola sat quietly, trying not to hurry Ed as she could see it was hard for him. Finally, he spoke.

"If there is anyone, I can tell this to without being judged, it's you Nola." He paused again. "Anyone else would say I was crazy, and I would agree with them to have me locked up, but you will understand."

Nola didn't know what to do, so she just nodded her head. "Okay, here goes. Jolene was gone and one night I woke having problems breathing. I think my heart stopped beating for an instant and then it was like there was nothing, no one, just a blank nothingness. That's the best I can do to describe how I felt. In any case, I finally composed myself and was able to breathe again. And that's when I heard it."

Nola stared straight at Ed, making him nervous. Seeing that look in his eyes, she forced herself to lower hers and squeezing her finger, managed to sit quietly as she waited for him to continue.

"It was so quietly spoken I could barely hear the words at first, but recognizing the voice, my ears perked up. It was Jolene and she said, "Matthew, give the pages to

Nola. Give the pages to Nola." Then I felt a light touch on my hand."

Neves was having a hard time believing this. "Are you sure, she said that?"

"Yes, but when I asked Matthew about it, he seemed to draw a blank."

Nola, now quite good at putting things together was working mentally on this. She told it to Ed but called out Matthews name. What was she trying to say? While Neves and Ed talked, she continued to concentrate and then she had an idea.

"Ed, maybe she told you, but the papers are in Matthews room, or on his computer, or…"

"Ed was nodding. I think you have something there. I have looked for these papers and found nothing, but I didn't check Matthews room or his computer."

As if one, all three got up and headed toward the stairs. They moved quickly and followed as Ed led the way to Matthews room. Once inside, they dispersed to different areas, going through everything, even on the floor of the closet they searched. "Oh, God, I hope Matt will forgive me for going through his things."

Without looking up, Nola consoled him. "I'm sure he will."

At one point Nola heard Ed say, "Forgive me Matt for invading your privacy."

It was Nola who went over to the computer and turned on the monitor. Just like at their home, the system was always on, but they turned off the monitor to conserve energy. As soon as the screen opened, she knew she had something.

Ed moved over to where she was seated and said, "Matt hasn't used this system for a long time. He tends to be on his pad or phone. Very rarely does he work on the computer anymore.

On the screen are the notes that Jolene had written. It seemed just random words until they finished reading to the end and then it all made sense. Ed had been reading over Nola's shoulder and had the same reaction as she did. "Oh my God!"

Neves hearing them, joined them, and started reading. He too could think of nothing to say, but, "Oh my God."

Sticking out from under the keyboard were some pages and Nola pulled them out. Carefully she unfolded them. Everything on the screen matched that which was on the pages, except that on the pages, how she came to each conclusion was scribbled randomly before she was able to put it all together.

Nola turned her head to look up at her father and then over to the other side to look at Ed.

"Print it out, Nola. It's connected to the system in my office."

Nola didn't hesitate but did exactly as asked.

"What about the pages," she said, holding up the sheets she had found under the keyboard.

"Take them with you too." Or, if you like, we can make a copy and maybe I can help figure it out?"

"Okay."

The three went back downstairs to get the printed copies and to make copies of the sheets. When they were done, they felt like they had run a race. Ed looked at his watch and then peered into the kitchen to look at the clock for confirmation. Neves seeing this, looked at his watch. "I don't believe it. We have been at this all day. It doesn't seem possible."

It was, for at that moment Matthew and Jennifer opened the door, coming back from school.

CHAPTER 25

Jolene's Notes

"Nola, before you start going over the notes, I have something I need to tell you. It will help explain why I didn't want you to involve your dad in this. I know I should have told you sooner, but I didn't want to add one more thing to the fire."

"Mom, it's okay. I know how hard this is for you and I didn't want to have dad go with me, but he wanted to, and I thought it would make Mr. Mann more comfortable." Nola paused and peered at May. "So, tell me."

May took a deep breath and started by assuring Nola that she did not blame her for anything she had done or what might happen. Maybe nothing would happen, but she had to know so that she would understand. With that said, she began.

"When your dad and I first started out, we lived in a haunted house. Strange things happened all the time, but mostly to me. One day though, your dad and I were alone in the kitchen making a snack like I do for you when you come home from school. We put a plate on the kitchen counter and walked together to the fridge. Your dad, from the day I met him has always made me feel safe and happy." May had a sweet smile on her face as she thought about Neves." Anyway, we were giggling like children and kept pushing each other to get what we craved as there was usually just enough for one in the items we saved for snacking."

"We got what we wanted out of the fridge, turned around to walk back to the counter and I saw the figure in the black hood standing next to the plates. By now I knew that they were part of a vision that only I could see so I didn't say a word. Your father went to the counter to pick up his plate, but before he could touch it, it flew off the kitchen counter and broke on the floor."

"Your dad just stood there at first, then twisted his body to look at me. He said, 'did you see that,' and I just said, 'what?' He turned back around, and the hooded figure held out a bony finger and pointed at your dad as if warning me."

May took a drink of her iced tea. "If I had any doubt that it was a warning to keep my mouth shut, that ended when the next morning I woke to see the same hooded figure standing at the bottom of the bed, closer to the side your dad slept on. It didn't say a word, just stood threateningly close to him and then disappeared. I think, no I know it was a warning to not tell Ned anything about it. And I never did."

"Oh, mom, I'm sor…"

"Nola, I said it wasn't your fault. It was mine for not telling you this. So, we need to move forward with assiduousness."

May didn't have to say anything more. Nola not only understood that her mother wanted her to as much as possible keep Neves from actively participating, but also to keep a watchful eye out for any danger. That she was more than willing to do. Nola nodded.

Nola waited the rest of the day for Joy to return home from school. They had decided to sit down together and work on deciphering the pages from Jolene, and though it was hard to just wait, she agreed with Joy. In Joy's opinion 'two heads were better than one' and she didn't want her mom or herself to get stuck on one translation. Besides it was easier for two people who help each other to solve a problem than it is for one person to solve a problem alone. Working together they could reach the right conclusion. Outside of that first look at the pages over at the Mann's home, neither one had studied Jolene's information, but instead had concentrated on what they knew and what they had experienced. Together with Jolene's information and their own, they would figure out what it all meant.

Joy bounced in from school, looked around for her mother and not seeing her, ran up the stairs to get changed. When she came back down, Nola was in the kitchen with a snack on the counter. Joy thanked her as she sat calmly eating while her mother drank a glass of iced tea.

The house was quiet with Ned still at work so there was time for the two to talk. Nola told Joy what her mother had told her and that they couldn't pull anyone into this anymore than they had already.

"Ah," Joy began hesitantly as she looked directly at her mom, "I confronted Jennifer today at school. It wasn't easy as she tries to pretend, she doesn't hear me when I call out to her and tries to hurry away. In any case, I managed to pull her aside and asked if she remembered the day we were playing in the yard and we grabbed hands to swing around. Jennifer had nodded her head, so I said, 'You pulled your hands away as if something frightened you.' Jennifer looked like she was going to cry, but I was persistent. I came right out and asked if she had seen the teenage girl dancing with her boyfriend when she suddenly

144

burst into flames. It took a while before she admitted she had seen it. I then tried to console her before asking if she had also seen the two hooded figures. The one in white and the other in black. She, I think, answered honestly when she said she wasn't sure she had seen them."

Nola could see that Joy was amazed even now, knowing that Jennifer had been part of her vision.

"I was shocked enough that she had seen anything. I have never had that happen with another person beyond you, mom."

Now it was Nola's turn. "Jolene, called me and told me that Jennifer felt something when you two held hands. She mentioned that she felt something go between us on that first evening we met; something she couldn't explain."

"Are they like us?"

"No, I don't think so. Jolene said that she has always been highly sensitive and grew up with people thinking there was something wrong with her, but there isn't. Somehow it seemed to have passed on to Jennifer since she is the same way. Jolene told her that sensitivity is a normal, healthy trait that comes with a lot of advantages because they are aware of the feelings that exist inside their body, as well as the feelings inside the bodies of every other person in their space at any given time.. Jennifer doesn't see it as anything but a curse; especially after what she saw when she touched you, but for Jolene, well it makes her work hard to help the person. Like she did with me." The thought of this, brings tears to Nola's eyes. "It's probably what really killed her."

Joy agreed with her mother. It was more likely that Jolene's trying to help them was what killed her and not that she had a heart attack.

"But I don't see the difference between our visions and their; what you call high sensitivity."

145

Nola thought for a moment before trying to explain this to Joy. "Well, as it turns out, there is actually research on this trait, high sensitivity. The scientific term is 'sensory-processing sensitivity'. People who are highly sensitive are born that way; it is not something they learned. Jolene told me there are good and bad points to it."

"Like what, for instance."

"Well Jolene said that she experiences the blueness of the oceans like nobody else does. When she enters a room, she is the first to notice odors, subtle sounds, and startles easily. When she watches TV series, she immerses herself in each of the characters. It takes her days to recalibrate her sense of self after watching a movie or reading a book."

"What you are saying is that her sensitivity makes her feel deeper, but not necessarily have visions like we do."

"That's it in a nutshell."

Joy gazed into the distance as if wanting to say more. To her, this was a good explanation, but Jennifer had seen her vision. Was that just sensitivity or more?

CHAPTER 26

Another Episode

Joy walked with her mother to the office where they had locked the pages in a drawer of the desk. Joy turned on the lights while Nola unlocked the drawer.

"Joy, close and latch the office door. I think we shouldn't let anyone in here while we are doing this."

"Good idea."

Finally, they can sit down with the notes in front of them. "Look at this," Nola says fondly as she looks at the pages. She has put page numbers on the printout. Makes it easy to know where she started and ended."

"She did the same to her handwritten notes," Joy added.

"Mom, do you think we are doing the right thing? I mean, this is Jolene's files, and these are meant for us. But..."

"I almost forgot!" Joy reached in her pocket and pulls out a flash drive. "I'm sorry, but I put some stuff that I thought might help on this drive. It may be personal and not what I thought it was, but..."

"It's okay Joy. We'll look at it if we need it. I think Jolene wouldn't mind. I believe she wanted to help us, no matter what it took."

Not thinking, Joy went over and hugged her mother. And just like that they were no longer in the office.

They were driving down a strange road. Nola asked her to see if she could see a street sign so they could get their bearing. Joy nodded and then leaned closer to the side window, staring out.

It was late, the evening dark as ink with no streetlights along the route. The windows fogged and the rain coming in a thin, dingy spat and drizzled made it impossible to see anything. Joy rolled down the window and leaned her head forward, the rain splashing against her face as she squinted to see anything that would identify their location.

Nola tried not to show Joy how scared she was as she drove cautiously. Joy said, "Mom, I think there is something up ahead. I think we are on the road to the grocery store."

Nola turned her head toward her daughter. "Good." She felt tired, but better now that she knew where they were. In that instance a dog appeared out of nowhere racing across the street and directly in front of their car. Nola tried to break but was unable to stop the car before it hit the dog.

"Oh my god. Oh my god."

"Take it easy mom. Pull over."

As soon as the car stopped, Joy and Nola climbed out and headed to where now stood a man with his son already leaning over the dog.

"I'm so sorry. So very sorry." Nola kept apologizing to the man and his son even before she got up to them.

"Don't worry, Madam, it wasn't your fault. There was no way you could have avoided hitting the dog."

Joy looked at the boy who was silent. His long hair plastered against his head and his shirt clinging to his body. He looked up and Joy could see, even with the rain falling on his face that he was crying. He had a hurt expression on his face and Joy wanted to take the pain away.

"Maybe he's all right." Joy turned toward her mother, "Is he all right?" When her mother didn't answer Joy reached out and touched her.

That touch reset the whole scene. They were back in the car driving. It was still dark and rainy as they approached the same location, but instead of a dog running out in front of them, it was a man, standing in the lane that they hit.

Nola pulled the car over and they quickly walked toward the figure lying in the street. Hurrying toward the prone figure, Nola stood over him. It was a man. Nola let out a scream. Joy was right on her heels and when she was next to her mother, she leaned over the body and started screaming and crying uncontrollably. It was Neves laying there on the ground. When they both moved closer and reached to touch Neves, they were channeled back to the original scene.

Nola heard herself say in a shaky voice, "I am so sorry sir." She turned to the boy and said, "So very sorry." Then she straightened and asked, "Is there anything I can do."

The man shook his head and again told them not to worry. They watched as the man leaned down and picked up the dog. He turned to the boy and said, "Come along son."

Joy and Nola stood there watching as they carried the dog across the street to the sidewalk. They remained transfixed as the man took out his cell and soon was talking to someone on the other end. When a car beeped, Joy and

Nola jumped and turned around. "Get out of the road Ladies!"

Confused, sensing that they were still caught up in their vision, they quickly walked back to the car and climbed in. This was not how it usually played out. Usually they would return to where the vision started, but not this time. It was all changing. Nola turned on the engine and then turned to her daughter and knew that they had to get home right away. The store was forgotten as they carefully drove back home.

It seemed like forever before they were finally pulling up into their driveway. They waited patiently until the garage door opened and they drove in. Nola pressed the button on the visor and the door started its way back down, but before it reached the drive, they had jumped out of the car and burst into the house as quickly as they could. In the mud room they slipped out of their wet boots and socks and pushed their coats off their shoulders and let them fall to the floor in a heap.

Neither one questioned the other as they called out to Ned. It was Nola who found him, sleeping on the couch in the living room.

Ned lay there, rubbing the sleep form his eyes and trying to wake up. "Dad, wake up, we have to tell you something."

"Okay, what is it." They could tell he was now fully awake as he sat staring at them with a quizzical look on his face until he saw the expression on theirs. "Oh, what has happened. Are you all right?"

It was Nola who spoke. "Honey, I think we hit a dog." Seeing his reaction, she quickly continued. "But that's not the problem. We apologized to the boy and his father and they took care of that. What happened before they took their dog off the street, is, that…"

150

Nola couldn't say it so Joy chimed in. "Dad, we saw Neves. We saw the dog change to Neves, and he was lying dead in the street." She was hiccupping her way through as she cried uncontrollably.

Ned was wide awake now. "Was it real or was it a vision?"

"That's it, we don't know for sure. We were in the office and then we were in the car and driving. Usually when the visions end, we are back where we started, instead we went into the second vision that changed the dog into Neves and we never returned to the office... I don't know how much was real and how much was vision."

He could hear the confusion in his wife's voice as she tried to tell him what happened. Though he didn't have all the details of what had taken place, Ned had sensed that things were changing, and it was getting dangerous. The spells or visions if you will, were never so vivid and alive like they had been recently and inside he had the feeling that no one was safe. And just like that a thought popped into his head.

"Listen girls, we must get Neves some place safe." They nodded in agreement.

CHAPTER 27

Working Through Jolene's Notes

Joy and Nola could sense that something or someone didn't want them to view Jolene's notes. But they had no choice, if they wanted to stop these visions.

"Shall we get started?"

Calmer now that they are back home, without saying a word, they decide to not stay in the office. Instead with the notes in hand, Nola and Joy make a beeline to the kitchen island. Seated side by side, they lean over the printouts trying to decipher what Jolene has entered in the computer.

Several times they glance at each other in amazement. Jolene had somehow been able to figure out the key. Though she hadn't mentioned anything about the number 7, she seems to have figured out something just as important to them.

Neves has been standing in the doorway watching his daughter and granddaughter as they study the papers. "So, what is it."

Both look up at the same time. "It's nothing. We haven't figured it out yet."

"Give me the handwritten notes and let me see if I can come up with something."

Hesitantly, they turn and then, instead of giving him the pages, they patiently say, "We need to do this ourselves."

There was no way of denying the hurt in Neve's eyes. He drops his head down and his shoulders droop as he turns and walks away. Nola has all she can do, to not follow him or to call him back and explain. Best to stick to the plan and not draw anyone else in.

Even though the vision had forced them to not want to be in the office, they know they have no choice as they start gathering the papers and carry them back to that room. They had been so frightened by that last vision; they didn't feel safe in there. They knew that but didn't want a repeat of anything. Only it was safer for them to be in that room to go over the pages.

Once in the office, they locked the door and got started. Every now and then one of them would reach up and stretch out as they continued to work diligently. It was all there, but in pieces as Jolene had jotted down each thought as it came to her. In between she had written notes that explained what she had done. When Nola found the first key, she looked up at Joy and said, "It's me. I am the special one."

"How do you figure mom."

"Well, she has written that down and next to it she put my name. Under that she wrote, 'reverse it'. I wasn't sure what she meant at first, but it means to reverse my name."

"Nola in reverse is alon; so, what does that mean?"

"No silly, my full name. Enolai Ceps. My full name before I became a Log. That's what was puzzling me. But anyway. My name in reverse is Special One."

"Under it she has written notes. It means there is a place in their heart that holds a special spot for you. You probably have a way of making them feel a certain way, or you add a certain value to their life that is not added by someone else."

"That doesn't help us, really."

Nola read on. "There are so many variables that would make you special to them. Angel number one is the angel number that you are likely to see often on your spiritual journey. As a spiritual person you are likely to encounter new beginnings all the time. Seeing angel number one repeatedly means that the universe is offering you a new beginning, or clean slate."

"Okay, that says something. You are the special one and that makes you an angel..." Seeing her mother is about to interrupt. "Hold on, I know that you have a hard time being considered an angel, but," Joy looks down at her notes. "Before you protest and say that the figure in white is the angel, listen to this. 'The angel number 111 is a symbol of spiritual awakening, providing you with the opportunity to determine what your purpose in life is. ... But when they send the angel number 111 to you, it means that the power of this number will manifest in your life soon. They want to make sure that you're paying attention.'"

Joy looks deep in thought. "Think about it. You are Angel number 1 and the figure in white is Angel number 111." Nola must agree, at least for now.

"One more thing. I was born with a caul."

"What is that?"

"It's a membrane over the face of the newborn. Some people call it a veil, but in any case, in many belief systems they say that being born with a veil is a sign of special destiny and psychic abilities, or good luck. Once I learned about it, I read about this and found that most born with this are female and believe themselves to be psychically gifted, while others show no advanced abilities nor interest."

Nola looked at Joy. "Okay, now we are getting somewhere. I can see that you agree with me now Mom." They smile, all excited.

"It's right. I would never have gotten that either. Okay so let's go on."

They continued through the pages and the next name to write in reverse was Ned Log.

"Oh, Joy, I remember my dad saying when he first met Ned, they were talking about something and were in agreement. Your dad had said, 'Ned you're golden'."

"Mom, that's just a saying."

"Yes, I know, but in reverse Ned Log is?"

Joy waited and realized her mother wanted her to answer that so she quickly wrote down her father's name so that she could see it as she wrote it backwards. "Oh wow, its Golden."

"What does it mean."

Nola stops to think for a bit. "I do know that your father lived a hard life, but was able to smile through it, which is probably why his family and people he came in contact with wanted to help him and did."

Joy has been looking through the notes and reads, "The Golden One is haughty and proud, and adores his special one. He is strong and sharp. At the start woman feel subservient to him almost immediately, but he seeks one who feels his equal and will not become his total possession. Because of this the Golden One is nevertheless superior to those around him because he suspects that there is more to the world than the collective equality enforced in the society. This will make him stand out from the faceless, nameless masses."

Joy turns the page over and says, "Ms. Mann takes another viewpoint in quoting the Bible. "So, in everything,

155

do to others what you would have them do to you, for this sums up the Law and the Prophets."

Joy tips the page upside down and reads, "The English Standard Version translates the Golden Rule like this: "Whatever you wish that others would do to you, do also to them, for this is the Law and the Prophets."

"Well, I think there is something in there so let's highlight it and come back. Let's just keep going."

They continued through the pages seeing where Jolene had written every family member's name in reverse but was coming up with nothing. Joy Ceps-Log, Jonathan Ceps-Log, May Ceps, and it wasn't until she hit Neves Ceps that she got something, but it was just using his first name. She got, 'Seven' when she wrote it in reverse. That was not following the pattern of before, but she continued with that searching for a meaning.

Nola flips through the papers she has and starts, "The number Seven is a highly spiritual number that is associated with intuition, mysticism and a deep inward knowing. Seven has had significance in almost every major religion. In the Old Testament the world was created in six days and God rested on the seventh, creating the basis of the seven-day-week. In the New Testament the number seven symbolizes the unity of the four corners of the Earth with the Holy Trinity. Scholars have found that the number seven often represents perfection or completeness in the Bible and in Judaism, there are seven heavens. Seven is also a prime number, which means it can only be divided by itself and one."

Joy sat listening to her mother read, taking it all in.

"Anything in the handwritten section Joy."

Joy looked down and began looking through the notes. She smiled and began. "In Christian numerology, the number 888 represents Jesus, or sometimes more specifically Christ the Redeemer. This representation may

156

be justified either through gematria, by counting the letter values of the Greek transliteration of Jesus' name, or as an opposing value to 666, the number of the beast. In modern popular culture, 666 has become one of the most widely recognized symbols for the Antichrist or, alternatively, the devil."

"What are you thinking?"

Joy looks puzzled for a minute and then says, "That the number 7 falls between them both is all."

Nola, not quite sure exactly, says, "Well, we have nothing else, so lets just write that down for now."

CHAPTER 28

Meeting with Dr. Memer

They had come a long way, thanks to Jolene, but it wasn't clear yet. They needed to work on the number seven and both of them thought that they needed Dr. Memer's help. Nola put in a call and set up an appointment for them.

In the meantime, Joy and Nola tried to be patient and go about their daily life, trying not to touch and set of another episode even though they had a feeling it wouldn't matter anyway. The forces were so strong now and the one that was in the black robes has almost moved ahead of the one in white. They saw them in their dreams and later felt their presence as they moved about their daily routines.

They had made it all perfectly clear to everyone. No one questioned them now. The family knew the rule was to keep it all inside them so that nothing bad happened. So, they did. Many times, Nola would think that Ned was smart and could probably figure out what it all meant, but she couldn't chance it. The only one they could turn to was Dr. Memer. On the day of their appointment, they anxiously arrived at his office.

It had been a while since they had been to see him, but as usual, they were comfortable from the moment they entered the room. Once seated and catching him up on all that had transpired since their last visit, they couldn't wait to share their reason for coming.

"Dr. Memer, our friend Jolene Mann died, but before she did, she had done some research to try and help us figure all this out. She came up with some interesting things".

That was Joy's clue to read to him what they had summarized from all the notes that Jolene had written. Dr. Memer listened carefully to what they presented. He frowned at some points and nodded at others, but he never spoke until Joy read the last word. "So, doctor. what do you think?"

"Well, like I told you, the psychic, Margarette mentioned the number seven. She said it is all tied up with the number seven and that something is happening, and it is going to take a circle of seven to stop it."

"I don't understand."

"Neither did I, but she said she would have to see you two before she could put it all together. But she thought that maybe you might be able to figure it out yourselves. It sounds like you have a good start at it."

"We do, but we don't know who is part of the circle of seven since there are only three with a reverse spelling that means anything. How do we decide who else should be part of the seven and the big question is what do we do once we are all identified."

"Yes, that is a big question to say the least."

"It's important we figure this out soon as the visions are now entering into real life situations and taking away people that have been part of what we see."

Dr. Memer rolls his chair in front of the desk so the three are closer together. "Is it fair to say that the two hooded figures are energizing—they're almost alive?"

159

Nola and Joy nod. "As scary as that is, yes, that is what we think."

Dr. Memer stares off in the distance and says, "Even people who are not fascinated by numbers have a soft spot for the number Seven. For various reasons, many of us find it fascinating, even magical. Slot machines have jackpots with the sequence of Sevens. There are the seven wonders of the world. Like you mentioned it has had significance in almost every major religion. The number seven is also featured in the Book of Revelation--seven churches, seven angels, seven seals, seven trumpets, and seven stars. The Koran speaks of seven heavens and Muslim pilgrims walk around the Kaaba in Mecca seven times. In Hinduism there are seven higher worlds and seven underworlds, and in Buddhism the newborn Buddha rises and takes seven steps."

Dr. Memer gets up and is walking around, thinking. "Seven is associated with luck and magical properties. He pauses, "Oh, yes, and various parts of the world had beliefs about the seventh son of a seventh son, legends that endowed him with magical powers of both."

He takes a sip of water before he continues. "It has been cited as our memory capacity. A George Miller of Harvard University wrote that most people can retain roughly seven items of information in their short-term memory." He looks at his audience. "That is why phone numbers in the U.S. and many other countries tend to have seven digits as it is the most digits most people are likely to recall." Dr. Memer walks back to his desk and takes a seat. "I could go on, but I think you get the picture.

Nola says slowly, "Yes, I see."

"Wow, so it is an important number in so many ways, but how in our way?

"What I think is that there are two forces, one good and one evil fighting to be the survivor and the woman in

160

the Ceps family are all chosen ones. Both sides are fighting for power and existence. I think only one of them is aware of the need for seven to form a circle."

"But we don't have seven. If the power is in the Cep women there is Joy and May and me."

"Well, bear with me because I don't think it is only family. I think this goes beyond the family members. I had a dream...not a vision...a dream. I dreamt that we were all standing in a circle, but I could only identify you two. Yet I had a sense that there were men as well as women in the circle just like you have figured out. I also saw a hooded figure in white and I am going to say that it was good and not evil. The good one realizes that men and non-family are to be part of the seven."

The women stare at him. "I think you've figured it out. But why you?"

"Well, mostly because of how close I have worked with you, but the other reason is in my name in reverse."

He can see the puzzled look on their faces and taking a moment to enjoy it, he finally says, "My name is Reb Memer. In reverse, it is Remember. I think I am to be part of this circle. I have felt a closeness to you since day one and I only recently figured it out."

Understanding it now, Nola nods. "So, the Circle of Seven is me, you, Dr Memer, Joy, Neves, Ned and May. That's only six."

Dr. Memer shrugs his shoulders.

CHAPTER 29

The Safers

Nan didn't like herself much these days. Not in her weaker moments could she excuse her actions. As much as she fought against it, she knew in the end she had no choice, that she was driven to do something or say something.

She knew right from wrong and she knew good from evil. She couldn't help feeling that if she kept ignoring the voices she would be pushed to the dark side, but if she listened to them, she would be doomed. Lucky for her, she was forced into action.

The phone rang. Nan peered over the top of her book to look at her husband who was reclining in his favorite chair, steps away from the phone.

"Are you going to get that?"

Ted's forehead creased as he turned his gaze from the game on the tv to look at his wife. "Could you?" He followed those brilliant words with a lift of his arm and a finger pointing at the game.

Nan shook her head, laid her book down beside her on the couch and stood up. She reached out and rubbed her husband's cheek as she passed him.

"Hello?"

Before the caller answers, Nan knew who was on the other line. "Is that you May?"

"Yes, Nan, it's me."

Once she started, May couldn't stop as she rushed ahead. "Nan, I hate to bother you, but were you serious when you said that I could call you if I needed help."

"Yes, May, what is it?"

May decided to come right out and tell the whole story. She shared the vision that she and Joy had and how in the retelling to Ned, he had said that they needed to get Neves out of the house.

"I didn't know who else to call. They would think I was crazy...you probably think I am crazy...but can we come over this evening?"

Nan didn't hesitate. She could feel Ted's eyes on her and turned to look at him. He had a worried expression on his face as he nodded his head as if he knew what was being discussed. "Yes, May. Oh yes. We are here for you."

Nan slowly hung up the phone and with a puzzled look walked slowly across the room until she was beside her husband. "How did you know?"

"I think you know how. Ever since the Ceps family moved in, I know you've been having dreams."

Ted waited for Nan to respond. She did by nodding her head. "Sit down Nan. I guess I got a premonition. I think we are attuned to our neighbors and our friends, but more vividly to the Ceps. Yesterday I was making coffee when May, not Neves popped into my mind. I felt that she was thinking about me and would be in contact and so she was." He raised his arm in a fluttering motion. "That's not odd, really most people are hardwired in that way, even if they aren't aware of it. But you, Nan, well, you are special."

"What are you saying Ted."

"You don't have premonitions."

"I don't?"

"No. I have waking visions of a future. I get a sense of nervous anxiety; a gut feeling that something is about to happen. You on the other hand see a future event in your dreams while sleeping and that is a precognition event."

Nan is quiet, thinking about what he has said. "You are right, and it scares me. It never really bothered me before, but now, since the Ceps arrived, I feel something." She frowns. "For lack of a better word. I feel that I am their protector. Is that silly or what."

Ted assures her that it is not. "I figured that whatever was happening was serious. I noticed that you always keep a notepad with you; even next to the bed. I saw you several mornings frantically writing before you got out of bed."

"Yes, I didn't want to forget any of what I dreamt or felt."

Ted reached out and grabbed Nan's hand. He could feel her shaking. "Am I going crazy, Ted?"

"No, dear. I think we are about to understand what has been happening soon. You are far from crazy."

While Nan and Ted were coming to terms with what they had been sensing for some time, Joy and Enolai had a change of mind.

The next morning, they sat down with Ned who advised them that Neves and May were already involved and for their own safety they needed to be included now.

Hesitantly, Nola went to get May and Neves. She didn't have to go far as they were standing at the entrance to the living room, eavesdropping on their conversation. Caught in the act, they tried to look innocent.

"Ah, we were just on our way to get something to drink."

"It's okay mom, dad, I was coming to get you. We want you to join us."

They started at the beginning, telling May and Neves about the name reversals that Jolene Mann had figured out during her attempts to help.

"Is she like you and Joy?" May asked.

"No, mom, I just think she senses things deeply. She said she knew there was something going on with me the first time she touched me and knew she had to help. It was like it was her mission to figure out what was happening because she felt it was getting stronger."

"I think she was right."

Quiet permeated the room as they each dealt with their own thoughts until Joy spoke up.

"Papa. Grandma. It gets worse. Jennifer not only sensed something; she actually saw what I was seeing." Joy went on to tell them of the vision she had that day and how Jennifer had reacted. "That's why she would never play with me again."

"It is becoming more frequent now and we are seeing friends and family in our visions. It scares us."

The four of them continue to share with each other and tried to decipher the meaning with it all mushed together. There were so many secrets unveiled, including the fact that May and Nola were both born on the seventh day, of the seventh month. Joy too shared this distinction, but Nola had thought that since she was a twin, she had hoped she would be spared the visions.

"What do we do?"

It was Ned's turn to speak. "We have discussed many angles and have decided that in order to break the visions we need to contact these spirits that Joy and Nola keep seeing in their dream."

"So how do you propose to do that?" May asked.

Ned didn't answer. Nola spoke up instead. "Mom let's fix some breakfast. I think we could all use some nourishment."

May, like Nola wanted to find the answer, but knew they needed to take a break, so she got up and started getting out the makings for breakfast, while Nola gathered the utensils.

While the men sat at the island, Nola and May soon had everything underway. Joy set the table and the men moved over to sit there while May and Nola brought the food over.

Every member of the family could feel the tension in the air as Joy filled their water glasses and May poured the coffee. When they finally sat down, there was silence, except for the sound of the silverware against the china. It wasn't until the meal was over and the table cleared, did they pick up the conversation.

Before addressing May's question, they shared the fact that Jolene had mentioned the number seven in her notes and to decipher what that meant, they went to see Dr. Memer.

"Mom, do you remember how surprise you were when Dr. Memer decided to move here from New Jersey?"

"Yes, I remember."

"Well, there was a reason. It seems in his exploration of all this, he went to see a psychic who told him that there was something about the number Seven."

"Great, so what did that mean."

166

"Well the psychic said she couldn't figure that out without meeting with us. Only we think that we have figured it out. In talking with Dr. Memer we realized that he is also part of the equation. His name in reverse is 'Remember'. He thinks that he is to remember all that we have told him and all that he has learned, and he was to share it with us. We think he is part of what we determined to be a circle of Seven."

Nola can see the puzzled expression on her parent's faces. "What it seems to mean is that it will take a circle of Seven to stop these spirits who are always part of our visions. These spirits we now determine represent good and evil. At the start the one that was evil was in the back and the one who was good stood in front. Now they are almost even and that means the evil one is gaining on the good."

"I don't understand daughter."

"Simply put it is the change in their position, that is why our visions are more frequent and are causing harm to those we love."

Nola can see that her mother is beginning to understand as she nods and then says, "How does Dr. Memer fit in as the one to bring it all together."

"Well, his name is Reb Memer. In reverse it is 'remember'.

"Oh my God."

Nola wondered what to do next. Since it had helped Joy and her to understand, she decided to share a vision. She pondered for a moment and then it came to her exactly what she should share.

"Mom, my earlier visions were always about someone I had no connection to, and I could never understand why I dreamt or was a part of them. Now I think it was that I was in training."

167

"What do you mean, Nola."

"Well that I had visions that were not pleasant, but because they weren't about anyone I know, it was less personal and I didn't worry what was going to happen to whom; if you know what I mean..., so I could let it go. The one that was most disturbing and probably the only one that I visualized at different stages was the one I want to tell you now."

May looked at her daughter, understanding what she is trying to say.

"I saw this woman with her two children; a boy and a girl. The little girl wore a plaid button-down shirt over slim pressed blue jeans. Her brother had on denim jeans with a plaid vest. It looked to be a special occasion as the woman wore a tight-fitting dress crafted from a soft, stretch fabric in red, along with high heels and nylon stockings. In this vision, the woman dressed in her best finery prepared to sit down to eat with the father of the children. It was easy to see how the woman adored the man just by the look in her eyes. When she looks at him, her eyes look calm and kind and sweet. They even seem to sparkle."

Nola paused in the telling and turned toward Ned. "It's how we look at each other," she said with a smile. Then she continued.

"Once the meal was over and the children put to bed, the man took advantage of this time with the woman. Like many times before, she couldn't help herself as she asked him when would he marry her? The man never gave her a direct answer, but instead he'd kissed her deeply and she took that to mean he would."

"Any way, the next time I saw her I heard the clock strike midnight and I hear an eerie cry that echoed throughout the night. The same woman, I think, and it could have been happening in the sixties, at least that's the style of clothing she wore. She wandered about the town stricken with grief wearing a red and white stripe stretch knit top with a fabulous fold over that extended to her arms for a retro off shoulder neckline. With it she wore a gathered A-line swing skirt in a navy-blue color, cinched at the waist with an elastic buckle belt. As I watched her crying and screaming, I saw dark stains on her skirt and blotches of red on her top and I realized she was covered in blood!"

Nola paused to reflect before continuing. "What I gathered from conversations she had, the man grew tired of her and stopped coming to see her. She had been dependent upon him for financial support, but now he neglected to send her money."

"She was lonely and the need to know what had happened to change him, put a nasty taste in her belly until she made the mistake of going to his home to beg him to come back to her. She arrived at the home and did find him, but to her horror he was in the midst of celebrating his marriage to another woman. All she could do was rush to him in tears, but he pushed her away, coldly telling her that he had never told her he would marry her."

"The woman was hysterical as she ran home. She felt helpless and alone, unable to think what she could do. That evening she sat in the tiny apartment with her lights out, brooding over how hopeless she felt. She fixed herself a drink and paced as she downed first one, and then another until she could barely walk anymore. At that point, she went into the kitchen and taking the largest knife from the holder, she walked stolidly into her children's room. They were asleep, caught up in their dreams. She covered her daughter's mouth and began stabbing her repeatedly. When she was done, she went to her son and repeatedly stabbed him. She stood over them, glancing from one to the other until she realized what she had done. With that apprehension and covered with the blood of her own children, she fled from the house and dashed screaming through the streets, until she was arrested and thrown into prison."

By the time she finished, Nola was in tears. She kept wiping her eyes, but the tears kept forming on her cheeks. Finally, she was able to get herself under control and looked at her mother. Instantly she could see that the visions affected her deeply.

May couldn't speak as she stared at her daughter.

Nola sensed it was more than her visions affecting her mother now. "What is it mother?"

"I used to have that same vision because it happened. I was about fourteen and we lived in an apartment building. The sound of her screaming woke up everybody in the neighborhood. Someone called the police and they came. I watched through the window as they took her away and taped off the house. I was afraid to go back to sleep because I knew what would happen before it actually happened because I dreamt it."

"Oh mom, I wish I hadn't chosen that vision."

"No, we just learned something by that. You shared something I saw that haunted me as a vision. That to me means there is a connection between us that goes deeper."

Nola thought about it, nodded. "Yes, you're right. She wrote her mom's reference down.

When everyone calmed, Joy told of one of her visions.

Joy told that on an evening in October she went to a Halloween party with some friends. "We were encouraged to dress in scary costumes, so I decided to be a witch. You helped with the costume, remember?" Nola nodded. "I had on purple and black striped leotards, a black loose-fitting short dress with a ruffled off the shoulder top and a pointed hat. You found some huge buckles that we attached to the top of my high heeled shoes and I put on dark lipstick and shadow with long eye lashes. I won second prize in the contest."

"It was the most amazing party with foods like peeled grapes, because they looked like eyeballs, cooked thin spaghetti to appear like guts, steamed whole cauliflower to represent brains."

"The party room and garage were decorated to look like a haunted house with strips of black crepe paper to walk through. The lights were dimmed, and the walls were covered with black sheets with fake spiders and other creepy crawlers. They had some kind of spooky music playing and ghosts hanging around the rooms along with an area made to look like a graveyard. It was the perfect atmosphere to initiate a scary vision."

Joy paused as if reliving the scene. "Peter, that was his name, was dressed like a zombie. He wore some old, old jeans that had one leg ripped clear up to his hip and the other leg full of holes with what looked like blood and mold all around the holes. He even had fake blood running down his chin and coming out his eyes. He looked a real mess," she said with a smile on her face."

"I was dancing with Peter, when suddenly I wasn't there anymore and the boy that was holding me was not Peter—I didn't know who he was. He held me so tightly I could hardly breathe, and I fought to get out of his grasp."

Joy's whole demeanor changed as she began reliving that moment. It took her a while before she could continue.

"I could feel it. It was like I was driven by an inner storm. There were flames bursting furiously from my back and chest, enveloping my head, and igniting my hair. In seconds I was a human torch."

Again, she paused, confused, and scared. "I felt my partner let go as the skin on his hands began to melt, and then I was consumed by the flames and…"

"You died?"

"I did," Joy said to her mother. "I didn't tell you because I didn't want to scare you." It was the first and only time I died in my vision."

"Now what?" Neves asked.

"Now we get ourselves together and we fight. We fight for our family; we fight for our life."

CHAPTER 30

Taking The Final Plunge

The Ceps and Log now had a deeper understanding of what was happening to them. That evening, Nola could no longer deny that she was the chosen one, but knowing isn't as easy as being told, straight-up, that you're destined for greater things. So, she was chosen and so far, they had picked up subtle clues and come to terms with the fact that everyone is depending on her. This scared Nola to no end. She was not used to be a leader, but from all that had happened she should probably buckle up, because she had a date with destiny. Like it or not a higher power was sending her visions, ones she shared with her mother and others that she shared with her daughter. If she didn't act soon, the figure in the black cloak would kill everyone she cared about. She was the glue that held together this circle of seven. Oh, how she wishes she were just normal and not the figurehead of the rebellion that she never wanted to be a part of.

Nola sigh. At least she was not alone. There would be others to help her stop the impending disaster that threatened all life, though they were the only one's privy to it.

She knew what needed to be done first. Nola took a deep breath and said. "Dad, Mom, we need to talk with the Safers."

May looked at her daughter with empathy. Nola was glad she didn't ask why. Jolene had written in her notes about them. All she knew was that they had something to do with them, but what, she didn't know.

It was at Nola's request that May made the call to the Safers. When she hung up, she turned to Nola. "They have invited us to join them for dinner tonight."

That done, she was on to the next step to be taken. She and Joy were scheduled to meet with Dr. Memer. They both knew they needed to fill him in on all they had ascertained to date.

The time spent before the appointment was adding what they had learned through the recent conversations to all they had discovered earlier. As for their conclusions, that they would wait on until hearing what Dr. Memer had to say. Nothing was too insignificant to discuss.

When they entered the reception room, Dr. Memer was waiting for them. He could sense they were eager to begin so, he led them into the office and asked them to have a seat. They had barely sat down before they began. The words flew out of their mouths so fast that Dr. Memer, afraid he would miss something, had to turn on his tape recorder. When they finally stopped. He felt as breathless as they did.

"Well," he said. "Well."

"So, everyone is on the same page now. Whether that is a good thing or not, we had to get it all out in the open."

"I agree."

"There is something else," Joy added shyly.

174

"Jonathan! I know he is alive... somewhere... and I need to bring him home." She choked on the sobs she tried to hold back. Nola could only show her daughter with a nod that she agreed with her. If they touched, she was afraid of what might happen. Dr. Memer on the other hand, didn't agree. He was sure that Jonathan was dead, but he was not going to say it. Joy needed to hang on to that hope and he was not going to take that away from her.

Dr. Memer finished jotting down notes and looked at first Nola, and then Joy. He didn't say anything. He looked down at what he had written again and then lifted his head.

"I know that giving advice and opinions is my job, but I don't know what to do. I am too close to the situation and trying to take control of it I can put us all in jeopardy."

"No, that is not true. You have helped us to get to a point where we have an idea of what we need to do. This is a crisis situation and the stakes are high, and we may have only one shot at making a difference."

Dr. Memer smiled wanly. "Psychiatrists are not gurus with the answers to life's problems, but I feel I am experienced in treating patients in very difficult life circumstances because I have often heard variations of the same tragic stories many times. As relatively objective third parties with exposure to what has and hasn't worked for many other patients, I may have some helpful ideas. But should I share them? Are they right for this situation that is different from any circumstances I have encountered?"

"Yes, In my opinion, you should. I know this is not your typical situation. We are talking spirits. We are talking visions. What basis can you draw upon except your feelings. Besides, we know that you are part of us now, and probably was before we all knew how deep our connections went. But, in any case, you must go with us to

175

the Safers tonight. I think this is where are first step to solving this 'curse' will take place."

"So, do I have a choice?"

"Yes, you do, but I think it will be wise to come. Or maybe I should say, safer if you do come."

Neves and May were the first to arrive at the Safers home.

"Come in, come in, please. Where is the rest of the family?"

"Oh, they're running a little slow and I didn't want to be late."

They stood in the dramatic foyer with an arresting light fixture and a supersized tree sculpture in the distance that always made them feel as though they were entering a special, enchanted home. Nan hugged them both before showing them to the living room.

Ground level windows reach to the floor and can even be passed through for access to the porch are one of the unique features that make their home different from the others on the street. The enchantment continues throughout with twinkly fairy lights in the fireplace for a quirky touch in this neutral living room whose cool, modern feel comes from a large painting splashed with color and the oversized comfortable furniture.

On the side table is a tray of hors d'oeuvres.

"What can I get you to drink," Ted asked

"A red wine for me," May responded.

"Oh, what the heck, I'll have the same."

"Great, I'll be right back. On the way to the living room they had passed the drink station tucked into the side wall of the kitchen.

Ted was getting their drinks when the doorbell rang. Nan excused herself and went to answer it. If she was surprised, it didn't show on her face as she ushered Nola, Ned, Joy and Dr. Memer into the foyer. "She looked over her shoulder and said, "Ted, our other guests are here."

"Nan, this is Dr. Memer. We brought him because…"

"No need to explain. I know. Welcome Dr. Memer. Come join the rest of the group," she added as she led them into the living room.

Ted delivered May and Neves's drinks and then turned to the new company. "What can I get you?"

Nan excused herself and went with her husband to prepare the drinks. When they returned, they went around delivering the drinks and then Nan picked up the tray of hors d'oeuvres. "Come on folks, you have to try these. I made them myself."

No one refused as she made her way around the room. When she placed the tray back on the table, she sat down with her drink, nibbling nonchalantly on her hors d'oeuvre.

"We have had a great span of good weather lately," Ted said. "If it continues, Neves, want to join me tomorrow for a round of golf?"

That broke the ice of silence and everyone relaxed, adding to the conversation around them. It had already been decided that nothing about the recent exchanges they had would be discussed until after dinner. It would be cruel to ruin the meal because what they had to share would surely do that.

"Dr. Memer, how do you know the Ceps?"

"Well, I am a longtime friend of the family?"

"Can I ask what type of doctor you are?"

"Just your run of the mill doctor. Yes. Your run of the mill doctor."

Joy was taking a sip of her drink and it spurted out her mouth. "Oh, sorry."

Nan worked the corners of her cocktail napkin, folding them in and out as she smiled at her friends. She turned to her husband.

Ted added to his previous conversation. "I suppose Neves told you I have been teaching him golf. We go out every now and then, not as much as I'd like to though. Do you play, Dr. Memer?"

"Yes, I do." He paused. "But, please just call me Reb."

"Doc...Reb, we would love to have you join us on the course, wouldn't we Neves." He looked in Neves' direction.

"Sure, that would be nice."

Nan stood and excused herself. "I better check on dinner."

"Let me help you," Nola said.

"Me, too?" added Joy.

"Sure, the more the merrier."

All the women left the men to continue conversing, while they busied themselves with getting out the food and putting it into the serving dishes. Joy picked up a pile of dinner plates and started setting the table. They kept busy, smiling as they passed each other and making simple comments, "Oh, this looks delicious." "Thank you." "It smells heavenly." "Thank you."

It was Nan who returned to the living room and called the men into the dining room. May was always in awe of the gorgeous vintage shade of green that defined their elegant old-world dining room filled with antiques and linen dining chairs monogrammed with their initials. It was so perfect she was afraid to touch anything, but Nan would always say, "nothing is too precious that an accident would unnerve her".

Soon the sound of chairs sliding back and then forward on the floor filled the air until everyone was seated. Nan began passing the food. The sound of the serving utensils against the china replaced that of the chairs. When everyone had been served, they bowed their heads. Nan said a prayer. "Dear God, bless this food we are about to partake and let it nourish our bodies and mind, to prepare us for what lays ahead. Amen."

Whether noticed by the Safers or not, the guests slightly raised their heads with puzzled expressions on their face, but with a raise of an eyebrow or two, they lowered them and joined in with, "Amen."

The dishes were passed around the table. There was orzo salad, marinated chicken breasts, string beans, homemade rolls. Little was said while they ate until dessert was served. For dessert, Nan had prepared her specialty maple syrup cake and coffee.

"So, Doc...I mean Reb, have you gone on any exciting vacations lately?"

"Yes, matter of fact, I have. I went on a fishing trip with some friends."

"Where did you go?"

"Cairns, Australia. It's known for giant black marlin." He chuckled. I broke two rods and had nothing to show for it."

Everyone started laughing and soon the conversations flowed easily as they shared anecdotes from work and books they had read. In the background soft music played as their voices mingled with the songs until dinner was over.

"Why don't you all retire to the living room while I help Nan with the cleanup."

"No, we won't hear of that. We will all help."

Chairs pushed back and everyone carried their plate into the kitchen. Neves stood by the dishwasher and Ted scraped the dishes as they arrived. Nan pulled out storage containers. Joy and Nola helped empty the remaining food into them, making sure lids were on tight and zipper bags were sealed properly. In less than fifteen minutes, everything was back in order.

"Does anyone care for something to drink?"

"Sure." They spoke in unison. From the kitchen they made their way to the drink station. It was late when they finally sat down in the living room again. It was time.

CHAPTER 31

Bringing The Safers UpToDate

While the Ceps reviewed it all in their mind, they were surprised with the Safers began the conversation.

"We know. We know why you are here; or we at least know something of it."

"You do?"

"For some time, probably since the first day we met, we knew there was a connection. When we sat down and talked about it, we felt the same thing...well not as strongly...when we first met the Manns."

Nan looked around at the faces before her and her husband continued. "We are not psychic or anything like that. It is a feeling we got. Can't say that it ever happened before we met the Manns and not since we met you. But there is no denying it. Now we need to know what we are to do beyond opening our home and graciously having Neves stay with us."

"You've got to be kidding!" Joy said it aloud, before she could stop herself. "How did you know that? You must be psychic."

"I swear to you, we are not. Well, only with you and the Manns we do seem to be."

At that moment the doorbell rang. Everyone inhaled. It was Nola who finally came to her senses. "Oh, yes, that must be Ed Mann. I hope you don't mind Nan, but I thought he should be here."

Nan smiled. "But of course."

They all stood and followed her to the door. When she opened it, Ed Mann stood there his hair amiss and his soft blue eyes glowing between sympathy and puzzlement. He managed a smile and politely asked, "May I join you?"

"Yes, we have been waiting for you. Please come in."

Ted stepped into the foyer and greeted the group. "Can I get you something to drink," asked Ted.

"Sure, I'd love a cold beer."

Ted checked with the rest of the party and seeing that he needed help with the drinks, Neves stood and followed him.

In the meantime, everyone went back into the Living room and waited for Neves and Ted to join them. They waited patiently until the drinks were delivered and everyone was seated.

It was now time to begin. "I think I should start the discussion. I want to make sure that we all know everything there is to know so that we come to a group decision on what we need to do." Nola said, feeling comfortable for the first time with being in the spotlight. She took a deep breath and commenced.

"When mom first took me to see Dr. Memer it was really, the first time she had opened up about the possibility we were the same." Nola looked over at her mother who nodded. "Mom told him that she as well as me had been born with a veil. This had astounded Dr. Memer, since being born with what is medically called a caul occurred in

182

fewer than 1 in 80,000 births. Having a mother and her child born with one was unheard of."

"Though I felt different, I tried to ignore it and try to appear normal, but people noticed. It was not until around the age of twelve that I admitted to myself that I was not just dreaming, that there was a presence with me almost all the time. It somehow felt to be more than one, but I was not sure of this. I kept on trying to dismiss it and tried to deny its existence. But by the age of twelve the force was too strong to deny any longer."

"I always felt that mom didn't care for me as much as she did my brother, but I would learn that the real reason was because she dreaded my future once I became obsessed with IT. Her mother before her was born on the seventh day of the seventh month just like my mother and of course, Me. So, she knew that I would dread the day I was born. She had gone through the same thing. The entity had entered her life at just, past seven years of age and she had tried to ignore its existence but failed."

May turned at looked at Nola with an encouraging smile. "All of that which Nola shared is true. She followed the exact same pattern in life as I did being born also on the seventh day of the seventh month. I watched her turn from a happy, carefree little girl into a shy, quiet young woman. The change, as had been the pattern for so long, took place just after the passing of my seventh birthday." Again, May looked at Nola who gave her encouragement to go on. "I think that at first I was hoping that her daughter would be spared because she was born a twin, she would not have to go through all of this," she added as she spread her arms out, "but she did and she lost her twin..." Tears welted in May's eyes and she had to wait before she continued.

"What I know and what we have figured out thus far is that there are two forces. At first the good force was the strongest. But now the good force is weakening, and the evil force is becoming stronger. I know this because of the change in the visions that Nola has and the fact that Joy has them as well. I think that the reason they now share the visions is why the evil force is growing and taking command. I think it was this force that killed Jolene and took our Jonathan."

"What?" It was Ed who piped in. "What do you mean, killed Jolene. She died of a heart attack. That's what the doctor said…it was a heart attack."

Nola started to speak, but Nan, placing a finger to her mouth, paused her. Nan got up and went over to Ed and put an arm around him. "Ted, think about it. You know our Jolene. She wasn't fragile and she never had heart problems."

Ted looked up at Nan with tears forming in his eyes. "I know. I know. How could this happen. Why?"

Nan squeezed his shoulders before going back to her seat.

With her misery apparent in her voice, May added, "Moving from Salem New Jersey to Rochester, I thought the visions would stop but they didn't."

Joy has been listening closely so that she wouldn't just repeat what her mother and grandmother had shared. She allowed the silence to envelope her as she worked on what she wanted to say.

"I think it is now my turn to speak," she began. "First, have you ever seen a mist or fog that almost looks like it's swirling?" Ed Mann reacted with a slight tilt of his head as if he wasn't sure, while Ted Safer, raised his eyebrows in wonderment, but Nola, May and Nan seemed to understand. "Well, if you have, you witnessed an ecto-mist. It's a vaporous cloud that usually appears several feet off the ground and moves swiftly most of the time, but it may not move at all." Joy ran her hands across her eyes. "That ghostly mist can become a full-bodied apparition.

184

Most people who have seen this were outdoors somewhere, but we," she added as she leaned her head toward May and then toward her mother, "witness them most anywhere."

Joy sits quietly, looking at those in the room, then lowers her eyes, trying to hide the pain that welds in her from just the thought of what she is about to say. "Eelissa's ghost takes various forms and is known as The Lady in White. On that day I saw her as a youthful spirit who coalesce from the mists of Durand Lake." A breeze blew up and mom and I lifted our hands to protect our eyes. Our hands brushed each other on their way up and that was enough to start the vision. We see a lady dressed in white walking on top of the water. She heads toward Jonathan who is not aware of her. Once she has neared him, she begins talking to him, but we are too far to hear what is being said. Then we see Jonathan nod his head, saying yes to her and he grabs the lady's hand."

Joy's voice chokes and she tries to clear her throat. "We were paralyzed with fright when we realize that the lady is taking Jonathan away." Joy is sobbing now, and she tries desperately to control herself. When she can, she continues. "It was a vision, one that mom and I shared together, but when we touched again, the vision disappeared, and it all became real. Jonathan was gone and we still haven't found him. Yet, I feel he is alive...somewhere. I am his twin and that is why I know he is alive." Ned gets up and goes over to give Nola a hug. Slowly she gains control and offers him a weak smile.

"Okay, I'm all right. I need to share one more thing and that has to do with Jennifer Mann." At the mention of his daughter, Ed Mann sits up straight in his chair. "One day when we were playing a game, we grabbed hands to swing around and I saw something in the distance, something that frighten me so bad. I thought it was just me, but I saw that Jennifer couldn't move or breathe. At

185

first, I was afraid to reveal that I had seen something that I knew wasn't real, but when Jennifer snatched her hands away, I realized that she has seen something too. Only when I asked her what it was, she didn't respond. Instead she backed away from me."

"What did you girls see?" Asked Ed Mann.

"We saw a pretty teenage girl dancing with her boyfriend when she suddenly burst into flames. It was like it was driven by an inner storm that this fire bust furiously from her back and chest, enveloping her head, and igniting her hair. In seconds she was a human torch, and before her companion could beat out the flames, she was consumed, and he had to back off. We watched as she disappeared into a pile of ashes." Joy had embellished the story a little, but not so much that her main point of telling the tale was in question. When she looked at her mom, she gave her a slight nod.

"After that, I watched as Jennifer raised her hands as though she wanted to cover her eyes but couldn't. Then, when it was over, she never looked at me. She just stiffly walked away. She never played with me again."

"Oh, my dear, I am so sorry. Really sorry. Jennifer may have told her mother about that, or not. She never mentioned it to me, but now that you said that, I remember, she always seemed too busy whenever we were going to see you. I am so sorry."

"It's okay Mr. Mann. I understand. Really I do."

Dr. Memer cleared his throat. "I'd like to go next." He looked around the room and everyone nodded. "Okay. I am Dr. Reb Memer, I am a psychiatrist and I am from Salem, New Jersey, where the Logs and Ceps hail. I was introduced to Nola when she was a little girl. Neves and May brought her in to see me and without giving me much detail, I started from scratch. Nola was like my own child since she had been with me from her childhood days. At

186

first, she had been like any other patient who needed special assistance in understanding something happening in their life. But over the years this had changed. Nola's problem was indeed different from any I had dealt with in my 56 years of practice, something too that no one would believe."

Dr. Memer took a sip of his beer before continuing. "Oh yes, I had seen patients who had suffered from strange dreams, but nothing like Nola's. Nola's were not dreams. This I had determined long ago. Dreams were unconscious thoughts that could be dealt with in one way or another and resolved to some extent in a year or two of sessions. Nola's were like "spells" because they were more real than a dream. I even fancied that they actually took place as a reality, which we now know they do."

"Excuse me Dr. Memer, but is it caused by the veil," asked Ted.

"Please call me Reb. I think what we are sharing we need to be on first name basis." He took another sip of his beer. "Let me start by explaining that some call this condition 'born with a veil' but, it is a caul. A caul happens when a piece of the sac breaks away during gestation or during the birthing process and attaches itself to the baby's head. It is rare and is harmless and is immediately removed by the physician or midwife upon delivery."

Reb paused and slowly drank his beer, concentrating on how to phrase what he planned to share next. Finally, he sat is beer down. "As for whether all that is happening is caused by the veil, let me share with you that many cultures consider a baby born with a caul a sign of good luck. Many belief systems hold that being born with a veil is a sign of special destiny and psychic abilities, or good luck. Most who are born with a veil are female and believe themselves to be psychically gifted, while others show no advanced abilities nor interest."

Nola looked up and gave Dr. Memer a half smile, encouraging him to continue. "To be born with a caul, may go more to being Born with a Calling and where that takes a soul. It was considered an omen that the child was destined for greatness."

"When Nola brought Joy, they came separately, but when the visions changed and became stronger, they started coming to see me together. Shortly after that they informed me that they were having the same visions at the same time. In other words, they shared the visions together."

"It was at that point I think I knew the visions were more than just visions. They were working in their 'real' life. They gave hints at times of something about to happen as with a picture that kept changing to show Jolene's face until Jolene passed." He paused and stared directly at Ted. "I don't think for a minute that Jolene had a heart attack. Not for a minute. And," he said looking at Joy. "I believe that it was one of the hooded figures that you see in your visions that took the shape of the woman in white and took Jonathan away. Which one I dare not guess." Seeing Joy shake her head, he added, "That's my opinion, only."

Dr. Memer cleared his throat again. Then reached over and grabbed his beer, taking a long draw this time. "Best to drop the 'doctor' and call me Reb as I admit the following and psychiatrist do not believe in mediums." He paused again before continuing. "I spent evening after evening reviewing all the tapes and notes I had gathered since I first saw Nola and even at that I could not make head nor tail of what was happening. I finally had to admit this was not a psychiatric matter and I turned to a medium. But not just any medium. I wanted one with a proven record that I could trust their judgment. I don't know if you ever heard of the infamous Fox Sisters?" He looked to

188

see that there was no one in the room that hadn't heard of them."

"We learned about them from Jolene. It was one of the mysteries she shared when she was trying to educate us on the ghosts and spirits Rochester is famous for."

"Good, so it will allow me to say that though they are dead, I was able to locate one of their ancestors, a Marguerite Fox. She is the daughter of Leah Fox one of the Fox Sisters. She is single and still lives in Rochester. When I called and explained the situation, she agreed to see me. I sat up all night going over the notes and tapes I had, trying to organize it into something I could share with Marguerite. After listening to what I had to say she said that my patients were blessed, and that they must believe this if they are to have the strength to prosper. As she walked me to the door she added, and I quote, "Tell them to not talk to anyone else about their visions or it would be fatal. Most importantly, remember, the secret is in the seven." She said that something is happening, and it is going to take a circle of seven to stop it."

"What? What did she mean by the circle of seven?"

"She didn't say. She said to understand it further she needed to see Joy and May."

They had been at it for some time, though no one wanted to quit, they took a break. Ed, Neves, and Ned went out on the back deck for a breath of fresh air. No one spoke as they sat staring off into the distance. If anyone had seen them, they would have thought, there was three men who were at peace...little did they know.

While the men tried to relax, Joy, May and Nan emptied the dish washer and got out fresh drinks for everyone.

"Do you want to join the men out back?"

"No," Joy and May said together.

189

"It's just that we feel safe in your house and we don't want to spoil that. We'll wait for everyone in the living room."

"I think I'll take a bathroom break." Nola said as she headed in that direction.

"Me too."

"You can use the one by our bedroom, Joy." Nan said as she pointed the way.

Nan went out to get the men. When they came in, they also waited a turn to go to the bathroom. The conversation waited until everyone was back, seated in the Living room. At that point, Ed began.

"I guess I should start with the day of the arrival of the Ceps-Log to their home here was the day that Jolene had a vision. In her vision she saw seven heavenly bodies. The Sun, Moon, Mercury, Mars Venus, Jupiter, and Saturn and seven faceless figures floated with her in space. Upon waking from the vision, this was all she could remember, and she told me about it, asking what significance this vision had. I had just stared at her before bursting out in laughter. Now I wish I hadn't. I wish…"

Edward Mann picked up his beer and took a long draw before setting it back down. "The next instance was when we all met at the Logs home to welcome them to the neighborhood. Jolene told me that later at the door as we were leaving, she hugged Nola, withdrew quickly, and gave her a puzzled smile. Something had passed between them during that hug." When she told me, I again dismissed it.

"I remember." Nola paused. "I felt a closeness to Jolene even though we had just met. Yes, I believe something had passed between us during that hug, but as usual, I kept it to myself."

Ted nodded and started again. "From that point on you became an obsession with my wife. Remember how

190

she dragged you around to all the haunted places. She was on a mission. Night after night she told me she needed to talk to Nola and maybe the two of you could figure it out together. Somehow, she had figured out the names, how I don't know."

"What about the names?" Asked Ted. "Yes, what do you mean."

"Oh, well, she had figured out that some of the names meant something in reverse."

"Like what?"

"I don't have those notes. I gave them to Joy and Nola. Can you answer that?"

Nola cleared her throat, "Yes". My full name is Enolai Ceps. Leaving off the addition of 'Log', in reverse that is 'Special One'. Neves is 'Seven' and Ned Log is 'Golden'.

She told me she had notes, lots of them she had written down, even more than I shared with you earlier. I have them here." They all set tense and anxious as Ted reached into his pocket to withdraw some pages that he read to them.

Hearing a noise in the kitchen, I looked at the time on the bottom of the computer screen. It was after midnight. I smiled thinking; Edward must be looking for a snack. I shut down the internet and rubbing the back of my neck, headed toward the kitchen. The house was silent and dark as I felt my way until the glow of the night light in the dining room helped light my path until I stood at the island in the kitchen. It wasn't until that moment I realized, there was no light on in the room. As my eyes adjusted, I moved over to flip on the light switch. There was no one there. Softly I whispered, "Ed? Are you in here?"

Nothing, not a sound. I shook my head doubting myself now. 'That's what you get girl for looking up all that spooky shit at night.' I reached over to turn out the light, but it went out before I could touch the switch. Paralyzed I squinted trying to see in the darkness but could see nothing. Slowly a shape floated in front of me, and I tried to scream, but nothing came out.

Unable to move or make a sound I could only watch as the figure came up close and reached out to place darkness on my head. At that instance my mind started racing with thoughts that I barely was able to decipher until the shadowy figure moved back and disappeared.

I fell to the floor. I was quiet as I laid there motionless until slowly my body began to move. Never one to faint, but finding myself seated on the floor, the only hypothesis that worked was that I had fainted. Slowly I worked my way up to a standing position, turned and went into the office. I made sure I wrote everything down. I then opened Word and studiously began typing information into the program.

Ed stopped trying to gain control of his feelings so that he could continue because he knew he must. Finally, he was ready.

The next few days, I felt different. I couldn't put my finger on it, but something had changed. I just didn't feel right. It had to be something simple and would pass so I just ignored it. I didn't tell Ed as I didn't want him to worry, but when the puzzling symptoms included a burning in my chest, fatigue, neck pain, and a tendency to sweat profusely after just a short workout I decided I needed to get a checkup. I needn't have worried. Dr. Matthew said that all the test came back negative. When I asked why I was feeling this way. He told me I had all the symptoms that preluded menopause.

I was shocked and told him I wasn't that old. He said that the average age for menopause was approximately fifty-one for most women. However, it is possible for perimenopause to start in the late thirties and early forties. Which makes the average age for perimenopause around your mid to late forties. To ease the symptoms, he said he can give me something, but he knew I would prefer not to take anything unless it was really necessary. He said they checked the x-rays done on my lungs, looking for pneumonia and bronchitis and they were clear.

"Well, that was what she wrote on that day. Her doctor told me she had left the office, feeling good about the tests results and something happened because she reentered his office. She was almost up to the reception desk, steps away when she fell to the floor, grabbing her chest. One moment she was gazing at the office door, breathing in air, the next she was gone. The attack gave her perhaps a half second of confusion and then it was "lights out."

"Refills anyone?"

"Yes. Let me help Nan."

May and Nan left the room. "What do you think," Nan asked. May shook her head. "I don't know what to think. I feel so guilty. If we hadn't come here, none of this would have happened."

"You don't know that. It might have happened differently, but something would have happened. It is not your fault and one other thing…"

"What's that."

"May," Nan said as she put her glasses down and took the one's that May was holding and set them down beside hers. Grasping both her hands, Nan stood in front of her, looking into May's eyes and said. "It is not your fault."

As she stood there with her hands in Nan's, May registered the same sensation as when she hugged Jolene that first evening they met. May tilted her head and focused on Nan's face and she could see immediately that Nan felt it too.

No words were spoken as they released their hands and picked up the drinks. They walked into the room and distributed the drinks before each took their seat. Seated in the room, May picked up her drink and as she sipped it, looked over at Nan, who was looking at her. There was a twinkling in Nan's eyes as she nodded.

Nan said, "I believe it is my turn to share." She smiled at her friends as she began.

"I can't add much. I first learned of something extraordinary going on with Nola and Joy when I was at the neighborhood gas station. Peter Reed who runs the station knows everyone in the neighborhood as he is very personable. Everyone likes him and he likes us as well. Pete likes to interact so when it isn't busy, he will pump the gas. The only fault, if you can call it that, is he likes to talk." She could see everyone nodding in agreement. "Well, on this day as I sat in my car with the window down, he walked over, and I immediately sensed something was wrong." Knowing straightaway what everyone was thinking, she added, "No, I don't have premonitions, but I am in tune at times with what my friends are feeling. I asked Peter, what was wrong. He hesitated but then told me that the other day, Nola and Joy came to get gas and something weird happened."

Nola looked at Joy. Both were trying to remember what could possibly have happened. They turned and stared at Nan.

" When I asked him to explain he said he was pumping the gas into your car," Nan added as she looked over at Nola and Joy, "when the light from the sun hit the rim of his cap, then everything went blank. When he became conscious again the gas was spilling on his shoes and the tank of the car was full. He didn't remember even

194

putting the pump into the gas tank." Nan gazed over at May before adding, "Later I told May about the incident."

May didn't have to say anything, because from the expressions on Nola's and Joy's faces, she hadn't shared that with them.

"Beyond that experience, was the one that I knew that you were going to call and ask me to allow Neves to stay here. I knew it before you told me, but I don't understand how."

"That's it, unless you," she said turning toward her husband, "have something more to add."

"No, that about covers it."

Nola took a moment to explain what had happened at the gas station and then said, "As we mentioned before, from what we know we have determined that there are two forces, one good and one evil fighting to be the survivor. We think that the women in the Ceps family are the chosen ones and through us both sides fight for power and existence."

"To what end?" Asked Ted.

"We don't know that. We do know that only one of the forces is aware of the magical number seven." She paused then added, "The number doesn't quite work since the family does not have quota for a circle of seven. So, it is our guess that other than family some of you seated here are part of the seven."

CHAPTER 32

Making Decisions

As they prepared to leave the Safers that evening it was still with questions on their mind. They did not know for sure who was part of the Circle, or what they were to do. But they were all tired and ready to call it an evening.

At the door, Nan turned to Nola. "Neves? Aren't you staying?"

"Not tonight Nan, he needs to get his things together. It's so late now. We'll come by tomorrow."

"That sounds good. Make it early, Neves and we can get an early morning golf game."

"Sure, Ted, you're going to be up early," Neves replied with a twinkle in his eye.

"We'll play it by ear."

"I'm sorry Nola, but we never got a chance to ask you why Neves, and not May too. Aren't you worried about May as well? And not that we aren't more than happy to have them, but there must be a reason you chose our house."

Nola was quiet, trying to figure out how much to say on the subject, but decided to stick with their original plan of telling everything so no matter what happened everyone would be prepared.

"Mom and I had a vision together. In this vision we were driving, and we hit a dog. We stopped the car and got out and stood by a man and his son who were leaning over the dog. We apologized to them and they said there was no way we could have avoided hitting him. When I touched mom as we were about to leave, we were thrown into another vision and instead of the dog laying there before us, it was Neves. There was no doubt in our mind. Neves was there on the ground, dead before us."

"Oh, honey, that must have been hard to see, vision or not."

"And that is it. Now the visions are more real and have people we know. That was not the case before. It was always somewhere or something but never a loved one."

"Why not have May stay too."

"I don't think she is in danger because she is a Cep woman and we are the 'chosen ones', or at least we think that is true. We need her to help solve this puzzle."

Nan was nodding her head. "Why here Nola," Ted asked.

And just like that Nola understood it. "Oh my gosh!" All heads turned toward her. "What is it, Nola. What did you see?"

"Sorry. I didn't see anything, but I did figure out something. I was only aware that it had something to do with you two, but I was hooked on the face your last name was 'safer', but even thought that may be a part of it, it is not all of it. Since early on we had been seeing this group of seven as being only made up of women. I even played with the ideal of your name, Nan being a palindrome. But that's not it."

The words were rushing out and Nola had to take a breath and relax. Standing with half of them in and have standing on the porch, they were like statutes. No one moved or breathed for at least five seconds as they waited for Nola to tell them what she had figured out.

"It has to do with my husband, Ned in reverse is Den."

"Wait. I don't understand. So, Ned Log is the Golden One and has the clue for a safe haven being a den?"

Nola could see the puzzled expressions as eyes turned to her in wonder. "I don't think there are rules to this, but I think there may be just hints as well as other meanings. I think that Nan, Ted, you are the 'safer' place. Jolene had written in her notes about you as being part of this though she wasn't sure how and we didn't see it because we didn't expect any type of overlap in the names."

"You are saying that are home is the safe haven, in a sense."

"Yes, Nan, but more than that. I know why."

"Tell us, please. What did you figure out?"

"Okay, but it isn't all of it, but it gets us one step closer to know what must be done. The safe place is your den, Nan. Your den is the safe spot. This is where we will be safe from visions, and evil and where the final key of the seven will be revealed."

The words were rushing out so fast that Nola sounded as though she had just finished a marathon. "It's Ned, in reverse, Den, then add the last name, Safer. The Den is safer."

"Wow, Nola." That was all anyone could think to say as they stared at her.

"Yes, wow, added Nola. I think that you and Ted are, for a lack of a better word, 'surface helpers' and whatever we are to do as a circle, I think; with emphasis on 'think' it must be done here in your den."

198

They could all see the exhaustion on Nola's face as she wiped a hand across the beads of sweat on her brow. "Okay, I think that is enough for now. Let's go home."

The troupe headed toward home. They were drained of conversation and ready for bed. Once inside, Joy headed straight upstairs while Neves and May went around making sure windows and doors were shut and locked. Nola gave Ned a kiss and sent him up to bed saying, "I'll be up shortly."

While the family dispersed, Nola went in the kitchen and got a glass of water.

Nola was deep in thought. She had not shared with everyone that evening what happened when they were going to leave. The closer they got to the door, the less confident she felt. She could feel a presence, but didn't dare turn to see if something, anything was following them.

She wondered if Joy or her mother had sensed it or was it just her. That is when she realized the importance of the den at the Safers and that was when she found herself worried for her mother's safety as well.

Over and over she concentrated on this wondering what to do. Looking over and seeing the laptop on the island, Nola pulled it to her and started a word document to jot down all they had talked about that evening. Doing it now why it was still fresh in her mind, might help her to see between the lines and know what needed to be done next. There was an urgency for her to put the pieces together quickly before anything else happened. So, Nola said a prayer, asking for guidance and then began typing.

With her mother frantically typing, Joy readied herself for bed. She climbed between the sheets, closed her eyes and she soon was dreaming or was it a vision.

Joy sat up, but instead of being in her bed, she was seated on an overstuffed chair in what looked to be a formal area. Across from where she was seated was an overstuffed sofa with two wooden tables at either end. Trying to get her bearings, Joy stood up. Looking down at the floor she saw it was of rough grey wood planks and at several points light shown through the boards.

It had been a while since she was caught up in a vision alone and she was afraid as she looked about her hoping to see her mother. She was in the front room of what appeared to be an old house. She cautiously walked to the back, passing a wooden staircase, and found herself in a very large kitchen. Every area was neat and clean though the furnishings were worn from years of use. Joy returned to the front of the house, but hearing voices, she looked around for a place to hide.

She heard two female voices that she easily surmised to be a mother and daughter. The mother's voice was raised in concern for her daughter who did not seem to understand that her mother was just trying to protect her.

"Dear, it's not safe for you to be out alone at night. What if someone attacks you. We are a distance from our neighbors, and no one would hear you."

"Oh, mom, I am not a child. I can take care of myself. Besides I have been helping you on the farm all day and I just want to go down by the lake and breathe in some fresh air."

Shortly after that, Joy heard the front door open and close and knew the daughter had her way. It was getting hot in her hiding place and she wanted to come out but didn't dare do so until the woman went to bed. But that didn't happen. Joy's arms and legs ached from being so confined in the closet until she decided to take a chance and opened the door. If the woman saw her, she would ... she didn't know what she would do, but she had to get out of this closet. As she tiptoed toward the front of the house, she kept her body close to the wall. She cautiously kept her eyes moving from side to side and in front of her until she was at the edge of the wall that led to the front room. She leaned there for a moment as she took a deep breath, then peered around the corner of the wall. The woman sat on the couch. She was young, small, and delicate-featured. Joy could see the side of her face and thought she was pretty and looked accessible in a way, but she did not dare approach her. She looked as though she had been in a fight with her eyes peering out through a wild tangle of hair. She could feel a tenseness about her and thought better of revealing herself. This woman, she was sure, was planning to wait up all night for her daughter. Joy was forced to wait too.

Time crept forward and Joy saw the woman was dressed in a gauzy white flowing gown with a hood of the same material. She watched as the woman rose and went over to open the front door. Joy heard her calling out and soon two large white dogs appeared in front of her.

Joy who had been leaning forward, quickly pulled back and pushed her whole body against the wall, praying the dogs would not sense her presence. She waited, tense and alert, then leaned forward to see what was going on. The woman had put leashes on both the dogs and putting them on either side of her, she started to lead them forward. Only they weren't allowing it as they fought against the leash, looking into the house, and barking madly.

Joy didn't know what to do. Frantically she looked around for somewhere to hide and was heading back to the closet when the dogs stopped barking. She turned thinking they would be there, ready to rip her apart, but the front door was closed, and she was alone. Cautiously she crept into the front room. She walked to the side of one of the windows and looking out could see the dogs as they walked quietly at the sides of their master. "Thank you, God, thank you."

She remained in the room watching until she could no longer see the trio and then she made her escape.

As she stepped outside, the coolness of the evening sent a chill through her already stunned body. She stood there trying to get her bearings. Then cautiously she stepped out into the darkness, barely able to see a foot in front of her. She could smell the scent of manure and the scent of pines as she walked unsteady through a poorly constructed gate of wooden planks and chicken wire that flex and bow when she opened and closed it behind her. At first, she felt the softness of the grass under her feet, but then that changed as she stepped into the rugged terrain of the farmland. There were small rocks and wayward weeds that brushed against her ankles from time to time as she trudged forward. When her foot landed on uneven ground, she had to steady herself, then test the ground in front before moving forward again.

It was slow going and she wished she had a flashlight or even her cell phone, but neither one were with her in this vision. Her eyes began to adjust to the darkness, and she was able to make out shapes. She saw bushes off to her left that, in a pinch she could hide behind, if necessary, but so far, she hadn't seen the lady in white or her dogs; or anyone else for that matter. It was like she was alone on the planet, and then she heard it. She paused to listen. There was no doubt that she was hearing the sound of waves lapping ashore and it was coming from somewhere up ahead.

Anxiously she began to hurry and stumbled as her feet hit the sand, throwing her off balance and before she knew it, she was down on her knees. Joy felt around her and managed to stand up. She could see shadows of trees off to the right of her and she thought she may be where

202

they had picnicked that day when Jonathan had disappeared. She tried to control her excitement, tried to pay attention as she hurried toward the water.

There she was, the woman was just ahead of her, calling out as she made her way along the beach with the dogs at her side. Joy no longer cared if she was seen, no longer cared about anything because as she stared out toward the water, she could see another shape and she knew without a doubt it was Jonathan.

Nothing mattered now as Joy stood unable to move as their conversation floated toward her.

"Tell me, please, what have you done with my daughter?" The woman in white asked Jonathan.

Jonathan replied, "Nothing. I haven't seen your daughter. I don't know who she is."

The woman in white bent over and Joy could hear her sobbing loudly.

"Please lady, I don't know where your daughter is, but I will help you find her."

"You will?"

"Yes."

Joy tried to advance, but her body wouldn't move. She tried to yell out to warn her brother, but her voice was silenced. All she could do was watch as the woman in white walked off with Jonathan until they disappeared in the midst coming off the lake.

"Oh my god," Joy whispered. He's here. I knew he was here, and he probably can't get back.

As that thought came to her, Joy realized that she didn't know how to bring him back either. That was when she heard her mother's voice, calling her and she was back in her bed.

CHAPTER 33

Neves & May Move To The Safers

Joy woke to the sound of footsteps. Cautiously she peeked through half closed eyes, stretching her arms over her head, afraid of what she would see. She sat up, rubbed her eyes with her balled fist and then peeked slowly through half closed eyelids. She sighed loudly. She was in her room, in her bed. The only sound was that of movement beyond her bedroom door. Joy slid out of bed and grabbing a robe, went to the door. She opened it slowly and glanced about the hallway where the voices had come. It was her grandmother talking.

"Ned, can you talk some sense into that husband of mine?" Before Ned can answer May turns to Neves. "Neves, will you listen to me? You need to get a move on. The Safers are waiting breakfast for you." Not getting the reaction she wanted she added, "What's wrong with you?"

"May, calm down. I know you're scared, but we have time."

"I don't know that, Ned, nor do you. He could be gone just like that!" She tried to snap her fingers.

"Good morning, family," Joy interrupted.

"Ah, good morning Joy. Maybe you can get your grandfather moving. He thinks he has all the time in the world."

Joy smiled and went over to Neves. "Granddad, I know you like sleeping in your own bed, but mom is right. You two need to get over to the Safers this morning. Besides, it will be like being on vacation. You don't have to do anything but relax."

Neves tilted his head to the side. "Okay Joy. You're right. I just need a few things." He disappeared into the bedroom, his wife clicking her tongue and watching the hallway clock. When Neves reappeared, he walked over to the stairs and turned to say, "Well, May, are you ready?"

Ned turned to Joy. "Get dressed. I'll walk them over to the Safers and come right back. I think we have some work to do."

Joy nodded and went back down the hall to her bedroom. She pulled out shirt and capris from the closet and then went to the dresser to get out underclothes. She laid them on the lounge chair in the room and quickly made the bed, then she headed into the bathroom to get ready.

When she returned to the bedroom, she dressed, ran a brush through her hair and headed downstairs to find her mother had started the coffee. She leaned against the island waiting for her father to return.

It was quiet. She missed the sounds of her grandparents moving about and decided she would go over to the Safers. She was on her way to the front door, when it opened.

Joy leaped back, her heart racing as she caught her breath.

"Sorry, sweetie. It's just me."

"Not your fault. I am just so jumpy."

Ned put his arm around her shoulders and guided her to the kitchen, making her sit while he went to get them coffee. As he passed Nola, he gave her a peck on the cheek. "Good morning dear."

"Good morning sweetheart." Ned put his arms around her, and they walked back to the island with their coffee in hand. All three sat, taking in the waking power of the fresh coffee.

After several sips, Ned smiled at his daughter and then turned to Nola. "Nola, we need to figure out something to do. I have been thinking about it all night and have an idea, but I want your opinion."

Nola had been studying the swirl of the coffee in her cup as she gently tilted it back and forth. "Okay. I could use some help. Tell us, what did you come up with?"

Ned stared across the kitchen, sipping his coffee. As he slowly began. "First of all, we know a lot more than we did. We know that those who know are in danger. So that means, all of us including the Manns and the Safers are in danger. We know that the Den in the Safer's home is the safe spot. In that room we are assuming you and May are safe from vision and the rest of us are safe from whatever evil is to befall us. This is good. It is good that we figured all this out and I believe we are right on with our translation. I also believe we are right in assuming that my name in reverse and the Safers was brilliant, to say the least. If either of you think any of this is just a coincidence, forget that now. Nothing is a coincidence. We must believe it is all fact if we are to figure out what needs to be done."

"Yes, you are right." Nola paused. "And yes, knowing the Den is safer to me means that is where we must be when we work through all this. Ted and Nan, I'm sure do not fully understand, but they understand enough so that they will be cautious as well as accommodating. They are, ah, for lack of a better explanation, 'surface helpers', that I am sure of. What I mean by that is they are not the ones that evil will attack."

Ned nodded his head.

"Dad, I have to tell you something." Ned turned toward his daughter; he could hear the pain in her voice and there was no doubt that what she was about to tell them, hurt her deeply. Both Nola and Ned seemed to prepare themselves for the worst as they leaned toward their daughter.

Taking a deep breath, Joy stumbled through the events of her last vision where she had been in the home of Eelissa, the lady in white. She told them she wasn't a spectral, but a real woman. She recited how she had hidden in the house until Eelissa left to find her daughter and then she had managed to find her way to the lake. She had to stop at that point to control the choking sobs that kept trying to take over her voice. When she was sure she could continue, she said, "I saw him. I saw Jonathan. He was there with her out on the lake."

Stunned, Nola and Ned stared at their daughter, their mouths hung open and their eyebrows raised. Tears rolled down their cheeks as they tried to grasp all that Joy had articulated. Jonathan was alive; or at least he had been in her vision. Their son was alive.

"Oh, thank God, thank God. He's alive," Nola kept saying over and over again as she hugged Ned.

"Now, Nola, I believe he is too, but we have to calm down. Why don't you get us a refill?"

Nola nodded and got up from the island. Joy noticed a lightness in her step as she moved across the kitchen to fill their cups. Joy picked her cup up, downed the final contents and went over to fill her cup.

While Nola went to fill their coffee cups, Ned let it all sink in. He had hoped to figure out what to do to save Neves and the Manns from any further incidents, but now here was another issue. They had to figure out how to get Jonathan back. Ned had no doubt that Joy was right. That vision put it all in perspective for him. Jonathan was alive and it was up to them to figure out how to bring him back.

A small smile is plastered on Ned's lips at the idea he is going to propose. Nola, walking across the kitchen to hand him his coffee, catches the look. "What? What is it?"

"Well, you are going to think I am crazy, but so what. All of this is crazy so why not add one more layer to it." He takes a deep breath and then looking directly at his wife says, "A séance! Yes, that's what I was thinking. We need to hold a séance!"

Nola is reflecting. That was unexpected; especially coming from her sensible husband. As she mulls it over, she excuses herself. When she returns, she has her laptop. Moving her stool closer to her husband, she begins searching the internet.

Ned and Nola sit, reading information from different sites that they find in the google lists. When they come across one on Carl Gustav Jung, their interest peaks. The article is long and full of information, but it is near the end when they stop and stare at each other, smile and continue. This was a psychologist who had a near-death experience that transformed his psychologist's attitude to the world of mysticism and magic; a world-renowned living psychologist.

Joy points to a passage. "He called it 'active imagination', a kind of waking dreaming. Sort of like what we have been experiencing."

They continue through the article to the end, noting a change from believing to almost disbelief until finally the article ends saying that in a letter he wrote to Fritz Kunkel, a psychotherapist, Jung admitted: "Metapsychic phenomena could be explained better by the hypothesis of spirits than by the qualities and peculiarities of the unconscious." She printed the article.

Nola next did a google search on the world of spirits. She tried to find one to cover bringing someone back from the spirit world, but nothing came up except how to bring your lover back to you. Finally, she did a search on crossing over and got better results. She clicked on one article that told about crossing over to the spirit world.

Ned tapped her on the shoulder. "We want the reverse of that, Nola."

"Yes, I know, but we can't get anything that way so let's do this and see what they are saying."

Joy leaned in and they read it together, their eyes brightened as it was interesting. It was about the book by a person named Swedenborg who said that he experienced the process of dying and being awakened in the spiritual world so that he could tell people on earth what it was like. He describes how angels sat beside him, unseen by most because angels are in the spiritual world. These angels stayed with him throughout the entire transition, surrounding him with loving thoughts. He experienced the transition from a physical existence to a spiritual one as though his eyes were being opened for the first time. He was then able to see into the spiritual world. It went on to cover the world of the spirits as an intermediate realm before souls transferred to heaven or hell.

"Jonathan is in that holding realm because Eelissa took him there. But he doesn't belong which means that he can be returned.

"I agree with that," Ned said

"Me to," added Nola. So now that we have confidence that he is alive and able to move back to the living, let's check out how to hold a séance.

That was much easier to find and soon they had a screen full of websites with information. They went through several, sending information to the printer before going to the next. Joy was filled with hope as she read the following:

All of us, at some point in time, have desperately wished to bring the dead back to life, to contact a lost loved one, to say the final goodbye, properly and well. It doesn't matter if we're rational skeptics or followers of Spiritualism. It doesn't matter if scientists have tried to debunk psychic theories and fraudsters have taken advantage of innocent people. As Ted Dekker says, 'The power of belief alone could change the course of history', and that is what magic and manifesting your desires is all about.

And the truth is, if we believe hard enough, we can make the impossible come true.

Finished with their research they stood with confidence that this is what they needed to do.

Nola looked at her husband. "Let's print this information out and show it to Dr. Memer. See what he thinks."

Nola picked up her cell and called the doctor. He answered on the second ring. She explained that she needed to talk to him as soon as he was free. There was silence on the line while she waited for him to respond. "Doctor, is everything all right?"

Dr. Memer didn't want to put more on their plate. Since they were last together, something had happened. From the minute he climbed into his car to drive away, he felt like he wasn't alone. He had found himself turning to check the back seat several times but saw nothing. By the time he arrived home he was so sure that someone or something was right behind him as he walked up to his front door and he could barely put the key in the lock, his hand was shaking so bad. When he finally did, he stepped over the threshold and slammed and locked the door quickly. The next morning, he woke with this pain in his stomach, thinking that it was the result of being scared, but now he wondered. The pain never stopped, it was a constant ache and he couldn't shake the feeling he was still not alone.

"Doctor!" The worry escalated in Nola's voice, causing Ned to rush over to stand by her side.

"Sorry. Forgive me. I was just thinking, ah, checking my calendar. I'm free the rest of the day. I have no appointments." He decided not to say more. He had asked his receptionist to clear his calendar so that he could go to his doctor.

"Oh, that's great. We could come there, or have you come here…whichever works best for you."

Reb Memer had a feeling it would not be good to bring them here; that whatever was going on with him might harm them. As much as he didn't want to admit it, something strange was happening to him. "No, I'll come there. See you soon."

Joy and Nola looked up at Ned. "Okay, that's done."

Joy and Nola went about putting the kitchen back in order, while Ned gathered the papers from the printer.

While they readied themselves, Dr. Memer had kept his appointment with his doctor. Several tests were done before he left for the Ceps home. In less than an hour, Dr. Memer was at the door and Joy went to let him in. The minute she saw him she recognized something was wrong. "Doctor, are you all right?"

"Yes, my dear, I'm fine. What is it you wanted to see me about?"

Nola showed Dr. Memer to a chair in the living room and offered him some coffee. It was now after noon and so it wasn't surprising for him to decline the coffee and ask for a glass of wine. Ned helped her open a bottle and filled three glasses.

Nola and Ned sat down in the living room and started right off telling Dr. Memer about what they had read on the internet. When they were finished, they waited for him to reply.

Dr. Memer cleared his throat and looked at their anxious faces. "I am going to be honest and say, that before all of this happened, I would have said that it was a farfetched idea and not even hearing about Dr. Jung would have changed my mind. But after what I have seen and felt and heard from you Joy, over the years, my mind is wide open to any suggestion. Yes, I will contact Marguerite Fox and if she is willing, we will have a séance.

Nola relaxed. "I know this is a lot to ask, but we are out of options here and I think that if we are successful in getting my brother back, we will be able to figure out the rest.

"I hope so Nola. I really hope so because I think this is going beyond the realm of logic for a solution. Should I call her now?"

Both Ned and Joy nodded. Dr. Memer took out his cell and placed a call to Marguerite. When she answered, he first reintroduced himself. "Marguerite, I don't know if you remember me..."

"I do, Reb."

"Great. Well, I am sitting here with Joy, Nola and Ned Log and they have asked me to ask you if you would conduct a séance for them."

There is silence on the line and Dr. Memer waits patiently. "How do you feel about that Dr. Memer?"

"Please call me Reb. I am fine with it."

There is another few seconds of silence. "Yes, I will do it. How many will be coming to participate in the séance?"

Joy, hearing this, touched Dr. Memer's shoulder. "No, we can't do it there."

"Marguerite?"

"Yes, Reb."

I'm putting Joy on the phone. He hands Joy his cell. "Hello Ms. Fox. My name is Joy Ceps-Log and I am the one asking for the séance."

"Hello Joy, it's nice to hear your voice. I understand you would like a séance?"

"Yes, but we can't do it there. We have to do it at our neighbors house, the Safers."

Joy goes on to fill her in on what has taken place and why they must have it at the Safers house. "I hope this isn't inconvenient for you, but I am sure that it must be held there."

"No problem dear. I think you are right, and I am glad to oblige. I will bring what we need with me. Will eight o'clock in the evening tomorrow work for you?"

"Yes, but..."

"What is it."

"I think we have to do this quick. I think my brother is lost and I think seeing him in that vision means that I must provide him a way back to us and I need to do it quickly. Could we do it tonight?"

"Ah, Just a minute." Joy unknowingly squeezes the sides of the cell as she waits. "Yes, we'll do it tonight."

Joy, relieved, handed the phone back to Dr. Memer and he gave Marguerite the directions.

CHAPTER 34

Opening Up

Reb looked at his companions. "So, we are about to have a séance."

Joy and Nola smiled at him. "Yes, we are. A séance is really just about calling up energy and trying to communicate with it." Reb nodded.

Joy continued. "We can't think of any other way to reach Jonathan and believe me we have tried."

"I don't disagree. If you are looking for me to come up with a reason you shouldn't do this, well, it's not forthcoming. I think we have exhausted all sane avenues and I truly believe that what has been happening has nothing to do with sanity."

Joy smiled. "One more thing. We think it must take place in the Den at the Safers so as soon as I clean up here, we will go over there and fill them in.

"Well, I will join you, if you don't mind."

"I think we all feel safe when we are together, so, yes, please come with us."

While Joy cleaned up, Ned and Nola showed Reb what they had found on the internet. They sat going over the information and when Joy was ready, they were too.

They locked up and went over to the Safers. When Nan opened the door, she didn't seem surprised to see Reb as she stood back to let them in.

"We're in the family room," she said as she led the way.

Ted offered them drinks, but they declined, anxious to tell them of the plans for the evening. Joy sat next to Ned and Nola on the sofa and Reb went over to the winged chair near the back of the room, away from any doors or windows.

May and Neves sat on the other sofa facing them, while Ted sat in his recliner and Nan took a seat by May. When everyone was seated, Joy began.

"Last night I went to bed and fell asleep but woke to find myself in a whole new place that had old fashion furnishings in a room with rough grey wood plank floors. I started walking around trying to figure out where I was but hearing voices, I quickly found a place to hide. It was two female voices; I was pretty sure they were a mother and her daughter. The mother's voice was raised in concern for her daughter who did not seem to understand that she was just trying to protect her. From what I heard I surmised that I was in a farmhouse and from the mother's complaint, it was in a sparsely populated area. After a while I heard the front door open and close and figured the girl had left. It was getting hot in my hiding place and I wanted to come out but didn't dare do so until the woman went to bed. But that didn't happen, so I chanced it. What I saw was a woman seated on a couch, staring out the window. From her body language and the earlier conversations, I could tell she was planning to wait up all night for her daughter. I was forced to wait too."

Joy took a drink of her water as she gazed about the room, now, after all that had happened, she was pretty sure they believed her. She decided to skip ahead. "Anyway, I next was at Ontario Beach and I saw the woman now dressed in a gauzy white flowing gown with a hood of the same material with two dogs at her side. And then I saw him. Jonathan was there like he was that day at the beach and the woman was saying something as she approached until she stood right next to him." Joy paused. Don't you cry, she said silently. She took a deep breath and continued. "I only heard pieces of the conversation, but it was enough to know that she was asking him what he had done with her daughter. Jonathan was telling her he hadn't seen her daughter so the woman had asked if he would help her find her. Jonathan had agreed and they had disappeared in the midst."

Joy stared at the faces around her then added, "I think that Jonathan is in that house and unlike me he can't get back. I know the house and I think if we can reach him, I can guide him home."

No one said a word, trying to absorb what they had heard.

"What we are proposing is that we do a séance here in your den because this is the safe place."

More silence followed. Finally, Ted spoke. "I don't know what the rest of you are thinking, but I am in. I think this is at least something, whether it works or not. We should do it."

"Yes, oh yes, we should," Nan agreed, and Joy saw May and Neves nod their approval.

"Okay so what do we do."

"Well, first we need to figure out who should be part of it. I think for sure all of us here. And, we have invited Marguerite, to host the séance."

Joy saw the questioning looks on the Safers. She looked over at Reb. "Please, can you fill them in on that?"

"Sure, no problem."

216

"I think Ed Mann should be part of this." May paused before adding, "and what about Jennifer and Matthew?"

"Yes, all of them. They knew…know Jonathan and I think they should be here if they can come."

Ted said, "I'll go over to the Manns with Nola and we'll fill them in. I think everyone else should stay put. I don't want us to take any chances."

"We'll figure out what we need to do to get ready while you do that."

With their jobs given, they didn't waste time. After Ted and Nola left, they all gathered around Ned who shared the information they had printed out. They headed to the den and began the preparations.

"Are you going to do the séance, Reb?"

"Oh no, not me. I will be part of the group, but the séance will be conducted by Marguerite Fox."

Nan and Ted looked up. "You've got to be kidding! Is she related to the famous Fox sisters?"

"Yes, that she is."

"Wow, one of the Fox sister's offspring is coming to our house." Nan looked at Reb and asked, "Do you know how she is related, Reb."

Reb smiled. "Yes, I do. She is the daughter of Leah Fox who was one of the famous Fox Sisters. She is single and still lives in Rochester."

"Does she do this kind of thing for a living?"

Reb hesitated. "You know, I am not sure, but it is part of what she does."

As Reb Memer moved about the house, he suddenly realized he wasn't feeling any pain in his stomach. Not only was the pain gone, that feeling that he wasn't alone passed as well. Since entering the Safer's house he hadn't felt the pain at all. He looked at everyone in the room and thought Are we they all caught up in some crazy hallucination? What they planned to do his profession would say was the act of a medically unbalanced person. Was he going crazy? He tried to rationalize what he was doing and after a few minutes, it came to him. James Hervey Hyslop was a professor of ethics and logic, a psychologist, and a psychical researcher. He was one of the first American psychologists to connect psychology with psychic phenomena. What was it he said? Oh, yes, he said that he regarded the existence of discarnate spirits as scientifically proven. He believed that any man who did not accept the existence of discarnate spirits and the proof of it is either ignorant or a moral coward. Reb smiled, feeling more at ease with the matter.

"It says here we need a round or oval table and I see that is what you already have in here, but it doesn't look big enough for all of us to sit around."

"Oh, it is," Nan responded. "It has two leaves. Ted, help Reb with the leaves for the table, please dear."

"Grandma, it says we should put some food in the middle of the table?"

May looked at Joy and then said, "I don't think that is necessary, really. We'll check with Marguerite, but let's forget that for now."

"What about the candles?"

"I'll pull some out and put then on the credenza, but I have a feeling she will be bringing her own."

While Nan went to procure the candles, and the others were in the process of gathering the chairs Nola and Ted returned.

"The Manns won't be joining us."

"Why, what happened?"

218

"He feels that he would be no help and he doesn't want to expose Jennifer and Matthew. He says he understands why we are going to this extent, and wishes us luck, but he would rather not be a part of it."

They gave each other sympathetic looks, understanding why he declined. So, they surrounded the table with nine chairs.

"Oh my god, that's as it should be?"

"What are you saying, Joy," her mother asked.

"It says here the number around the table should be divisible by three. This is how it should be.

CHAPTER 35

Meeting Marguerite Fox

At a half hour before eight, Marguerite arrived. Those in the room couldn't hide their interest in the woman. They took in her flawless complexion. If asked, they would have agreed that the fact that she parted her dark hair in the middle and pulled it back into a bun, fit the image they had pictured in their mind of a psychic.

Marguerite knew what people expected to see when they approached her, and it humored her to play the part. She wore a high neck blouse, tucked securely into the waist of her long, flowing black skirt, and for extra emphasis she wore a black shawl. Ted welcomed her into their home and showed her to the den. She wasted no time getting out what she would need for the séance.

"I have candles over there," Nan said smiling. "If you need them, they are there." Nan couldn't contain herself as she went over to Marguerite and grasping both her hands added, "Oh, it is a great pleasure to meet you. A great, great pleasure."

Marguerite use to this by now, patted Nan's shoulder. "No, the pleasure is all mine." She paused and reached into her bag, bringing out candles. "I have my own candles, but I would appreciate it if you could light them for me."

"Oh, sure, anything. Anything at all."

While Nan lit candles, Marguerite introduced herself to the other members in the room. She shook hands with each of them, but a funny expression came on her face when she shook Nola's hand. The same happened when she held Joy's.

CHAPTER 36

The Séance

Marguerite moved about the room, lighting candles. She asked Nan and Ted to lower the blinds and close the drapes while she continued. When Nan and Ted were done, they went to sit at the table.

"No, please, not just yet. I want to position you in the right place."

There was a puzzled expression on Nan and Ted's faces, but they complied, waiting as Marguerite guided each person to their seat until all were around the table.

"Now before we begin there is much we need to do." She cleared her throat as she looked around the table at the eight sets of eyes on her. "Seances are a means of communicating with spirits that have passed and for safety and results, they must be led by a medium or other spiritual guide, like myself. It is important that each of you believe in me and I in you, so we need to know and feel comfortable with each other. I'll start first."

Marguerite moved her chair up closer to the table. "The Fox sisters were three sisters from New York and my mother, Leah was the oldest. She had two sisters Margaretta and Catherine. My mother was the one who took care of them and managed their careers. They became famous when Margaretta, then 14 and Catherine was 11 told a neighbor that every night around bedtime, they heard a series of raps on the walls and furniture. The neighbor, skeptical, came to see for herself, joining the girls in the chamber they shared with their parents. The neighbor was not disappointed. Later the family left that house and Margaretta and Catherine came to live with my mother here in Rochester." She paused looking around at the faces before she continued. "So, the two sisters were famous, but my mother Leah never revealed her 'gift'. While her sisters were able to conjure up spirits, Leah could do much more, she could bring back the lost..." She stood up staring at those at the table. "I don't mean bring back the dead, no, if the dead have taken someone who is living, then she could reach out and bring them back."

Marguerite sat back down. "I come by my, shall we say talents, hereditarily." She looked at those gathered and said, "Who wants to go next?"

Each one in turn gave a brief description of themselves and that they were believers in what they were about to do. Satisfied with what she had heard, Marguerite spoke again. "I have been told by Reb that you have lost a loved one and want him back." There were nods this time. So, I need to know what happened."

Surprisingly, Nola spoke up first. It shocked her how comfortable she was with these people and with Marguerite. In the past she wouldn't have dared to share her secret with anyone and now she was anxious to do just that.

The pain evident on her face, Nola begins. "Eelissa took my son." Tears roll unchecked down her cheeks as she continues knowing she doesn't have to explain who this woman is to Marguerite. "We had gone to the lake for a picnic with the family. Everyone was off doing their own thing and Jonathan decided to go swimming. On that day I

223

saw her she was young. I was caught up in one of my visions when I looked out at the lake and saw a mist. A breeze blew up and my hand brushed Joy's," she turned to look at her daughter, "and then we both entered the vision. That's what we call them…visions. We saw a lady dressed in white walking on top of the water. She headed toward Jonathan and once she was near him, she seemed to be talking to him, but we were too far to hear what she said. Then we saw Jonathan nod his head, saying yes to her and we watched as he grabbed the lady's hand." Nola chokes up, but manages to say, "Then Jonathan was gone."

There is silence around the table. Joy wants to hug her mother, but doesn't dare, afraid they will be swept away and not able to complete the séance. It is Marguerite who finally speaks. "I understand your sadness and hopefully we will change that. Now I need to know what happened to lead you to me."

It was now Joy's turn. She glanced around the table and started out by telling them that Jonathan was gone, and we still haven't found him. "I felt he was alive…somewhere. I am his twin and have always been able to feel what he feels. That is why I know he is alive." She paused. "That and because of what happened to me the other night."

Joy lowered her eyes as she spoke. "I had gone up to bed and something woke me, and I found myself in a strange room, in a strange house that turned out to be the home of the woman in white; the same woman who took our Jonathan. I was there and when she left the house, I followed her to Ontario Beach where she walked, calling out to her daughter." She looked at Marguerite. "She was the Lady In White who roams the beach as a ghost." Joy couldn't hold back her sobs and had to stop to get control before she continued. "I saw Jonathan. She was asking him what he had done with her daughter and Jonathan was telling her he hadn't seen her daughter so the woman had asked if he would help her find her. Jonathan had agreed and they had disappeared in the midst coming off the lake." She managed to say, "That's it. That's all I know." Before she broke down again.

Everyone was quiet. Nan asked, "Can I get anyone something to drink?" She looked at Marguerite. "Yes, Nan, that would be wonderful, but make it water. We must have clear channels.

Nan got up and when Ted rose, she pressed her hand down, indicating he should remain. She walked steadily into the kitchen and in the refrigerator took out nine bottles of water. She placed them on the counter while she went to the cabinet next to the refrigerator to pull out a tray.

She stayed in that leaned over position for some time, before finally standing. Her mind was racing, and she was scared. She wanted to call this whole thing off, but she couldn't do that. It had to be done and deep down she knew she had to be here as much as it had to take place in her home. When she had herself back under control, Nan placed the bottles of water on the tray and headed back to the den.

As Nan walked around the table, her friends each took a bottle off the tray until she stood beside Marguerite. Marguerite reached out and first, touched Nan's shaking hand. She smiled at her and said, "Don't be afraid Nan. It will be all right, I promise."

Nan managed a smile as Marguerite took a bottle and immediately opened it. She took a sip. A drop of sweat on the bottle clung to her chin when she lowered the bottle, and Nan, always the thoughtful host, handed her a napkin.

Marguerite gave them a chance to quench their thirst and then prepared them. "We are all going to hold hands and no matter what, we cannot let go of each other. Does everyone understand?"

The group nodded in agreement. "Good, there may be some flickering of the candles and do not let that draw your concentration away from the circle."

"No, no, this is wrong. The circle is to be seven. There are too many of us," Joy butted in.

Marguerite paused for a moment to go back over what Reb had shared with her. When she was sure, she spoke. "Joy, honey, that circle of seven is not for the return of Jonathan. The circle of seven has to do with relinquishing those two hooded figures that are part of your visions. Your vision of Jonathan had nothing to do with them. It had to do with the Lady In White."

That made sense to Joy. "Sorry, please go ahead."

"It's all right dear."

After a bit, Marguerite continued. "Now this is very important. You cannot speak. None of you can speak during the séance. And you need to close your eyes. Close your eyes tightly closed and no matter what, do not open them. Even if you hear someone calling your name or feel someone near, do not speak. You will be tempted, but it will break the connection if you do."

She pauses wondering if she should add to that and decided she must. "Not every attempt at communication with the beyond goes according to plan. Even experienced mediums may run into a nasty spirit from time to time, and those who have no experience whatsoever may find themselves overwhelmed by a strong-willed entity with an inclination to do harm."

That did it. She could tell by the expressions on the faces that focused on her. She didn't like scaring them, but she had to make sure they truly understood and did only what they were told to do.

"First we need to make contact with Eelissa. We will do that together with a chant we will all say. When I say stop, you will stop chanting because I have reached her. She will either be in me or talk to me and I will tell her what she needs to know to release Jonathan to us. Then, she will agree or not agree. We must wait and find out. But as not to shock you. I have done a little mystic checking and believe that Eelissa's teenage daughter that disappeared was indeed murdered by a neighboring farmer. He buried her body in the field, close to the fence that runs along the woods. She will finally have her daughter's body and know that she had been abducted and murdered."

There is a sophistication about Marguerite. Her voice is soft, but there is strength in it encouraging us to support her decisions. Everyone at the table feels a closeness to her and they trust her.

"Okay, please hold the hand of the person on your left and on your right. Hold tightly. Now close your eyes." When all hands are held, and she can see all eyes are closed, Marguerite held the hands of those on either side of her and closed her eyes as she says, "When I squeeze the hands I hold, they will squeeze the hands they hold and that will be the message to stop the chant. Now, repeat after me. "Eelissa course through time, we are in need of assistance, Oh spirit come, we beckon you."

The chanting begins. "Eelissa course through time, we are in need of assistance, Oh spirit come, we beckon you."

They say it in unison repeatedly. It feels like it goes on forever when finally, the hand squeeze comes, and it goes around the room.

There is silence and then Marguerite speaks. "Eelissa, I have a message for you." Nothing. Then they hear it. A sob that sounds distance away. Then the question, "What is the message."

Joy almost groans aloud but manages to stop it before it escapes her lips.

"Eelissa, you have our son, Jonathan. He is not dead and does not belong with you. He is from our time and had nothing to do with the disappearance of your daughter."

Silence again. Just the sound of loud breathing around the table before finally words are spoken. "If this is true, what happened to my daughter?"

"Eelissa, you were right. Your daughter did not run away but was murdered by the neighboring farmer up the road from your place. He buried her body in the field, close to the fence that runs along the woods."

Sobbing, loud sobbing follows as Eelissa's heart breaks. There is a tenseness in the silent room. Each person around the table is wondering what this ghost of a person will do. Will she take it out on Jonathan just the same?

Finally, Marguerite speaks. "Eelissa. I want you to release Jonathan and let him come home. He is not to blame. He was not even born when it happened. Will you do that?"

A muddled reply of agreement follows. "Thank you. Oh, thank you for giving me my daughter back. Jonathan is yours." Then there is nothing.

"Everyone, open your eyes." Eyes fly open, hoping to see Jonathan. Joy twists around looking about the room. "Where is he. I don't see him. Where is he?"

"He's where you left him. I'm sure he is confused so I would suggest that the men waste no time in going to get him."

"I want to go," Joy says.

"You can too. The rest of us will wait here for you.

CHAPTER 37

Retrieving Jonathan

Joy stood up and Ned stood too. "We should go."

"Maybe I should go with you," Reb added."

That's fine. The rest stood and walked to the door with them as they hurried out to the car. They heard Reb say, "We can take my car," as they rushed down the driveway. Those staying behind stood watching as they pulled out of the drive and headed north.

It was only an eight-minute drive to Durand Eastman Beach where they had last seen Jonathan. They headed west and turned onto List, making their way to Kings Highway North. It was late so there wasn't much traffic to contend with and in minutes they arrived at their destination.

Ned eased the car into a parking space close to the beach area where they had been picnicking and as soon as the car stopped, the doors opened, and they climbed out.

Joy saw him first. He stood near the edge of the lake walking back and forth as if trying to figure which way to go. It took a second or two for it to register, even though he was right before her eyes, larger than life. She felt her lips stretch wider into a gaping grin when her mind caught up with her sight. He made it. He's here.

"Jonathan! Jonathan! We're here. We're here." Joy was stumbling across the sand making her way to her twin. Hearing her voice, Jonathan turned, and a big smile crossed his face. "Joy, where have you been," he asked as he moved toward her. I have been waiting for you guys. You picked up our stuff and left me here. Why did you do that."

It was at that point she knew he didn't know what had happened or where he had been. Not wanting to frighten him. She stopped in her tracks and turned to Ned and Reb. "He doesn't know he was gone. He thinks we left him." She moved closer to Reb. "Can you handle this for us?"

He nodded.

"So?" Hearing her brother's voice close to her she turned and grabbed hold of him. "Come on, we're going home. You can sit up front with Reb and Dad and I will climb in the back."

As they drove, Reb talked slowly to Jonathan. By the time they reached home, Jonathan was aware of what had happened though he had no memory of it at all. When they reached the home of the Safers, he looked puzzled. "I thought we were going home."

"Later, Jonathan. Everyone is waiting for us here."

He didn't ask any more questions as they climbed out of the car and went to the front door, that opened before they had a chance to knock. Jonathan was practically dragged inside.

It was an exhausting evening with everyone trying to tell Jonathan how much he was missed and hug or shake his hand. Through it all, Jonathan kept looking at Reb. He had never gone to see him but knew that this was the man that Joy and his mother saw often so when Reb finally found his way again to Jonathan's side, he walked with him

230

into the living room and sat him down. The rest of the party followed.

"I know this is a lot to take in. It was a lot to take in for all of us. We were afraid we would never see you again, son, but here you are." Reb paused before adding. "There is someone I want you to meet." He turned his head around trying to locate her and when he did, he gestured to Marguerite as he said, "Marguerite, please join us."

Marguerite Fox went over to Jonathan and stood in front of him. "Please to meet you Jonathan. I've heard a lot about you."

Jonathan gasped her outstretched hand and expressed his gratitude. "Reb told me that you brought me back. Thank you so much."

"You are welcomed Jonathan. Can you tell me anything about what happened to you, where you were, how did it feel?"

Jonathan took a deep breath. "Sorry, but I don't know. I can't remember anything. Until I saw my sister and Reb, I didn't know that I was gone. I thought they had left me on the beach." He stopped and looked at his family. "I know they would never do that, but what could I think. They were there and then they were gone."

"Jonathan do you remember talking to The Lady In White?"

An undefinable expression passed over his face for just a second before he said, "No, I think there was something, but I just don't know. I can't remember anything beyond going for a swim. Sorry."

"It's okay. I don't think it matters. What does is you are back with your family."

Marguerite stepped back and the family immediately circled around him. Marguerite and Reb moved out of earshot of the group.

"I didn't expect that he would have no memory of what happened," said Reb.

"I did," replied Marguerite. "I've seen it before. It's like when someone crosses over into another time or space in the universe, sometimes they are in a void where they are no longer in either place. I once hypnotized a man who returned and said exactly what Jonathan did. He couldn't remember being gone at all."

Reb looked at Marguerite questioningly. "What is it that you're not saying?"

Marguerite started, then with a smile replied. "Nothing, Reb. Nothing."

He knew there was something, but before he could question her more, they heard May say, "Come on everyone. It's late. I don't know about you, but I need to get some sleep. It has been an exhausting day."

Marguerite was the first one at the door. She had her hand on the knob as she turned to say her goodbyes. Reb stood beside her, in the midst of hugging Nola when Marguerite opened the door.

Outside it was pitch black, no stars or moonlight visible from the open doorway. Marguerite stepped over the threshold, her hand still on the door handle when suddenly flashes of light came towards her. Reb acted quickly, pulling her back inside, but not before the rod of light reached her and not before Nola, who stood behind them, saw the two hooded figures now side by side, battling for entry.

"Close the door."

While May and Neves tried to move forward to see what was happening, Nan and Ted moved backwards, not wanting to know.

Reb's quick action of pulling Marguerite back inside and slamming the door shut had saved them. Once they had the door between them and whatever was out there, Reb, realizing he was holding his breath, let it out. He stood there with his arms around Marguerite for several minutes before realizing she wasn't moving.

"Help me with her."

It was Ned who hurried forward and standing on the other side, helped Reb. Her head hung down and her hair covered her face as they took her over to lay her on the sofa. "Can someone get me a glass of water."

Nan reacted first, as she hurried into the kitchen and returned with a fresh bottle of water. She handed it to Reb and stood next to him as he brushed Marguerite's hair off her face.

"Oh, my God!" The words flew uncontrolled from her lips as she stared at the reclining Marguerite.

Dr. Member turned toward Nan, a look of fear spreading over his face that caused the others in the room to move closer.

Gasps of despondency passed like a quick spreading disease as each one was able to see Marguerite's face. Looking from one to the other, they whispered in awe, "It's a seven!"

Marguerite's pale face was ashen, her unblemished skin now clearly showed the figure seven deeply etched into the surface of one cheek. Her normally perfectly coifed hair was tangled and dull as it spread out on the pillow around her.

Joy looked at Marguerite. "I think we should go home. Now!"

Ned hearing his daughter, moved up beside her. He had always been the rock emanating undeniable self-confidence and managed to lower tension with his quick wit. "I'll take a "No way," with a side order of "no way in hell" and an "absolutely not" to go, please and thank you.

233

"I second that!"

Slowly the room came to life with everyone moving into the living room and sitting down.

May went over to the side of Marguerite. "Is it okay to move her?"

"Yes," replied Reb. "I think she just fainted."

May lifted Marguerite's head and sat down. She put Marguerite's head in her lap and took the bottle of water. Slowly she forced some of the liquid between Marguerite's lips. Sluggishly, Marguerite finally became conscious. They had no problem interpreting the expression on her face. "What happened?"

We're not sure. It was a flash of light, we thought.

"Like lightening?"

"Ah, no, because it didn't come from the sky."

Hearing that, Marguerite remembered. She managed to swing her legs over the side of the couch and sit up. Everyone watched as she lifted her hands to smooth back her hair and as she went to tuck it behind her ear, she felt it. "What?"

Marguerite tried to jump up from the sofa but fell back down. She looked pleadingly at Reb who knew what she wanted and helped her up, taking her out to the foyer where a mirror hung.

Marguerite stood there, turning her head left and then right. He watched as she ran a finger along the scar embedded in her cheek as if she wasn't sure it was really there. Then, she turned to Reb.

"I think we are all stuck here now. No one can leave this place."

CHAPTER 38

Gathering The Information

Nola stood aghast. Her mouth hung open as she stared hard at Marguerite. For perhaps a split second her shock was suspended, the surprise shattered like glass. She was sure of what she was seeing once she passed that first fraction of a second of an inability to compute. "You saw them Marguerite. You saw them?"

Amazement doesn't quite cover it, Marguerite thought as she tried to identify what she was feeling. It was like every neutron of her brain was trying to fire in both directions at once. She tried to release her face muscles not wanting Nola to see shock registered on her face, but she couldn't hide it. She had been witness to a lot of weird things, but this...

Marguerite tried to pull herself together and managed to nod in response to Nola's question.

That didn't seem to be enough. She could hear the wonderment in Nola's voice as she asked the direct question. "You saw the two hooded figures?"

"Yes, Nola."

"Do you think it is because you're psychic?"

Marguerite pondered that for a moment before answering. "I can't say for sure, that is the reason."

Slowly as she recovered Marguerite had a question of her own. "From your reaction, I am beginning to think that I am the only one other than you and your daughter who has seen these figures?"

"Yes. Even my mother hasn't seen them, or she just hasn't mentioned that she has! I believe they came when Joy and I started having visions together. At first the one in white was way in front, miles I would say, but every time they have appeared, the one in the black robes gets closer. I believe that the one in white represents good and the one in black represents evil; but that is just my assumption. I don't know if that's true, but for some reason that's what I believe. The last time we saw them they were side by side. That scares me because I don't know what to do to defeat the evil one."

Marguerite looked perplexed. Carefully she said, "when I saw them, they were side by side with a space between them that might mean there is another that can't be seen."

"What do you mean? A third figure. Why do you think that? It could be they don't like each other and keep space between them." The thought of there being one more figure stunned Nola.

"I'm not saying it's the case, only that it's possible that it could be." Marguerite stared off into the distance, "But I have always found that it is never as simple as it seems. There is always the unexpected to contend with." She reached out and put her hands on Nola's shoulders. "I know you are worried, but if we are to figure this out, I am going to need you and Joy well rested. I think we all know how important it is that we figure out what to do as quickly as we can. But not tonight. Tonight, we forget and rest."

Nola reached up and squeezed the hand on her shoulder. "You're right. See you in the morning."

As Nola turned to leave, Marguerite stopped her. "Nola, one more thing. Did you ever see the figures inside? I mean did they appear in your home or any enclosed space?"

Nola thought for a moment. "No, I don't think so." She saw Joy at the kitchen island. "Joy, honey, can you come here for a minute."

Joy walked over to join Marguerite and her mother. "Joy, have you ever seen the two hooded figures inside or always outside in the open?"

"No, never inside." Looking from one to the other, Joy felt there was more to this question than safety. She also knew so much, and her intuition was so great that her opinion would never be dismissed without giving it some consideration. However, in this case she was wrong. "Why, what does that mean?"

"It means what you are thinking. As long as we are inside, we are safe. So, we can all relax and get some rest."

May helped Nan prepare for their new overnight guest that grew from two to eight. Having four spare bedrooms in their home, Nan armed each of them with two sets of sheets and they went their separate ways, making up the beds.

With that done, Nan and May stood in the hallway staring at each other, at first afraid to say what was on their minds.

"Nan, I'm so sorry we got you into this."

"No, May, don't be. You had no choice. I believe that you were all right. This is the safe place and if I can help keep you safe, well, I want to." They hugged each other and when they pulled back, May asked, "What about Reb and Marguerite? Don't think they will sleep together…"

Nan laughed as she said, "No, I have a pull-out sofa in the office and there are sheets there. That's where we will put Reb.

"Guess what?"

"What Nan?" May asked hearing that sly sound in her voice.

"I am a pack rat. Every time I got toothpaste and toothbrushes from the dentist, I put them in the spare rooms. Even those small samples of mouthwash I saved as well." May looked at her friend and started laughing. Still chuckling, they headed downstairs.

Everyone was in the kitchen. Nola and Joy had found pasta in the pantry. They had that on the stove boiling. Ted had given them some of Nan's frozen sauce and that was on the stove heating up while the rest of them were busy setting the table in the dining room.

Nan and May jumped in to make a salad and fill water glasses and with everyone pitching in, they soon sat down to eat.

At first the only sound that could be heard was that of the utensils against the china and an occasional slurp to get the strands of pasta into their mouth.

Reb was the first to break the silence. "That was wonderful."

The group nodded, leaning back in their chairs.

No one wanted to disturb the comfort that had settled over the room, but there was no getting around it. They had to talk about it.

It was Marguerite who spoke next. She began by saying that this was a serious matter. "I have never had this happen to me before," she said as she lightly touched the new branded seven on her cheek. "What is happening here is a powerful force and we will need our strength and our heads clear if we are to defeat whatever is out there. I suggest we clean up and then get a good night's sleep." She looked around the room and saw the worried looks on their faces, but where she might try to ease the stress, this time she felt she should not. It was best that they were aware of the seriousness of the matter so that no one tried anything foolish.

"So, my friends, I think we know the next rule. No one is to leave this house. No one is to open any doors or windows of this house, because to do that will put all of us in jeopardy."

No one protested as they went about cleaning up after the meal they had shared. When they were done, Nan showed everyone to their rooms, offering pajama bottoms and tops and a few nighties she had in drawers Soon the sound of running water in all five bathrooms ran at once and Nan had to smile. Her house had never been so full.

Once everyone was settled in, Nan walked with her husband to the office door. They knocked.

"Come in."

"Reb, are you comfortable? Can we get you anything?"

"Oh, yes, I'm fine."

"Do you mind if we check the windows. They should be locked, but it doesn't hurt to check."

"No, please do."

Reb was seated in the chair, reading. His eyes stayed lowered as his hosts went about checking the windows. They lowered the blinds and closed the curtains before turning to say goodnight.

"Goodnight. And thank you for your hospitality."

"You are so welcome. Sleep well, doctor." With that they walked to the door, exited, and closed it behind them.

Nan and Ted paused outside the door. They looked at each other. Ted reached over and pulled his wife to him. "It's going to be all right dear. We are going to be fine." Nan tried to smile as she nodded, but she was still not convinced of their safety as they went about closing the shades and curtains, checking locks on all the windows and doors. They turned off all the lights and finally turned in for the night.

CHAPTER 39

Nan Safer

Nan was the first to wake. She sat up in the bed, listening and staring around the bedroom that was now bathe in light. She had slept soundly through the night and now was a little disoriented. Could all of that have happened just the day before, she wondered. She looked over at Ted who was still sleeping soundly as if he hadn't a care in the world. Just seeing him gave her the confidence to put her feet over the edge of the bed and head to the bathroom.

She took her time showering and getting ready for the day, feeling that this would be the only time she would have when everything was as it used to be. When she was done, she went into the bedroom, tiptoeing around and slowly opening and closing drawers and closets until she had gathered her clothes. When she turned to lay them on the bed, she jolted backwards.

Ted, who had just sat up in bed, read the expression of horror on his wife's face and quickly leaped out of the bed and went over to her side. "What's wrong?"

Nan let out a gasp before leaning into her husband. "I'm so sorry. I thought you were asleep and then seeing you sitting there…"

"Oh, Nan, don't apologize, we are all going to be jumpy today." He held her closer. He could feel her body shaking, so he held her longer. When she seemed calm, he pulled back and putting his fist under her chin, lifted her face up so that he could kiss her soundly on the lips. He smiled. "Go on and get dress. I'm headed for the bathroom."

Nan watched her husband as he disappeared into their bathroom and feeling a little foolish now, she got dressed and walked across the bedroom to the door. She paused, gazing back into the room for a second then stepped over the threshold and closed the door behind her, she stood there in the hallway enjoying the silence of the house before shaking her body into action. She walked slowly down the stairs, looking off to the side and in front until she reached the landing. Standing there, she listened, but there wasn't a sound to be heard. She stepped down and proceeded to the kitchen to begin preparations for breakfast.

Nan moved about the kitchen with ease pulling out the preparations for a big hearty breakfast. She hummed to herself as she glided from the pantry to the counter and back again. Then she made several trips to the refrigerator bringing back the rest of her supplies. She was just getting started when May walked in.

"Oh, my God," Nan spurted out as she turned and saw May.

"I'm sorry," May cried. "I should have said something instead of just suddenly standing here.

Nan grinned. "It's okay, I am just a little jumpy this morning." Nan looked up at her friend. "Did you sleep well?"

"Like a rock. I have never been so tired in all my life."

"I hear you. Here, come help me."

Soon they were both at work putting the meal together. When Joy came in, they had her set the table and fill water and juice glasses while they prepared hash brown potatoes, bacon and sausage, pancakes and waffles, toast, and eggs. If this was to be their last meal, it was going to be a good one.

One by one the guest arrived in the kitchen and greeted each other, making small conversation, and getting their own coffee.

"Okay everyone, breakfast is served." As if on command, everyone in the room made their way to the kitchen to carry in a plate of food to sit on the table. When it was all laid out in front of them, they made approving sounds before being seated. And, without anyone saying a word, they grabbed their neighbors' hand and bowed their head.

May began the prayer. "Loving God bless all those gathered here today as we come together in friendship and fellowship. Thank you for the blessings of our individual and collective God-given gifts. Place in our hearts the desire to make a difference to our families, to our community, to our country, and to the many cultures and inhabitants worldwide. Give us balance in times of distraction and uncertainty. Help us move towards our goals with determination and always with an abundant sense of humor. Please bless this food we are about to share, those who prepared it, those who serve it, and those who have bounded together to give us strength to face whatever is before us. For all of this we give you thanks."

For a moment, all heads remained bowed as they said, "Amen." Slowly each person lifted their heads and turn from side to side to greet each other and to smile confidently.

The meal was a joyous occasion with laughter and praises to the cooks, who demurely replied, it was nothing. After the meal was over, they lingered at the table drinking coffee. It was Marguerite who spoke first about what laid ahead.

"I wish we could just sit here and enjoy each other's company, but we can't. We need to start working on what needs to be done.

"What is that?" Joy said with hope in her voice that Marguerite knew the next step.

Marguerite sensed the feeling that those at the table were looking to her to guide them, but she couldn't and was not about to take that burden on. "I don't know what's next, yet, that is why we need to use our collective brains to first figure out what this all means and then find a way to combat it and whatever comes next."

Everyone nodded. May asked, "Who has the knowledge to figure this out. I mean, besides you Marguerite."

Marguerite turned her head to the left and proceeded to look at each one of the occupants around the table until her eyes reached the end of the right. "It's everyone. We all, whether we know it or not, hold a piece of the key and if we can find each piece, we can come up with a plan."

"What's first?"

Marguerite smiled. "That's easy. We clean up our mess."

That lightened the mood. Everyone picked up their plates and carried them to the kitchen. Nan and May stayed in the kitchen, putting things away, scraping dishes and handing them to Ted who stood by the dishwasher. Joy and Ned carried out the rest of the dishes and utensils, while

Marguerite and Reb got sponges and cleaned the surface of the table.

Neves went about opening the blinds and pulling back the curtains, mumbling as he did, loud enough for those in the dining room to hear. "Going to enjoy the light why I can, damn it." They looked at each other and smiled fondly before continuing with their jobs. When all was cleared away and clean, those who wanted it, went to the Keurig, and fixed a cup of coffee. With no more delay it began.

All eyes turned to Marguerite. She didn't have all the answers, but she could see they were depending on her so feeling the pressure she began. "Okay, first we need some supplies. Pens, Pencils, Paper, cell phones, laptops, computers, and a copier. She tapped the table with each announcement. Did I forget anything?"

"The TV. We could turn on the television and see what's happening in the world," Neves said.

"Sure. But keep the sound low so it doesn't interfere."

"The notes. We need to gather our notes so we can refer to them," added Nola.

"Great. Anything else?"

She could see everyone thinking it through and then shaking their heads.

"Okay, let's get moving, people."

People were going in many directions trying to get everything together. "Don't forget your plugs. We can't have power drained before we reach our goal." She smiled as several people turned around and retraced their steps. When everyone had everything they could contribute, they sat back down.

"The computer is in the office, but it would be tight in there for all of us to sit. Plus, the printer is connected. But it's on and ready."

Marguerite nodded. "That's fine. If we can't find it on the laptop, we can go in there and look it up."

"Ah, Marguerite. No laptop."

"Sorry, but besides our computer, all we have is a tablet." Ted added.

"I could run home and get ours?" Joy replied.

"NO!" they said in unison. Marguerite added, "no one leaves the house. We'll be fine. Nan, the tablet will do fine. That and the computer will be fine. You do have the internet?"

"Oh, yes, we do have the internet." Let me get the tablet. It's upstairs. I use it for reading my books online. I'll be right back."

While Nan went to retrieve the tablet, Marguerite began. "Okay, we'll start by finding out what each of us knows and has experienced. Ted, would you like to go first."

Ted thought a bit and then said, "Nothing, directly that is, but just that Jennifer had an experience when she played with Joy. She didn't tell her parents because, I don't know why for sure, maybe she thought they would think she made it up. But she told me. "

"Excuse me, who's Jennifer?"

"Oh, sorry, Marguerite. She's the Mann's daughter. They live on the other side of the Ceps-Log."

She looked at them. "Don't you think we should have her here. She may be in danger."

"She's not there. After Jolene died, Edward was so beside himself he hadn't wanted to let Jennifer and Matthew go to stay at their grandparents, but he was in no shape to be around anyone at that point."

246

"What about Edward Mann. Where is he now."

"He's in their house, but I don't think he is aware of all this." May spread her hands out to include the group. Jolene never told him and none of us did. All she had said to him was that he had to give us her notes and that he did."

Marguerite looked satisfied with that. "Well, let's begin. Remember we need to tell everything we know or have experienced. I know less about what has happened than any of you and each of you have knowledge of things, but not everything so think and try to share everything. Reb, Reb will you begin."

"Sure. I'm going to touch on just about everything. Last night before I went to sleep, I worked on trying to figure it out with what I had. It's like a long mini summary so bear with me." He started by reciting almost verbatim what he has been saying repeatedly. "Well, for my part I have been with the Ceps for a very long time. I treated May first and then Nola and finally Joy. I always had the feeling as though I was part of the family until we later figured out why."

"Dr. Matthews, Jolene's doctor, shared with me the events leading up to the death of Jolene. Jolene had told him she was feeling ill but was sure it was nothing. He had given her a complete physical and didn't find anything. This heart attack, which is what the medical examiner claimed caused her death, needed to be investigated further. Because he had just finished examining her and had her other medical records, it was in all probability just a heart attack. He just felt better having an autopsy performed to collaborate the cause. But Ed would not hear of it and I can't blame him. It was senseless and unexplainable how Jolene had just died. She was healthy and took care of herself so how could this have happened. We couldn't understand it no more than her doctor could."

"I told Marguerite about Jonathan and how from individual visions, it became visions that Joy and Nola both participated in. The visions affected physically their life beyond the vision. They were seeing spirits, ghost, whatever we should call them, which is not odd for Rochester has it shares of ghosts. But then one ghost called, the Lady in White, took Joy's twin, Jonathan who, thanks to Marguerite is with us now."

"When all these strange happenings took place, I did research. I theorized that there are two forces, one good and one evil fighting to be the survivor and the woman in the Ceps family are all chosen ones. Both sides are fighting for power and existence. I think only one of them is aware of the need for seven to form a circle. When it was pointed out that there were not seven women, I told them I didn't think it was only family. I think it goes beyond the family members. I had a dream...not a vision...a dream. I dreamt that we were all standing in a circle, but I could only identify Joy and Nola. Yet I had a sense that there were men as well as women in the circle. I also saw a hooded figure in white and I am going to say that it was good and not evil. The good one realizes that men and non-family are to be part of the seven."

"When I told them that I thought I might be one of the seven they were puzzled at first until I explained my name. My name is Reb Memer and in reverse it is REMEMBER. What I am to remember I am unsure of yet, but I think there is something. In any case, we determined that the circle of seven was to include myself, Nola, Joy, Neves, Ned, and May. Only that's only six."

Marguerite had the tablet and was quickly entering information into it. When she finished, she looked up and asked Joy to share.

"Of course. I had many visions, but I learned how to accept that. It was the day I played with Jennifer Mann that changed everything. That day we were playing a game, we grabbed hands to swing around and I saw something in the distance, something that frighten me so bad. I thought it was just me, but Jennifer couldn't move or breathe so I knew she saw something. It was much later when I approached her and came right out and asked if she had seen the teenage girl dancing with her boyfriend when she suddenly burst into flames. It took a while before she admitted she had seen it. I then asked if she had also seen the two hooded figures. The one in white and the other in black. She, I think, answered honestly when she said she wasn't sure she had seen them."

"The first time I saw them they were far away and the one in white stood way ahead of the one in black. It remained that way until that day that Jennifer saw my vision. Then they were almost side by side. I think the one in black is evil and is now gaining control over the one in white who is trying to help us."

"Later I learned that Jolene Mann, Jennifer's mother had always been highly sensitive and grew up with people thinking there was something wrong with her. I think she passed it on to Jennifer since she is the same way. Jolene didn't try to ignore her sensitivity. Like when she touched my Mom on that first day we met, she sensed something and wanted to help. Which is why she took mom on the ghost tour."

"Jolene was the first to begin doing research and was the one who figured out the reversal of our names."

"The day that Jonathan was taken was when we were at Durand Beach. My father suggested we go there. Everyone did their own thing. When sand blew up in our faces, our hands touched and that is when mom and I saw the Lady in White down on the Beach, talking with Jonathan. We didn't know what they said, but she grabbed his hand and they both disappeared. It was much later when I had that vision of being back in the past in the home of the Lady In White before she became the Lady In White and heard her asking Jonathan what he had done with her daughter. Jonathan told her he hadn't seen her daughter so the woman had asked if he would help her find her. Jonathan had agreed and they had disappeared in the midst."

"Joy shared a vision she had alone where she and Nola where driving down the street she simply burst into flames. Another time she was in bed asleep and she knew she had burned to death. She could feel the intense heat yet nothing else in her room was burned. She laid their burned and took in the areas around her. Her clothes, her sheets and blankets were not even scorched while still in the vision. The room was as it had always been, just she lay there burned beyond belief."

"Well that's it for me."

Again, they waited while Marguerite completed her notes. "Great. So, May, will you go next."

May cleared her throat and feeling Neves squeeze her hand under the table, gave her the strength to tell it all. May was about to shake up one theory as she began telling her story.

"I and Nola were born on the seventh day of the seventh month. It was when Nola was seven that I first witnessed the change that I dreaded because I knew Nola would be plagued with visions. It was subtle at first, but after the birth of Joy it became more obvious. "

"When Nola met Ned, they were so happy. People always adored Ned so when an old woman in the neighborhood offered a vacant house for the wedding, I willingly accepted. Later that woman told me she had no reason, none at all to think the house was haunted, but she swore that day she saw two figures. Both figures were tall and concealed every inch of their body in large ominous capes with hoods. The hood shaded their faces so that she could not even describe the face. She watched as the two figures faded, but she swore they described themselves in a way that made her think one represented evil and the other good. Only she wasn't sure it was words or thoughts that made her think that. The one who remained the longest actually spoke, saying, "The woman in the Ceps family are the chosen ones." When I was able, I had asked exactly what that meant, but the old woman couldn't tell me anymore then she had."

"It was later that Joy and Nola started sharing visions. If they touch it happened, and when they released contact the vision ended, but then it changed to when they touch it happens and may or may not end when they touched again."

"For some time I hadn't had visions and had a feeling that what I had seen was nothing compared to Nola's and Joy's and it may be due to the fact they were direct descendants of the Ceps and I was one by marriage."

"As for the two figures. I first saw the two figures clearly when I was in my teens. It happened when my dad had taken me to go on a helicopter ride that he had been given as a reward for something he did at the plant where he worked. I was as excited as my dad and glad my mother didn't want to go. On that day we arrived early. I heard one of the men say he thought something was wrong with the helicopter and then I saw it. The main rotor blades struck one of the men in the head. That was all I saw as I started screaming because there were two hooded figures blocking my view, coming slowly toward me and my father. I screamed and screamed until my father picked me up. It had been a vision, a powerful one and I could not get on the helicopter. When my father asked what happened, I never told him."

"Later, I saw the one in black, standing at the bottom of the bed, closer to the side Neves slept on. It didn't say a word, just stood threateningly close to him and then disappeared. I think, no I know it was a warning to not tell Neves anything about it. And I never did."

"Sorry folks, but I guess you are glad I didn't tell this last night or no one would have gotten any sleep."

Marguerite continued to write and without stopping asked, "Can someone get me a glass of water, please."

Like magic, the water appeared and without looking up, Marguerite said, "Thank you."

Without asking, Joy rose and went in the kitchen. She returned with a tray of glasses filled with water and set them in the middle of the table. It was then that Marguerite spoke. "Okay, Neves will you go next."

Neves nodded his head, thought for a moment, and then began. "There was the time we lived in a haunted house. Strange things happened all the time, but mostly to May. One day though, I was alone in the kitchen making a snack I put a plate on the kitchen counter and walked to the fridge. Later May told me she had seen a hooded figure dressed in black and it had held out a bony finger and pointed at me as if warning me. I didn't see that, but what I did see was that when I went to pick up my plate, it flew off the kitchen counter and broke on the floor."

"That was the only experience I think I had." He looked at his wife who nodded in agreement. "Yes, that's it for me."

Marguerite looked over at Nola. "Okay, Nola you are up."

"Well, because it is important, I should specify first that my full name is Enolai Cep and what Jolene figured out our names in reverse was, mind being 'Special One', Reb. Memer being as he said, 'Remember', Neves being

252

'Seven'; Ned being 'Den' which is why we are here because the last name is 'Safer'.

She took a deep breath. Okay, let's go on. "Joy and I shared a vision of May and Jolene. I never told mom about it. It was a vision we had before Jonathan disappeared. We saw you in a picture. First it is a picture of you mom, then it changes to a picture of Jolene. It keeps changing back and forth until finally it is a picture of both you and Jolene together before blood starts spurting out of your eyes, your mouths and ears."

"Back when we first met the Manns, I remembered Jolene giving me a hug and withdrawing quickly. She had this confused look and I disregarded it but couldn't ignore a feeling of closeness to her. Something had passed between us during that hug, but as usual, I dismissed it.

"Now I think all the time that Jolene is the key. Jolene was the one who took me around to see the scary places in Rochester. George Eastman House, Auditorium theater, The Main Street Armory, Rush Rhees Library in the University of Rochester, and the Rochester Public Library. She would have taken me to the rest of the places, but she didn't get a chance. Anyway, going to Durand Eastman was Ned's idea. It was Ned who suggested that it might be fun to spend the day at the beach during the upcoming weekend."

"Then there was the incident with the dog. Joy and I went for a drive and along the way we hit a dog. We stopped We got out and told the man we were sorry, and he said it wasn't our fault. The dog got away from them and ran into the street. When we turned to go, we touched, and the scene became a vision with us back in the car. It was still dark and rainy as we approached the same location, but instead of a dog running out in front of us, it was a man, standing in the lane that we hit. Again, we pulled over and got out. When we leaned over and saw it was Neves, we both screamed and when we leaned in to touch him, we were back at the original scene."

"As I said earlier, it was Jolene who figured out the name reversals. We went through the pages seeing where Jolene had written every family member's name in reverse but was coming up with nothing. Joy Ceps-Log, Jonathan Ceps-Log, May Ceps, and it wasn't until she hit Neves Ceps that she got something, but it was just using his first name. She got, Seven when she wrote it in reverse. That was not following the pattern of before, but she continued searching for a meaning. When she had my full name, Enolai Ceps, she got Special One in reverse and finally Ned Log as Golden."

"We were having visions that were of family and that hadn't happened before. And the fact that Jolene had taken it upon herself to try and expose me to all the haunts in Rochester was not just by chance. There was something more to it, but maybe even Jolene was not aware."

"Then the fact that Jolene's daughter shared a vision with Joy. Well, that was, she thought impossible. Unless again there was something, they had missed that conjoined them beyond the friendship. Who was it that said, 'all things happen for a reason'? Well their coming here and finding this house next door to the Manns was a sign. The fact that Reb who had been in our lives for so long was willing to move to continue to be our doctor, was another sign. But what did it all mean? How did they all connect."

Without being asked, Nan spoke up saying that beyond what has been mentioned, they had nothing more to add. They were ignorant to all that had happened, but they truly accept the fact that their house is the safe spot for all concerned. Ted nodded in agreement with his wife.

Marguerite completed her notes and laid her pen down. She stood up, stretching and rolled her head from side to side. She looked at the group around the table.

"This is a lot. I think we need to break for a bit, have something to eat and drink and go back at it. We need to all think about what was said and try to look for clues." She turned toward Ted, "Can you help me scan these notes to print and can we make copies for everyone to look over?"

"Sure, come with me."

While Ted and Marguerite made their way to the office, the rest of the group went towards the kitchen to prepare lunch. They chatted away, the conversation light, with no mention of the current situation as they moved about with ease, familiar and comfortable with the Safer home. By the time they finished and carried sandwiches and chips to the table, Ted and Marguerite had completed their task. In front of each seat there were copies, but no one reached for them as they tried to enjoy their lunch.

A heavy silence fell over the room as each said a prayer. After a united 'Amen', the only sound was the crunching of chips, and an occasional loud sound of chewing. Eventually it couldn't be put off any longer as one, than another reached across their plates and picked up the papers. They sat, they ate, they read. It remained that way for at least a half-hour before the sound of chairs being pushed back so that the occupant could get up followed. Footsteps permeated the room as the table was again cleared and the kitchen put back in order. Once everyone was seated again, Marguerite began.

"Well, first off there is the fact that we can't assume that the hooded figures will not, or cannot, enter the home after what May shared. I think that here at the Safers they can't though, or they would have already."

There were nods of heads all around as Marguerite continued. "The other definite is that the circle must be seven individuals."

"Why do you think that the number seven was chosen; I mean, beyond the fact that Neves is 'Seven' in reverse." This was asked by May who was feeling uneasy. To her, Neves was becoming the center of all this and she was afraid for him.

Marguerite understood and knew the importance of that number, so she shared it with them. "The number seven is a highly spiritual number associated with intuition, mysticism, and inner wisdom. That's the meaning of Angel number 7. In the Old Testament the world was created in six days and God rested on the seventh, creating the basis of the seven-day-week we use to this day. In the New Testament the number seven symbolizes the unity of the four corners of the Earth with the Holy Trinity. Scholars have found that the number seven often represents perfection or completeness in the Bible. In Judaism, there are seven heavens." Marguerite gave them a moment to digest this.

Ted added to what she had said. "Seven is also a prime number, which means it can only be divided by itself and one."

"Yes, all that is true." It was Nan speaking now. All heads turned to stare as Nan was usually the quiet one, absorbing instead of talking. "It is my belief now that the hooded figure in white is actually Angel number seven and just like one of you mentioned, Angel number seven is aware of the significance in that number." Heads bobbed in agreement.

"The next step is to figure out the seven for the circle."

"Well," Nola says hesitantly. At first, we thought that Circle of seven would be Reb, myself, Joy, Neves, Ned, Jonathan, and May, but now I am wondering if you, Marguerite, should be part of the seven."

"Anyone else want to say who they think who was meant to be in that circle? No one?" Marguerite while looking directly at her, asked, "Nan, have you anything to say?"

Nan Safer looked confused and shook her head. "I am unaware of most of this and beyond accepting this is the safe haven for my friends, I don't know what else I can say or do."

"It's understandable. You may not even know, but, Nan have you ever heard of Earth Angels?"

At first Nan has a puzzled expression on her face, but then Marguerite catches a glimmer of understanding. "I remember my mother saying... No, that's just parental pride, is all."

"What is going on?" asked Ted. Nan? What are they talking about?"

"I don't think she really knows so let me explain it to everyone." Marguerite took a sip of her water and smiled at Nan.

"There are certain souls with certain characteristics making up what the Archangels call 'Earth Angels'. These Earth Angels are spiritual beings born into physical form. They are born into the physical world in order to serve humanity and the earth at a specific time."

"What does that mean?" Asked Nola

"It means they are programmed with a wake-up call. In other words, they were born with a time to awaken when there is a series of happenings, lessons, or events that requires their help."

"Are they human, or spiritual?" asked Joy.

"Definitely human. Although they are physical beings, they retain the connection to their higher Angelic counterparts. And you, my dear," she said looking at Nan, "You are an Earth Angel."

"I would know it if I were," said Nan.

"Not necessarily. Earth Angels are people whose soul origins are from beyond Earth, and who have spent a great deal of time in the higher spiritual dimensions and may not remember it." She paused. Let me ask you this. "Have you always felt an overarching desire to bring peace and love to the Earth, humanity and all beings."

"Yes, but so do others. I am far from perfect."

Marguerite nodded. "Being an Earth Angel doesn't mean you are perfect. Like all of humanity, Earth Angels make mistakes, experience challenges, and feel disconnected at times. The difference is that you are called at the soul level to help others, spread kindness, have compassion, and make a difference on Earth by bringing the light and love of the higher spiritual realms into physical reality. It means that you have spiritual powers above those of a human to solve difficult crises like we are facing now."

"But how can I. I don't know what to do?"

"You do know what to do because you are an Earth Angel and you're a powerful being with a long history of helping and healing throughout your lifetimes. You've received a divine assignment to come here now and share your energy and spread love. It's likely that you've, at a minimum, had some suspicions about your true origins – and most likely you've struggled a bit to adjust to life."

"Oh, my God," said Ted. "Nan, she's right. I know she's right."

"I agree," added May. "We were strangers and even on that first day, there was an immediate connection. You are special, Nan, and you have to believe it."

Everyone around the table agreed. Nan was feeling self-conscious under their watchful eyes, but she finally realized it was true. She just hoped she could help before it was too late.

CHAPTER 40

Preparing For Battle

No one spoke for some time. Everyone was busy trying to absorb what they had learned; especially Ted and Nan as he stared lovingly at his wife.

It was Nola who spoke up first. "I think we need to all think about the circle of seven and who is really meant to be in it. I think for sure, Nan." She saw everyone nod in agreement. "We can't take it for granted who we think it should be, we need to really consider everyone and come to a conclusion together."

"Yes, we only get one chance at this so let's do it," added Neves.

Looking over the notes, Nola piped up, "Definitely Neves. He is 'seven' in reverse and the key to us getting to that point. He has the power of the Ceps in his bones."

Everyone agreed with that. "So that makes two so far... Nan and Neves."

With hesitation, May said, "Joy. You have the visions of fire and maybe there is a reason for that. Maybe she has the power to bring fire and annihilate the evil figure." She looked around and said. "Do we annihilate them both or just one?"

"Let's wait on that right now. I am not sure," added Marguerite. "Now we have Nan, Joy and Neves. Does everyone feel these are the right choices?"

A sea of yesses followed.

Reb spoke next. "In working with May all these years, I would have to say that she has the power of sight. I mean that she sees beyond what is in front of her and may be the one to help us in preparing ahead of what is about to happen."

"I see this too in what she has shared."

"No question about it."

"Okay so it's now Nan, Joy, Neves and May. We need three more."

Reb suggested that the last two should be Marguerite and Nola. "Marguerite has the ability of seeing through to the truths as she did with Nan and Nola has lived with these visions for a long time. Whether she realizes it or not, she knows them and what they are capable of. That she can share with the circle."

"Excellent. We now have Nan, Joy, Neves, May, Marguerite and Nola. We need one more."

All eyes went to Dr. Reb Memer. "You know most of us inside and out and have dealt with the visions for some time. Your knowledge will help unify the circle. I say you are number seven."

This was presented by Joy and everyone agreed. It seemed so obvious now that they had thought deeply about the connection they felt on both sides. It was the reason they had asked him to move with them and he had accepted. Their lives were entwined, and he was meant to be part of the circle.

With that decision made, everyone opted for a short break before they continued to figure out a plan. Ted led Nan to their bedroom. Once inside, he closed the door. He

261

looked lovingly at his wife, understanding her so much better than he had before. As he embraced her, he could sense her nervousness and said, "Dear, I know you are scared, but I think they are right. I've told you often enough that your level of kindness and concern went beyond that of the 'normal' person. You are indeed a special human being."

"I thank you for that. But, surprising enough, I am not really scared. I feel confidence I have never felt before. It must be as Marguerite said, I have awakened to my true purpose for being here."

Ted hugged his wife and they went out to rejoin their guest.

While Ted and Nan were gone, Neves had taken May aside to give her assurance. "No matter what happens baby, I am going to be right there beside you. I will protect you, so you don't need to worry about anything."

May grabbed her husband's hands and stared into his eyes. "I know that, dear. You always have."

Marguerite, and the rest of the party were in the kitchen talking amongst themselves as they prepared a snack to take to the table. They were trying to console Jonathan who wanted to be part of the circle. After several explanations from them, he was soothed, but still not happy.

"Okay everybody, let's get started." Marguerite waited until everyone was once again seated in the dining room and then began. "I think that once we are in the circle, we need to ask our angel for guidance and pray to be open to the messages that are coming to you. I want to say that I think we just need to destroy the evil demon; the one wearing the black robes, but destroying demons takes skill, determination and nerves of steel." Seeing the puzzled stares around her, Marguerite turned to Nan. "Nan, can you add to this?"

Nan took a deep breath and surprising herself said, "First remember that they are wise about both sides where we are not. Demons are actually fallen angels and they attack you during the spiritual warfare of good versus evil that is constantly going on in the world. Fallen angels are real beings who have dangerous motives to harm humans when they interact with us."

May added, "Every day we have plenty of opportunities to get angry, stressed or offended. But what you're doing when you indulge these negative emotions is giving something outside yourself power. We can't be angry or upset during our battle."

"Being a man and like many others I've made a conscious effort to be the best man that I can be. I take this seriously and I know that I'm worth the effort. I, like you have my own demons. We all do and I'm not immune to being beaten, battered and bruised. The difference is I haven't seen them walking on this earth like my daughter, wife and granddaughter have. I think my part is to provide the strength to withstand whatever the evil spirit throws our way."

"For me, all my life I have trained my clients to kill the quitter inside them," says Reb. "I have told them that they must look their demons in the eye, be in a position of strength, calm and well rested and like we have done, be totally prepared for what we need to do. I will be making sure that we keep all this in mind."

Nan adds, "Realize That You're in a Spiritual Battle. We are not fighting against flesh and blood, but against a spiritual force of evil. Therefore, you must have faith in God in your heart in order to survive. I will help you keep that in your hearts as we battle."

Marguerite smiled. "I think we are ready. I think that it will be just the seven of us who will step outside the door to face them."

"But, why, we said they can come in whether we want them to or not?"

"Yes, but we want the others to be safe, so we have to meet them outside the house. "

"What about the den," said May. We said that was the safe place. What if everyone else goes in the den and they should be safe there. We can meet them in the living room then."

"But that is opening the door to evil. I think I read somewhere that was dangerous…"

"You're right Ted. I think you are right too May. Consequently, here is what I suggest. Everyone in the house will be in the den for safety. We will not allow them inside the house. We will meet them outside in the park across the street; that is if we can get that far before they show."

Everyone thought about it for a moment. Then nodded in agreement.

"Now, it will be important that when we see them that we start. We grab hands and make a circle and don't let go of each other, no matter what. We will keep our eyes closed at all times. We will be strong; keep the faith and we will chant and mean it."

"What will we chant?"

"First, imagine a white light around you and the rest of your space. Start by imagining this internal white light as coming from your center and radiating around you filling each part of your being with pure, white light. Once that is done, we will chant. "I ask the Universe to bless this circle and fill it with light and love. Negativity and darkness are not welcome here. This is a positive circle of seven. So, it is said, so it shall be. Amen." We will say this nonstop until they are gone. I believe both will depart. Okay, let's first clear our minds and see the white light around us.

They stood, holding hands in a circle in the living room and felt the strength of each other as it joined with them. Then they chanted, "I ask the Universe to bless this circle and fill it with light and love. Negativity and darkness are not welcome here. This is a positive circle of seven. So, it is said, so it shall be. Amen."

They continued for several minutes and when they had it memorized, they stopped, opened their eyes, and stared confidently at each other.

"Ready?"

"Yes," was the response.

Nan Safer, Joy Ceps-Log, Neves Ceps, May Ceps, Marguerite Fox, Nola Ceps-Log and Dr. Reb Memer stood in front of the door. Marguerite stepped forward and hesitantly, reached out and opened the door. The others moved up closer as she paused, looking around. The vast, seemingly empty sky stretched out for infinity. They saw nothing, not a hint of a shadowy figure. Tentatively, she stepped over the threshold, paused to look around again. Nothing. She walked forward and the others followed close behind her.

Down the street, a car door slammed, and a motor whined, causing the group to recoil in unison. Their hearing heightened as they stood transfixed taking it all in. They could hear the wind whisper through the branches and rustled the leaves. They could see across the street there was light from a row of streetlamps along the pathway in the park.

There was no traffic as the party walked briskly down the sidewalk and hurried across the street. They paused on the sidewalk and again looked around. They were alone.

They moved swiftly up the lighted path to a spot in the park, not far away from their home, but far enough so that they would not be seen. There they grasp hands and closed their eyes. Marguerite waited for each to clear their minds before beginning the chant.

"I ask the Universe to bless this circle and fill it with light and love. Negativity and darkness are not welcome here. This is a positive circle of seven. So, it is said, so it shall be. Amen."

The chanting began. "I ask the Universe to bless this circle and fill it with light and love. Negativity and darkness are not welcome here. This is a positive circle of seven. So, it is said, so it shall be. Amen."

With their eyes closed they didn't see the approach of the hooded figures, but through their connection now, they received the message as Nan mentally alerted them. They never stopped chanting.

Each one provided the strength they needed to keep going. It was only Marguerite who heard a voice in her ear saying, "Let go". She did not, but when she held on tighter, the message flowed through them.

They were as one, chanting nonstop. Suddenly rain fell in torrents, the wind blew with almost hurricane force, and they could hear the lightning as it flashed across the heavens, striking terror in the hearts of the circle. Thunder pealed until it seemed as if the clouds would burst and fall into them but they held tightly to each other, moving their bodies together to provide support as they fought to remain upright in the circle. The fury of the storm raged around their bodies as it drove leaves and stones against them with powerful force. But no one broke the circle and no one stopped chanting.

The volume of sound around them was so loud and constant that neither one could hear the chanting of the one

266

next to them, but that did not stop them or lessen their faith in what they were doing was right. So they kept their eyes close, chanted and hoped.

They felt it around them, and they felt it within, that push and swirl, that stirring but they did not weaken. They grew stronger against this wind; muscles working hard as they clung together.

"I ask the Universe to bless this circle and fill it with light and love. Negativity and darkness are not welcome here. This is a positive circle of seven. So, it is said, so it shall be. Amen."

For a few minutes the rain ceased to fall, then there were slight showers at frequent intervals, followed by a heavier shower which continued for a few minutes before the storm ceased altogether. The seven still chanted and held hands as rain dripped down their faces until silence settled around them. It was Nan who felt they had defeated their enemy first. "We did it. Open your eyes. We did it."

All eyes fluttered open. They turned their heads two and fro and could see nothing at all. They couldn't feel any presence anywhere. Slowly they released their hands and smiling they hugged each other tightly, and for the first time in a long time when Nola hugged her daughter, nothing happened. They had done it.

"Let's go home." Like children who had won the game, they headed toward the Safer home, laughing, and complimenting each other on their strength and perseverance. They were at the door when they realized there were only six of them.

Frantically, Neves looked at the faces around him to see who was missing. He then went back on the sidewalk and looked up and down the street, then across to the park. She was nowhere to be seen.

Slowly he joined the others and then entered the house.

"Where's Nan?" asked Ted. "Where's my Nan?"

Marguerite went over to him and put her arms around him. She's gone, Ted. I'm so sorry."

"What do you mean, she's gone? Where did she go?"

"Back… to."

Seeing the look on his face she knew he now understood. "Did you know this would happen."

"I wasn't sure, but I thought it might. She was here to fulfill a purpose and that purpose happened tonight. With it over, she was taken back to her spiritual life."

No one said a word. No one tried to console Ted, knowing there was nothing that could be said.

For Ted the rest of the evening was a blank spot in his mind. He didn't remember everyone leaving for their homes, nor the fact that he closed and locked the door behind them. He didn't feel a thing as he moved slowly through the house, having a hard time accepting that his wife would no longer be at his side. He would no longer wake to see her face or feel her touch. Finally, he climbed into bed, not bothering to brush his teeth or take off his clothes.

He laid there until exhaustion took over and he slept. The next morning, he woke, looked down at himself. "Well, old man, sleeping in your clothes!"

He smiled and went into the bathroom to shower and get ready for the day. When he was dressed, he put in a call to Neves and asked if he would like to go out for a round of golf. Neves was up for that.

Everyone went on with their day feeling great because no one remembered anything that had taken place. Not the visions, the hooded figures, or the battle. But more importantly, no one remembered a woman named Nan.

ABOUT THE AUTHOR

Juanita Tischendorf lives with her husband in the suburb of Irondequoit in Rochester New York. Juanita has written several works of fiction and nonfiction books. She completed a writing course at the University of Washington, have taken James Paterson masterclasses and one with Martin Scorsese. Juanita is a member of the Writers Guild of America and is listed in the 1991 edition of "2000 Notable American Women".

www.ingramcontent.com/pod-product-compliance
Lightning Source LLC
Chambersburg PA
CBHW021224250626
47155CB00008B/2926